LUMINOSITY

THE RAVEN CHRONICLES

LUMINOSITY

THE RAVEN CHRONICLES

STEPHANIE THOMAS

Entangled Publishing, LLC
2614 South Timberline Road
Suite 109
Fort Collins, CO 80525
Visit our website at www.entangledpublishing.com.

Edited by Kerry Vail and Liz Pelletier
Cover design by Liz Pelletier

Ebook ISBN   978-1-62061-128-9
Print ISBN   978-1-62061-127-2

Manufactured in the United States of America

First Edition November 2012

For my husband, who has both supported me and kept me grounded through this journey. I am nothing without you.

My name is Beatrice.

When I was born, I was blessed with the Sight. I was immediately removed from my parents and enrolled in the Institution. At the age of twelve, I had my first, true Vision, earning my raven's wings. And when I turned seventeen, one of my Visions came true. Things haven't been the same since.

CHAPTER ONE

At night, my room illuminates with an indescribable brilliance. The glow of a million City lights pours into the small space officially referred to as Bunk 34A. It's not a large bunk by any means—just enough space to harbor a twin bed tucked under an overhead compartment of drawers where I keep my jumpsuits and robes. Stacked in squares of black, it is hard to tell which article of clothing is which without touching them. Sometimes, it feels the same way in the Institution—you don't know one thing from the other, no matter how long you try to figure it out. The Institution is all about uniformity. Nothing has changed here in years.

I have a small desk where I finish my class work. Stacked books form little towers on the surface, mimicking the tall buildings just outside my window. Some books are about learning to survive in conditions that aren't ideal. Some are about our enemy, and others are about the history of the Seers and our gift. There's always something to be learned here.

My reflection stares back at me, and I try to peer through it and the tinted glass panel. I trace the image of the black raven's wings, one tattooed over each of my eyes. The wings are spread and ready for flight. These mark the maturation of my Visions. They are a rite of passage, a signal to everyone that I am truly gifted with the Sight. Most of us earn our raven's wings by the time we are teenagers, but there are still those who take a little longer to understand the images that come to us. It's not easy to decipher or pick out what is truth inside our minds.

Just outside my window, patrol helicopters hover high above the ground, their searchlights bright and unforgiving. If you are caught in one of those beams, there is no escaping. The Watch are beyond vigilant since the first sighting. They take no chances in the City, or in the Institution. Especially not since the Dreamcatchers came.

The Keeper mandated a curfew, demanding that every Seer be in their bunks by nine in the evening. The Dreamcatchers are double the threat to us. They are able to reach into the minds of normal humans—Citizens—through dreams or touch. From what I've been told, a Dreamcatcher can shatter a person's mind with just one touch. I once saw a picture of one of the unfortunate souls who was Caught. His eyes turned white, mouth open…gone. Like an oyster shell without any meat inside.

The Seers are trained to prevent this, to protect the Citizens at all costs. At seventeen years old, I am arguably the most revered Seer because my Vision is the clearest, next to that of the Keeper. I didn't understand the importance of that at the time. I had the Vision that would change everything. But we all do now.

A knock jars me out of my thoughts. "Who is it?"

The door slides open with a hiss and then disappears into the wall. Gabriel stands in the doorway, his uniform a black and grey one-piece jumpsuit with the lavender eye of the Seer sewn above the right breast pocket. It matches our eyes, all of which are the same hue of purple, the mark of a Seer. His combat boots are tied tightly and shined to perfection. Gabriel is always perfect. Always. "Just me, Bea. It's my turn to make the rounds tonight. I can't stay long here, though. Gotta keep moving."

I smile as I lie down in my bunk. "Okay, okay. I'll go to bed." It's not going to be easy to sleep tonight, though. Not with the thought of the Dreamcatcher girl on my mind. They arrested her yesterday after I saw her in a Vision. She looked so young…so innocent.

Gabe grins and steps back from the door, allowing it to slide into place. With a click, it locks from inside. I flick the lights off, and I'm left in the dark to think about how it will be now that the Dreamcatchers have actually made their appearance in the City. Already, the change in security is overwhelming, and I'm sure it won't be long until the Keeper is back at my door, ready to record my latest Vision.

In two days, our new training begins, and I am not ready. None of this feels real, and there are so many unknowns that it seems like I'm walking around a corner without any idea what'll be on the other side. Yesterday as we sat together at dinner, Gabe told me not to be afraid. I poked around at my mystery-sauce pasta, and just as he always does, he picked up on my worry. Gabriel has been by my side since before we could remember. We were in the same batch of infants brought to the Institution, ready to be inducted into a lifetime program that we didn't choose to be in. It is the law, though, and anyone caught harboring a rogue Seer is put to death.

He's my best friend, but not my only one. Lately, though, it's been different. When he comes around I feel like something is curling up in my core, ready to spring out in excitement or giddiness. I wait anxiously to see him every day, just to catch a glimpse of him before we go to class. It makes me feel like a silly little girl, so I try not to think about it. Especially when he is close.

Ready or not, neither I, nor any other Seer, have any choice but to step into this whole new Dreamcatcher conflict which we'd previously only read about in our school books. This is more than just words on a page now. The Dreamcatchers are here, and it's our job to keep them at bay. But how much will we have to sacrifice to keep the City safe?

CHAPTER TWO

It is dark. The whole City sleeps. But it is a blank sleep, a hollow sleep. The lights should be on, but nothing glows. The City should still be alive deep down in the alleys and shady buildings where guards keep the unwanted from getting in, but no one is outside. There should still be a pulse, a few cars left on the roads, racing to get home before the curfew bells begin to ring high in the City Tower, but the streets are bare.

It's cold. The rain doesn't stop falling. Then something interrupts its fall. Something invisible. The same something that shrouds the City and makes it sleep. I don't understand how I know it is there; I just do. Whatever it is, it is looking for me, snaking through the City, hugging the corners and shadows in order to not be found. It whispers my name, "Beatrice, Beatrice…"

I want to go to it. I want to step into the rain and show it that not all of the City is dormant. I want to capture it, ensnare it, bring it back to the Institute and prove myself to it.

"Beatrice… Beatrice."

No one else hears it. There is no one else. There is only me.

I wake up in a rush. My head pounds like it normally does after I have a Vision. It feels like my skull is going to crack right down the center, and right now, I wish it would so that the pressure could break free. My hand curls around the bunk, and I feel for the purple button underneath. The Keeper will come running, as she always does, only to find out that it's the same Vision I've been having over and over. Since *the* Vision. The one that set the City into the protective, alert overdrive that it's been in since.

I dim the lights in my bunk to protect my eyes. When I look into the mirror, my eyes still glow a vibrant, violet hue. As time passes, though, the luminance will begin to fade until they are dull once more.

The door slides open. The Keeper stands with her digipad in her hand and her raven companion sitting on her shoulder. She is tall and stern, her face long, expression serious. Her eyes are the same color as mine and every other Secr, but they are so light now that they almost look white. She wears a red robe that brushes the floor and covers her feet. The bird stares vacantly at nothing and everything as the Keeper waits for me to report.

"It is the same Vision as before. They are coming." I rub at my head with my knuckles to try and relieve the pain.

"There is no new information?" The Keeper touches the digipad's screen, and I don't have any idea what she is doing. And I don't care. Right now, I just want the throbbing in my head to subside before it really does crack my skull in two.

"No. No new information. Just the same things. Dark buildings. Something there calling my name…shad—"

"Shadows." The Keeper knows the Vision as well as I do. She's heard it at least two dozen times by now.

Gabe shows up behind her and stands tall and rigid, mocking

the Keeper's stoic pose. He crosses his arm over his chest and pretends to type on a mock digipad. It takes everything in me not to laugh at his antics. Laughing would hurt my head anyway.

"Very well, Seer Beatrice. Lie down until you recover." Turning, the Keeper nearly collides with Gabriel, but he sidesteps out of her way. "Seer Gabriel."

"My Keeper." The Keeper leaves as Gabe greets her.

"She scares me." I lie back in the bed and drape an arm over my eyes. "It's like she doesn't trust me."

"She probably doesn't. After all, you seem to have a better Sight than she does. She probably feels threatened." Gabe sits on the edge of the bed and wiggles my leg. "So you didn't See anything new this time?"

"No. Why would she be threatened? I helped protect the City, didn't I?" I scrunch my nose up in annoyance at Gabe shaking my leg, but really I don't mind it. I never mind when he touches me.

"Yes, you did. Will you be going to the execution today?"

The execution. I forgot. Of course I was invited, being the one who technically captured the girl in the first place. She is a Dreamcatcher, one who somehow snuck through the barrier and into the City. I had a Vision of her wandering the streets, preying on people, grabbing them by the arms and stealing their minds, leaving them hollowed out. Dead. The bodies crumple to the ground, but she keeps walking. Always walking, like she has somewhere she must end up. Like there is something she is hunting.

When I reported the Vision, the reaction was immediate. The Watch swept the City for any signs of the girl, whom I saw very clearly. She was beautiful, with wide, blue, almond-shaped eyes, and short light-blonde hair. She wore a bright sundress. White, with tiny pink flowers. Against the black and gunmetal grey of the City, she screamed of being out of place. It was the pretty sundress that was her downfall; they found her almost immediately. Her name is Paradigm. The Dreamcatchers always have strange names.

"I really don't want to see the execution." And I don't. I already see her face when I close my eyes. It floats against the brightness that comes with having a Vision. Why would I want to see it hanging at the end of a rope, or however she's going to be executed?

Gabe shakes my leg again. Sometimes I wonder if he touches me because he really wants to, or just to tease me. Or both. Either way, it doesn't bother me. He has always stood right by my side, mirroring my accomplishments. But when I Saw my recent Dreamcatcher Vision, it seemed like a rift tore between us as everyone, including the Keeper, started to pay more attention to me. The time we used to spend with each other, the time I used to spend with my friends, has slowly dwindled. Now that the original Vision has passed, it hasn't been so bad, but still, I miss being "normal." The more time I spend away from Gabe, the more I realize I need him.

"Come with me. You can look away, but I think it would be good for people to see you, Beatrice. You're like a legend now. A hero. You should be proud."

"I'm not proud of being someone that gets people killed."

"She's our enemy. A Dreamcatcher."

Our enemy. Then why do I care so much? "Fine, I'll go. But I'm leaving before they execute her. I don't want to see it."

Gabe stands and then slides his hands into his pockets. "After lunch. I'll see you there. Today's ham day."

I laugh because it's so pathetic that Gabriel looks forward to ham day. The cafeteria food is never good, but it's all we have. Ever since we were little, he's liked this day the best. Sometimes he even convinces me to give up my share for an extra ration of green beans.

Not that I like green beans, mind you, but Gabe is so pitiful on ham day it's hard not to feel bad for him.

"See you there." Gabe leaves, and I drape my arm back over my eyes. I'm not going anywhere until my head stops hurting.

◇

Before it's time for the execution, our interrogation instructor calls an emergency class. Everyone reports immediately, filling the dim lecture hall bit by bit. Gabe finds me, and we steal two seats next to each other. Once we are seated, he leans over and whispers, "Do you know what this is about?"

I shake my head. Rumor has it that the execution has been delayed, which doesn't make sense since the Keeper probably wants to be rid of this Dreamcatcher as soon as possible.

The Instructor steps up to her podium and holds it tightly in her hands, bent over slightly, mouth close to the microphone. "Seers. Thank you all for coming here today on such short notice."

I spot Brandon, Mae, and Connie scattered about the room of faces, and when Mae finds me staring at her, she turns and cheerfully waves. I wiggle my fingers back and would normally be happy to see them, but mostly I am focused on the Instructor.

"As you've all heard, yesterday a Dreamcatcher was found among us. This didn't entirely come as a surprise, thanks to Seer Beatrice's Visions." There's a pause, and people shift to turn and look at me. I stiffly stare ahead, even when Gabe nudges me in the arm and grins, "Did you hear that? She mentioned you!"

"Shh! This is embarrassing." I mutter the words through my clenched teeth, and then smile benignly at those who are still staring.

"Still, we've found some disturbing information during our interrogation, information that will be shared with all of you, so that you understand the gravity of the Dreamcatcher invasion." The Instructor pushes a button on the podium's stand, and a projector lights up the screen behind her with the image of a young girl wearing a white dress with flowers scattered all about it. Fair-haired with deep blue eyes, the Dreamcatcher stares up into the camera, right at us, and she seems entirely unafraid. I feel like she's looking beyond me, and I glance away elsewhere, discomforted.

"This is Paradigm. She claims she's a Princess of Aura, the Dreamcatcher City. We have no way of verifying this information." The Instructor taps her fingers on the podium and looks to the side of the stage. "With the permission of the Keeper, we wish you to watch the interview and learn from it. This is your first time seeing a modern Dreamcatcher, so listen and absorb how manipulative they can be." The Instructor nods her head, and pushes another button that sets the video in motion.

The Dreamcatcher's cell is small, and she sits at a metal table across from a black-robed Seer, the Interrogator. The Dreamcatcher's hands are bound behind her back with metal chains. The girl looks so helpless and innocent that it's hard to imagine her killing someone with just a touch.

"Who are you?" the Interrogator asks.

"Princess Paradigm of Aura."

"And why are you here?"

"To bring about the war." She looks back at the camera, staring at the audience. Does she know it will be us?

The Interrogator doesn't even blink and continues with her questions. "And how do you plan to do that?"

"How do I plan to bring about the war? I've already done it, Seer." Paradigm smiles.

"But how?"

"By coming here. They are looking for me."

"But you will be dead when they find you."

"And you will be standing at the doorstep of disaster."

The Interrogator laughs a brief, staccato laugh, and all at once she stops and silence fills the cell once more. "You say that you're a princess?"

"I am. Of Aura."

"That makes your mother the Queen of the Dreamcatchers?"

"Yes." Paradigm seems unfazed by the seemingly cold and bare cell, and the unrelenting questions of the interrogation.

"What made you come here? Why now?"

Paradigm doesn't answer. She doesn't look up at the camera. This is when, for the first time, the Interrogator uses other methods of producing answers from the girl. With one nod from the Interrogator, two large Watchmen step into the room with metal prods and they poke Paradigm in the sides, just under her ribs. The girl is filled with what looks like a jolt of energy, and her whole body abnormally tenses and contorts into something strange. When they take the rods away from her, her body goes slack and she falls forward onto the table.

"You will answer me. What made you come here? What made you choose now?"

"My...my mother...she'll...she'll make sure you all die..."

The Interrogator nods to the Watchmen. "Again."

This is when I turn my head toward Gabe, unable to watch as they electrocute Paradigm again.

"...he doesn't know better...he'll come for her...and he doesn't know any better..." Paradigm breathes through clenched teeth and stares up into the camera again. "Do you hear me, girl? He might come for you, but he doesn't know any better. You will all die!"

The Interrogator stands from the table. "Keep it up until she gives us an answer." With that said, she leaves the room. Screaming ensues. The video switches off.

I swallow a lump in my throat, wondering why they made us watch something like that.

"Who do you think she was talking to?" Gabe murmurs to me, one voice among the many that babble on about what we've all just witnessed.

"Huh?" I don't know what Gabe is referring to, mostly because all I can hear are the echoes of Paradigm's screaming in the back of my mind.

"Did you hear what she said? She mentioned a girl, and that someone is coming for her...I wonder who she is talking about, is all." Gabe's eyes meet mine and he frowns for a moment. "You don't think she means you, do you?"

"Why would she mean me?"

"Because you are the one who can See them coming...What if she means you?"

It becomes too real then, and I shut the screaming out of my head to wrap my thoughts around the idea that the Dreamcatchers might be coming for me. "I don't know..."

The Instructor takes the stage again and taps the microphone to command our attention. "That's all we are showing you today. This is your warning that they are targeting specific Seers, though we never found out who the Dreamcatcher meant by 'he' and the 'girl.' We must be ever-vigilant now. Today, a Dreamcatcher will die, and we will be entering a new phase of our preparation for the impending invasion." With a pregnant pause, the Instructor looks us over, and I swear that, for a brief moment, her eyes meet mine, as if warning me specifically. But then she issues her dismissal and everyone stands, blocking my view of the stage.

"Come on. We'll be late." Gabe insists, and I follow after him, numb from the interrogation video and the memory of Paradigm's writhing body.

◇

It is strangely quiet for an execution. The sun struggles to shine through the thick cover of grey clouds. Few people have seen a Dreamcatcher up close before, so when they march her onto the platform and position her against the brick wall, everyone stands attentive, mesmerized. Her hands are cuffed together and bound in an iron box to keep her from grabbing anyone.

Paradigm is not scared. She looks as though someone could be walking her from one room to the next. She holds her chin high, and her hair angles around her face. Both her cheeks and her white-flowered sundress are smudged with dirt. When she looks over the crowd, she stares at me. How she finds me in the midst of a hundred people, I don't know. I can feel a dull pain building in my head, and though I quickly glance away, the pain remains.

The Keeper rises onto the platform but keeps her distance from the accused. She has her raven with her, though the bird is quick to take off, landing on a nearby light post to watch from afar. Tapping on the microphone, she sends a muffled noise through the speakers, then steps closer. "Seers and Citizens. Today we will witness the execution of this vile Dreamcatcher. She is found guilty of killing three Citizens by seizing their minds."

The crowd erupts into jeers. Gabe boos along with them, taking care to be extra loud and annoying. I elbow him in the side, and he stops abruptly. "What?"

I look back at the Keeper and Paradigm. "Don't be stupid."

"I'm not being stupid. She killed people."

"You're being stupid." I leave it at that because the Keeper begins to speak once more. The sun beats down through the smog of the City, which smells like trash and something else that I can't decipher.

"Dreamcatcher." The Keeper doesn't give Paradigm the respect of calling her by her name. "Your sentence is execution by firing squad. Do you have any last words?"

My chest squeezes tight. For some reason, I don't want her to speak.

Paradigm's lips peel apart. "We're coming."

The Keeper steps off the platform. The captain of the firing squad calls them to arms. The black rifles rise one-by-one, all pointed toward the girl who could hardly be my age. She looks at me again. I'm still looking at her. I promised myself I would not watch, but I watch. I can't look away.

"Ready!" The captain calls. The firing squad's elbows rise. "Aim!"

"I thought you weren't going to watch." Gabe reminds me, but I still can't tear my eyes away.

"I wasn't."

But I am.

"Fire!"

Bullets slice through the air and into Paradigm. Where they hit, her sundress turns crimson, first in small circles, then bleeding into larger spots. Even after she is hit, she stands for a moment, her eyes on me. Then, all at once, she crumples onto the ground in a pool of her own blood. The raven is screeching somewhere in the background.

"It looked like she was looking at you, didn't it?" Gabe speaks over the cheer of the crowd. People clapping for the end of someone's – or something's – life.

Why was she looking at me? How did she know it was I who had the Vision? Standing in a sea of other Seers, it could have been any of us…but she knew it was me.

When it is clear that she's no longer alive, the pain in my head starts to fade away. Some poor soul tasked with removing the body hooks his arms under Paradigm's shoulders and begins to drag her off the platform. A trail of blood follows behind, even down the stairs as she is *thunked* down each step.

"No, she couldn't have been. There are too many of us here for her to have picked me out of the crowd." I don't want Gabe to worry. Of course she was looking at me.

The Keeper steps back up onto the platform after it has been washed clean of the blood. "Let this be an example to you all. The Dreamcatchers can be anywhere. They are coming, and we must be prepared." Her violet eyes seem to meet each and every one of our stares. "You are dismissed."

"We are sparring in the arena today, remember," Gabe says, and we start to walk back to the Institution. We have little choice as the crowd begins to push in that direction. "It's about time we bring down Team B. I hope you are on your toes today, Bea. If we lose again, they'll think we are hopeless."

"Maybe we are."

"Don't be ridiculous. We have you. We can't be hopeless." Gabe grins, and something inside of me flutters. He always knows the right things to say. But what will happen when he realizes I am not the solution?

As we turn and leave, I hear the voice from my Vision in my head again.

It whispers sadly, *"My sister…"*

And suddenly, I'm filled with an unbearable sadness. An overwhelming feeling of sorrow flows through my arms, my fingers, down my middle and through my legs. I stop walking and close my eyes.

"What's wrong?" Gabe pauses next to me.

I have to shake the feeling. Gabe would never understand. I pretend as if nothing is wrong and smile at him. "Nothing. I guess the execution kind of got to me, that's all."

Gabe smiles and puts his hand on the small of my back, ushering me forward. "Let's sneak off and go get something cool to drink before the Keeper can find us. That'll make you feel better."

But I know it won't.

CHAPTER THREE

The City is dark. Always dark. I am street level, not hovering above, omnipresent. I am walking down a side road, my boots wet from the damp sidewalks. It has just rained, and puddles are scattered in the dimpled places where the pavement isn't quite even. I know where I am going, yet I don't know where I am going. Something tugs me toward the barrier, past the towering scrap metal guard stations that remind me of the parapets of a castle.

The barrier is the edge of our City, heavily guarded and definitely off-limits. Gates lead to the outside, but they haven't opened in years. No one leaves the City. There is undeveloped nothingness beyond here, an undesirable and uninhabited wasteland that we are forbidden to see or know too much about. Everyone, Seer and Citizen alike, is taught from a young age that beyond our great City lies a terrible threat, and a world of nothingness that will suck you in and never spit you back out. No one ever approaches the barricades. No one ever has a reason to wander anywhere near the perimeter of the City. Until now.

Everything is quiet, like I have gone deaf. I cannot hear the rain, or the surge of electricity pumped through the barbed wire spirals that line the top of the barrier wall, but I know they are both there. It's eerie not being able to hear anything. It's like I'm underwater and everything is so muted and silent that I can't discern my own thoughts.

But, I do hear a voice—the voice of a young man.

"Beatrice…Beatrice…"

"What?" I whisper, afraid the guard in the tower will hear me and shoot me. There have been stories of Citizens who have gone crazy and run themselves into the fence—a death sentence of its own, as their whole bodies fry and convulse against the lines of metal links.

"Beatrice…"

"WHAT?" I whisper louder, as loud as I can without drawing attention to myself. I shoot a look back to the guard station, but nothing up there moves, so hopefully I am safe. For now.

"Meet me…meet me…"

"Where?"

"Meet me…"

"Why?"

There's a hesitation between my question and the next words that come from the nothingness around me. "My sister…they killed my little sister. We need your help, Beatrice. We need your help to stop this."

"You need me?"

"Meet me…"

◇

"A boy?"

"He sounded older than a boy. Like Gabe's age." I look at Gabe when I say that, because of course he is standing behind the Keeper, waiting to hear about my Vision. After our snack, I told Gabe I was going to go back to my bunk to rest before the Training Games. That is when the Vision came.

"And what did he say?" The Keeper types on her digipad, her brows knitted in concern.

"He said to meet him…but he never said where…or why." Everything is too bright. This Vision hurts my head more than the last. "Can we turn off the lights?"

Gabe hits the button by the door without being told, and the lights flicker off as the window shades close. The digipad is the only thing that glows in the bunk.

"Thanks, Gabe."

"Meet you? That is rather strange. And you were by the barrier?" The Keeper's finger pushes here and there on the flat screen.

"Yes, beside a guard station."

"Mmm." After typing a few things more, the Keeper's violet eyes lift away from the digipad and flit to me. "Interesting, Seer Beatrice. Very interesting." And without mentioning anything else, she leaves, brushing by Gabe as she does so. "You should be hurrying along to the Training Games, shouldn't you?" But she doesn't wait for an answer. The "suggestion" is enough.

"Interesting, Seer Beatrice. You should be hurrying along to the Training Games, shouldn't you?" Gabe mocks the Keeper when she's out of earshot. He's dead-on with his impersonation, staunch and stuck-up just like her. "It *is* interesting though. Funny that you should have a Vision that makes absolutely no sense after having one that was almost too clear for your own good."

"Yeah, I don't understand it either. I keep hearing him calling me. Even now, after the Vision, I can hear him…"

"You didn't tell the Keeper that."

"She didn't ask, did she?" I smile through the pain in my head.

"No, I guess she didn't." Gabe taps his fingers on the frame of the doorway, as if waiting for something. "So, when are you going to get dressed? We have to be at training in…oh, fifteen minutes? And I shouldn't stick around any longer than I have to."

I groan since the last thing I want to do with a splitting headache is any extra work. But I have no choice. We have the Training Games today, and if I let my team down and we fail, Team B will never let us get over it and there's no way I'm going to allow for them to get a one-up on us.

Rolling out of the bed, I stretch my arms over my head and glance into the mirror. My eyes are still glowing, which probably explains why I still hear the echo of my name reverberating through my mind. The Vision doesn't feel over, but at the same time I know it has to be, or I wouldn't be able to function. "Fine, fine. I'll meet you down in the lobby in fifteen."

"See you there, Bea." Gabe leaves me to get dressed. I pull on my black jumpsuit and fasten my name tag opposite the violet eye embroidered on the right chest. My black hair is tightly bound in a bun high at the crown of my head. I lace up my knee-high combat boots and head out of the bunk.

The halls of the Institution are all the same: dark with dim bulbs that line the floors, with beams of light striating up the walls. Other Seers, also dressed for the Training Games, are heading in the same direction I am. Every few feet, a new door opens to another bunk, one for each resident. Some doors are still sliding closed, filling the hall with hydraulic hissing that mingles with the other participants' excited murmuring.

The loudspeaker crackles as the Keeper's voice echoes through the building. "The Training Games will begin in five minutes. Those players not assembled at that time will forfeit, and their teams will take a point loss."

Rounding into the lobby, I spot Gabe and jog in his direction. "You ready for this?"

"Ready as I'll ever be. Just remember our new tactics…and stay out of the lights." Gabe looks at me in concern. Specifically, he looks at my forehead, as if trying to gauge the pain there. "Are you ready, though?"

"Do I have a choice?" I don't. The Training Games are mandatory, especially now with the City on lockdown.

Our team lines up in pairs in front of a large door marked with a big, silver "A." Everyone holds a machine gun. Instead of live ammunition, the guns are equipped with laser sights that when aimed and fired send a shock through the opponent's uniform. The better the shot, the more painful the shock. You are out when you can't take the pain anymore…in other words, when you are unconscious.

I don't plan on being unconscious, though. Team A has a pretty good record, truth be told. So far this year we are eighty-three and seven, those seven being the few, rare times that Team B or Team C managed to cut us down. The other teams are classified differently, made up of newer and less-trained Seers. For example, Team A would never go up against Team M, because poor Team M wouldn't stand a chance in the arena with us. They are still equipped with paintball guns loaded with red pellets that leave nice bruises that take weeks to heal.

Gabriel and I are the last pair to line up. In front of us, a girl named Rachelle turns and smirks. Rachelle is usually the captain for Team B. She has been striving to move up to Team A, doing whatever she can to get the attention of our trainers. Sometimes, she even resorts to dirty tactics, just skirting the definition of "cheating." Today, they are letting her play on the A team, testing her skills. "You two together again?"

"We were late," I say defensively.

"Yes." Gabe replies without any hint of being offended. He smiles at me and warmth floods my cheeks.

The red light over the massive doors begins to rotate, filling the hall with strobes of deep crimson. A loud buzzer goes off somewhere behind where we stand. At the last minute, I pull the sensor vest off the hook on the wall and wiggle it over my head. I'm not thrilled about the Games, especially when something is still pounding from inside my head, as if trying to get out.

"Ugh," I groan.

"No turning back now, Bea. Just stay out of the light."

"Yeah, don't screw it up for us, you hear?" Rachelle throws in for good measure. I hear her, but I certainly do not care. She has no idea how this team runs, and she's no one to talk to me like that.

I turn to the rest of the team and step up to try and take control of the situation. "Listen up, Team A! We have a lot to prove, and we can't let Team B beat us. Keep to the shadows as much as you can. We are going to break up today and each go in different directions so they can't focus on any group of us." Looking over the gathered Seers, I stare at their helmets, barely able to see their eyes through the tinted visors. I look for my friends, but they blend into the group. "Don't hesitate. There's no time for hesitating. Got it?"

They mumble their assent together, and Gabe gives me a thumbs up. His simple gesture fills me with even more confidence than I had before, and I somehow know that we're going to be okay.

The doors part, screeching under their own weight, and the

arena opens before us, a large space with too many walls and too little light. We are dressed in black in order to meld into the shadows. That is where the Dreamcatchers lurk, and in the end, we are being trained to become efficient Dreamcatcher-killing machines.

The arena is constructed around large holo-projectors that recreate any scene they are programmed to display. Sometimes, you can even go into the buildings, the lights shifting so that you are hidden inside, creating walls that almost seem real. The technology probably costs more than the whole Institution itself, and some of it isn't explainable, not just tricks of lights and mirrors. Other times, when it's not so serious, a stage is set up with real rooms made from particleboard walls, and we run around practicing hitting one another with our paintball guns, destroying the bland decor and marking it and ourselves with splotches of many different colors of paint.

The ten others in front of us quickly scatter into the maze of towering walls, and Gabe starts to make a run for it as well. I thought we were going to stick together, but when he disappears into the dark I am left alone in the red light. *Damn you, Gabe.* I don't need him to move forward. I need to protect myself. I heft my weapon, duck, then scurry into the shadows with everyone else.

A large scoreboard strategically hangs from the top center of the arena. Under "A" and "B" there are two red zeroes. I hear someone scream from far to my left and the zero under the "B" changes to a "1." *Damn it.* They are already winning.

As I run, I nearly trip over a handle on the floor. Dipping into a crouch, I pull on it, opening a trapdoor that leads under the arena. I find this to be fair game. The Institution is always trying to sway the results of the Training Games one way or another, or at least it feels like it most of the time. The Keeper wants to see which of us is strong enough to survive, and she'll push us to our limits to find out.

Quickly, I drop into the space under the arena and carefully pull the door closed over me. Just in time, too, as the sound of footsteps bangs down on the hatch.

The room is dark, of course, so I flick on the flashlight at the end of my gun, flooding the area with brightness. It's a tunnel, and where the tunnel leads, I have no idea. I'm at the far end of it, stuck in a corner. Not ideal, especially if someone from Team B found a hatch on their end and is heading in my direction. I have to move.

As I snake through the narrow corridors, I hear people running above me, the soles of their shoes slapping on the ground. Mixed in are muffled screams and the sounds of bodies hitting the floor. Hopefully, we are winning.

At last, I find a place where the floorboards of the arena are loose, allowing a peek up through a crack. It's enough for me to aim the laser sight of the machine gun through the hole as well, so I crouch down low and switch the light of my gun off. Maybe five minutes have gone by and already it sounds as if seventy-five percent of the players have been rendered unconscious. Footfalls are scarce now, and the arena is eerily silent.

That's when I hear him.

"Bea? Beatrice! I need your help!"

Gabe.

He needs my help, but I have no idea how to get out of the tunnels. If I go back, I will be running away from the sound of his voice and not toward it. If I go forward, I could end up Maker-knows-where. He is not far away from me either, and it sounds like he is in pain.

"There's only one more, Bea! Where *are* you?"

I can't stay trapped in the tunnels the whole time, and I can't leave Gabriel to be "killed" either, even if he ran off without me.

 With the end of my gun, I bash away at the crack in the floor until it splinters open. After a few more adrenaline-powered thrusts, I am able to sling my gun around my back and climb up through the hole. Scrambling to my feet, my head still pounding along with my heart, I start to sprint in the direction of Gabe's voice.

I am afraid I am lost in the maze of walls when I find him. He is kneeling on the ground, his hands behind his back with a machine gun pointed at his head. And who else but Rachelle is holding the weapon?

She smirks and pushes the end of the gun closer to Gabe. "Bang, bang." Rachelle squeezes the trigger, and Gabe's body jolts with electricity. Because of the proximity, it's enough to knock him into unconsciousness and his body falls forward. Isn't she supposed to be on our team?

I jerk my gun up and shoot, but it's too late. I'm filled with an intense shock that brings me to my knees, and my palms hit the floor. I gasp for air and glance up, trying to find the source. It occurs to me that Rachelle is still shooting.

The arena lights come on.

My world fades to black.

CHAPTER FOUR

While I am out cold, I think of Gabe. We are around seven years old, and we are sitting in a classroom—a dim little room with long tables, each with four chairs, and two holoboards at the front, behind a small, metal desk for the instructor. Gabe and I always sit together. It's as if we naturally gravitate to one another, inseparable. I haven't ever thought of my life without him in it, because I've never had a moment when Gabe wasn't a part of what I was doing.

It is history day in our class, and the boards flicker on, words appearing across the length. The instructor taps one board with her hand, her eyes on us. "Today we are going to learn about the roles of Seers and Citizens. Please start copying notes." The first thing we ever did for this particular teacher was to copy a ton of notes that I never read again. Even today, this woman still insists on making us take copious amounts of notes, and one-by-one we all pull out our holopads and begin keying in the novella of background about Seers and Citizens.

Sometime later, when it looks like most of us are done, the instructor stands from behind her desk and approaches her podium.

Fingers curl around the edges as she regards us with her unforgiving stare. "We are, of course, superior to Citizens. They are normal people who depend on our gift to make sure the Dreamcatchers do not come back and take them. Without us, they would always live in fear, never feeling safe, always looking behind them and at one another in suspicion. Who could be the Dreamcatcher?" She speaks as if she is setting up the plot line to a story, and Gabe giggles at the ominous tone she uses.

"Seer Gabriel, do you think something is funny?" The teacher asks, pausing her lesson to address the squeaky laughter that erupts from Gabe.

But he explains himself, nonetheless, as if he's not remiss for laughing during the middle of a lesson. "It's just that…you make it sound like a story, Instructor. Like it isn't something that is real. How do we know how they'd live without us anyway? Haven't they always lived with us?"

"This is not a laughing matter, Seer Gabriel, and I am assigning you a demerit for your behavior." She taps the screen of her holopad and Gabe's responds, the display brightening as the little number in the corner goes from a stellar 216 down to 215. Gabe has been saving up those credits for a treat from the snack room. Two hundred and fifty of them would maybe earn him some chocolate, which is a big treat in the Institution. "But you do present a good question. Have the Citizens always lived with the Seers? The answer is yes, they have, but we've not always been in charge."

With another finger-push to her holopad, the image on the holoboard flips to a picture of the City. This picture was taken in the daytime, though the sky was still dim and foggy, like overcast weather that never quite went away. "The Citizens did not believe in our gifts at first. They would condemn those with the violet eyes for claiming they could See into the future. Some said we were paid by others to forecast one's life, especially when those Visions included something a person did not want to hear.

"The Citizens always knew that there was a threat of the Dreamcatchers' return, though, and one day, a great Seer, Seer Alene, had a Vision so clear and vivid that she could not bring herself to leave her own bunk."

I lean forward on my seat and wave my hand into the air. "What was the Vision about?" My Vision hasn't peaked yet. I am still just an ordinary Seer like the next seven-year-old, nothing special to add to the mix.

"It was about a Dreamcatcher army that came and stole hundreds of Citizens by ship, taking them from the City and disappearing forever." The Instructor pauses, letting the horrifying truth of this sink in. We all know that Seer Alene's Vision eventually came true. We already learned this last year, about the invasion that took hundreds of lives. "If the Citizens would have listened to the Seers instead of condemning them, then something could have been done. It was decided on that day, that in order to protect the City, all those who were born with the gift should be raised and trained to be the best Seers they can be. They must learn how to use their Vision to keep the City and its Citizens safe. So the Institution was created, Seer Alene was made the first Keeper, and here we are today."

My dream flickers, threatening to fade away. The last thing I remember is Gabe pouting at the red 215 that blinks in the corner of his holopad, reminding him of his terrible mistake of giggling during a lesson. I pat him on his arm and smile, "Did you hear that? We are going to save the City."

But Gabe doesn't care. He worked hard for those credits, and losing even one of them is a terrible blow. The instructor turns the holoboard off and dismisses the class, but Gabe doesn't move. I stay with him until the lunch tone sounds, and the only thing that gets him off his behind is the fact that it's ham day in the cafeteria.

◇

Gabe is standing over me when I come to. I'm no longer in the arena, but outside of it, hunkered in the corner of a busy hallway. There's little time between each Training Game, so they probably dumped me in the first place they could in order to clear the floor for the next pair of teams.

"That was dirty of her." Gabe kneels beside me, offering a hand to help me sit. I curl my fingers around his and pull myself up. "The trainer said that it goes to show us that you can't trust anyone, not even your own teammates. They wanted her to do it."

"That's because she's a jealous brat." Anger boils inside my veins. "Rachelle is worthless. She always has been. And then she has the nerve to cheat?"

"It wasn't exactly cheating if she was doing what she was told, Bea."

Gabe sounds a little too much like he's defending her, so I frown. "It's cheating. We're on teams for a damned reason."

"But the Dreamcatchers can always infiltrate a Seer and then what? They'd be on our team too, and we'd never know it."

"I don't know, Gabriel." By using his whole name, I let him know that I am pissed. "And you don't know what happens when a Dreamcatcher catches a Seer. No one's ever told us past the fact that it's not a good thing."

He backs off and rises to his feet. "Well, it's over now, and they won. There's other stuff to be done, and we still have our debriefing to go to."

"Whatever." I pull myself up and stand.

Beatrice.

Closing my eyes, I try to hide from Gabe that the Vision is coming back. It isn't normal for me to get two of them in one day, and it immediately makes me feel weak and exhausted. I can't hide it from him, though. He already knows by the way my eyes begin to glow.

"Bea?"

"I don't know…it's coming back."

"Now?" Gabe moves behind me and puts a hand on my elbow. "Let's get you seated. Are you Seeing anything yet?"

"No, I just hear him. He's calling my name again." A whirlwind begins to spin inside of my head. I feel as if the ground is slanting, and I can't stay steady. Gabe sits me down just in time, because I'm certain that my feet are no longer on the floor.

Beatrice.

When the Vision should come, it doesn't. My sight narrows into a tunnel of black with a pinprick of light. The light slowly becomes brighter and wider, eventually erasing the darkness, and my sight returns.

"What's happening?" Gabe stands in front of me, hands on his knees, peering into my eyes. His face is ruddy, slightly swollen from the jolt of electricity shot through his head. Somehow, though, he still looks attractive, like a war-torn soldier fresh from the battlegrounds.

"It went away." I rub at my eyes until everything is clear again.

"Should we report it?"

"No, there's nothing to report. I didn't have a Vision. Nothing ever came."

Gabe is just as confused as I am. His eyebrows tilt downward, furrowing curiously. "That's strange. You didn't See anything, but you heard something?"

"Just my name."

Gabe glances around us, watching combat-booted Seers gear up and get ready for their time in the Training Games. They aren't paying any mind to what we are doing. I don't think anyone saw. Or at least, I hope not.

"This is probably something we should keep to ourselves," Gabe suggests.

"Okay." I try to stand again, but my balance is still shaky. Gabe is right there to help me. Again. "Let's go get cleaned up. The debriefing is in a half hour."

Gabe links his arm through mine and we start down the hallway back to our bunks. Gabe's is on a different floor, but he takes care to see me all the way to my door. We pass by Seers dressed in jumpsuits and some in their traditional black robes.

I feel like time isn't quite as it should be, and sometimes I swear I hear the voice still calling my name. The edges of my sight are blurry, like the foggy condensation spreading over the windows lining the hall. Each one offers a view out toward the City, its buildings tall and covered with soot from the exhaust of all the traffic.

I barely make it to my room before collapsing inside the door. The sudden shift of weight nearly drags Gabe down with me. He reaches out and catches the closet handle to pull himself back up.

"Whoa, there."

"I'm sorry. I don't know what's wrong. Something doesn't feel right." I'm still on the floor where I want to be. I know if I get back up, I'll just fall right down again. In fact, I don't even bother to open my eyes because the world is spinning, and I'm somehow grounded in its center, surrounded by thoughts and voices.

"Maybe I should call for someone."

"No! No. Don't. Just…get me to my bed. I'll say I'm sick. Go to the debriefing without me."

"Obviously something is wrong. We should get someone in here to check on you." Gabe half carries me to the bed, where I flop down and prop my head up on a pillow. "Or take you to the infirmary. That's what the Keeper is going to order when she finds out you are missing."

"Clearly something is wrong, yes, but I don't want to be checked up on. They will quarantine me and keep me under observation. I won't get out for days, and then I'll fall behind in my training. It's just not worth it." I dare to open my eyes. After squinting, Gabe becomes less fuzzy. He doesn't look happy with my suggestion, his lips turned downwards and pressed together into a line.

After a pause, Gabe responds, "Fine. I'll leave you here, but if something else happens, I'm going to report it, and you can't do anything to stop me."

"That's a lame threat."

Gabe grins. "Not as lame as you look right now."

"Ha. Ha. Ha." I don't find this amusing, especially since I am, in all sense of the word, lame at the moment. "Get out of here before you are late for the debriefing. Tell me what they say, especially about that little cheater, Rachelle."

"Aye, aye, Captain." Gabe mock salutes me with two fingers to his forehead before he leaves. As soon as he is gone, I want him to come back.

But I have to figure out what is going on. I close my eyes to try and start the Vision again, but I know as well as anyone else that there's no way to bring on Visions. No Seer possesses the power to bring on the Sight; the Visions come whenever they want, wherever you are.

I feign sickness for the rest of the day. No one comes and bothers me, not even Gabe, since he knows it will draw attention. As time passes, my head begins to feel better, but the strangeness inside of me doesn't change. I feel like a cat stuck in a pouncing motion, except I never come back down, and my heart remains in my throat.

I want to know who is calling me. And most importantly, *why*? I need to find out from someone who knows the ins and outs of the Institution. Someone who is not the Keeper, and someone who won't report back to her.

I know the perfect person, though I've never even met her.

CHAPTER FIVE

It's past curfew, and they will kill me if I am caught. Gabe makes the rounds tonight, checking each bunk to make sure everybody is in bed, and according to plan, though he has no idea where I am heading, he lets me slip out of my room and leave the Institution.

Wearing my black robes, I slink through the shadows of the streets, staying close to the damp, brick walls of the buildings. It's easy to slip into the emptiness of the City. Even easier when the curfew wasn't in place. It's always so dark and dismal that my black shape is easily swallowed up by the baleful, urban surroundings. Most of the buildings are tall and loom over me by hundreds of floors that must take minutes to reach, even by elevator. Their windows are made to reflect their surroundings; each building mirrors another, which mirrors another and so on and so forth. Even if the sun shone very brightly in the City, the buildings would blot it out. But mostly, the sun never penetrates the fog of a million cars and cycles, or the search helicopters that are constantly keeping surveillance over our precious town. Or the force field that arches over the towering buildings.

There are still puddles on the ground from the previous rainstorm, some of which reflect the light, which winks in the ripples. I must be careful because even in these shadows any little noise can give me away.

When I get to the end of a row of stores or houses, I press myself against the cool stone facade of the building and peek around the corner. Down the street, a huddle of soldiers gathers, machine guns slung over their backs. These are the Watch, a team of militiamen who are assigned to uphold curfew and maintain order on the streets. Their commands: shoot to kill. They are unforgiving, especially now with the City's heightened security against the Dreamcatcher invasion.

I have to be careful or I will end up on the ground, bleeding out onto the moist concrete. They do not know who I am. They don't know I am the Seer who saved the City—or rather, alerted them to an impending attack. They won't care when they shoot me either. I am just another person who should be inside her home, nestled in a bed, tucked away against the threats of the Watch and Dreamcatchers alike.

But I need to find the Widow, and she's somewhere across the street.

When I'm mostly certain that the Watch is no longer looking, I sprint across the pavement, avoiding the puddles as I run. My shadow flickers against the street lamps, and just before I melt back into the safety of an alley's darkness, the Watch turns and heads in my direction. Their boots fall heavily on the ground, slowly at first, but then quicker as they close in. "Hey! Who's there?"

Now I must keep running.

I only vaguely know where I am going. The Widow is rumored to live in the basement of an abandoned bar called Lucky's.

Unfortunately, I haven't a clue where Lucky's is. All I know is it is on the east side of the City by the park, and so that is where I start to sprint with the sound of at least a half dozen sets of footsteps behind me.

I'm drawing too much attention to myself. No one should be running at this time of night. Especially not a girl with about six men behind her. It doesn't take long for other Watchmen to realize that something isn't right. As I fly by another corner, their beady little eyes follow the blur of my form, running eastward. Soon, the half dozen men behind me turns into a full dozen, and probably even more than that. I have to lose them, but where?

I hardly even know where I am. Seers very rarely set out into the City. The City is meant for the Citizens, and the Seers are meant to stay in the Institution. It's just how things are expected to be, with the exception of the Widow. I don't know how she got to live outside of the Institution, or why, but if I manage to live through this, I'll have to remember to ask her.

I pass a stairwell that descends into the depths of the subway, and I duck inside. The trains have no passengers at this hour, so the tunnels beneath the City are quiet, the silence interrupted only by the occasional sound of water dripping from the ceilings. Some of the dim lights flicker on and off, and the sound of electricity shorting in and out mixes with the hollow quiet of a vast space. I swear I can feel the floor tremble, as if one of the trains were coming into the station, but maybe it's just expectation or even hopeful eagerness that makes me think so. I've never seen a subway in person before, but I don't have any time to waste standing here thinking about it.

Behind me, feet begin to stomp down the stairs. There is little time to breathe before I find myself jumping down onto the tracks and sprinting through the eastbound lane. The shock from the impact of my shoes hitting the ground surges up my ankles and into my legs. I attempt to stay close to the wall, trying to blend into the deep shadows that swallow up the light as I disappear into the tunnel. One of the rails is bigger than the other two, and the white bolt of lightning printed on it warns me to stay away.

Eventually, I think I lose the Watch. I don't hear their feet anymore, and I'm coming up on another station. It's the stop I need: City Park. I pray as I climb up the platform that the stairwell exit gates are not pulled shut. Luckily, they aren't, and I slip back into the cool, night air and take care not to draw any more attention to myself. The Watch is probably still searching for me, and if I am not careful, I'll end up caught. This time, though, I decide not to run. No matter what, I am not going to take flight again and draw more attention to myself. I can make it to my goal if I use some patience, which reminds me of a lesson taught to us in combat class. Sometimes, the best way to defeat your enemy is to just be patient.

I look to my left and to my right. The left leads to the park, and to the right is a small neighborhood. I seriously doubt that Lucky's bar is in City Park, so I turn to the right and start in the direction of the houses. I'm so close to where I need to be, I can feel it.

After sneaking through the streets, I get to a corner where I can see an old wooden sign protruding from the face of a house. The sign reads "Lucky's"—and I am sure in luck. I reach the door just as a group of Watchmen turns the corner. Without knocking, I turn the handle and slip across the threshold. The door clicks shut behind me and I am alone.

I press my back against the wall and stand clear of the windows. Outside, I can hear the Watch marching by, and some of them are whispering about where I could be. Their shadows hesitate against the dirty windowpanes. Their hands move, pointing in many

different directions before they turn and all head the same way—
away from here.

"You're a brave little one." A gruff voice breaks the daunting
silence the Watch leaves behind.

I squint in an effort to see through the blackness. It is the first
time I've taken a moment to actually look around the room, which
is cloaked in black, lightless. Chairs have been turned upside down
and hung on the edges of the tables. The floor is dull and wooden,
with darker knots the size of fists. A splintery bar top stretches the
length of the far wall, and abandoned, unused stools still stand in
front of it, like people waiting to be served. Behind the bar, tucked
in a corner, is the Widow. Even in the darkness, her violet eyes are
bright. She must have recently had a Vision.

"I have questions."

"I know. I've Seen."

This surprises me. I've never been in anyone else's Visions
before, at least, not that I know of. "You Saw me?"

"I did." The Widow leans forward so I can see her face. It's
wrinkled and wizened, like the trunk of a tree. Her skin is a dark
tan, as if she's spent her whole life out in the sun. "Those Watchmen
were close, weren't they? In my Vision, I couldn't see if you broke
free or not. Looks like you have."

"Thankfully." I wrap the robes around my form. The hem is
dirtied and soaked through with grime and rain that is creeping up
and into the thread. "And barely. At one point, I didn't think I'd
make it here."

"Well, you are here, young one. Tell me what you need." She
pats the bar top in an invitation for me to join her.

I peel myself off the wall. After pulling one of the bar stools out,
I climb up and sit, crossing my legs in front of me. "It's about one of

my Visions. It's not normal, and I don't know what to think about it. If I tell the Keeper, she'll quarantine me."

"She will." The Widow laughs and uncomfortably stares into my eyes. "What is strange about it?"

"When it is over, I can still hear it. Someone calls my name over and over again. The boy from the Vision."

The Widow flinches. It no longer seems as if she is looking at me, but rather looking through me. "Are you sure?"

"Yes, Ma'am."

"This is troubling news indeed."

"It is?"

The Widow nods and glances away. "Many years ago, when I was still a student at the Institution, something happened. A Dreamcatcher scare. And it happened to me."

"What does this have to do with my Vision?" I ask, though I try not to be rude about it.

"Everything, my dear. Everything. You see, after my Visions, I had a very peculiar symptom. I could hear the people in them, though the Vision was over. Eventually, the Dreams became so similar to the Visions, I couldn't tell the difference. I reported what was happening to our Keeper at the time, and immediately I was quarantined. For months, they kept me locked away in a padded cell, and as long as I was there, the Vision never returned.

"But the second they let me out, something happened. I crumpled to the ground as another Vision came to me. I felt like I was being attacked from the inside out. It was violating."

"What was the Vision about?"

The Widow looks at me then looks back at the window. "It was the same one I'd had before. I saw a black bird, a raven, and it flew over the City. Then the bird disappeared. But I could hear it speaking, and it called my name before telling me to 'Beware what you cannot See. Trust what you cannot trust.'"

I hook strands of my black hair behind my ear. "So, what happened?"

"The Keeper put me back in the cell. Eventually, I was dismissed from the Institution. They told me that it had to be that way and wouldn't say anything more. I found out later that what I was hearing was the voice of a Dreamcatcher, channeling into my Vision. The enemy had figured out a way of infiltrating the Institution, but it only worked with me. To rid themselves of any pending invasion, the Seers let me go." The Widow lowered her violet gaze, looking away from the door and everything around us.

I could sense her sorrow, because for a Seer, the Institution is our only home. We do not have families, for once we are born and display the traits of those who can See, they take us away and raise us together. I never knew my parents, never will, and I don't really care. The only semblance of family that I do have is Gabe and a few others whom I call friends: Constance, Brandon, and Mae. If I got put out of the Institution as well, I can only imagine myself missing them.

"You cannot let them know, young one. Keep this to yourself. Find out what it is the Dreamcatcher wants, and maybe you can help to prevent these sorts of attacks—"

"Attacks?" I put a hand to my head, imagining something burrowing into my brain, taking control. I remember Paradigm and how she looked at me—right at me—and no one else.

"That is what it is, my dear. This is an attack. We have been preparing for an ambush, and they have started with you," the Widow says. I imagine Paradigm again, this time in the interrogation room, so sure of herself and unafraid. I can hear her words: *Do you hear me, girl? He might come for you, but he doesn't know any better…*

"And if you can figure out what they want, you might even be able to help us all. The Widow lays a hand over mine, and her touch is cold. I want to pull my hand away, but I know it will be rude, so I keep still. "But you have to find out."

The thought of this already weighs heavily on me. I do not want to be any more involved in this war than I am. I want to blend in with the other Seers and prepare to fight alongside everyone else. I want to stay with Gabe.

I can't let the Keeper find out.

"You have not told me…what is your name?" The Widow finally takes her hand off of mine.

"Beatrice."

The Widow smiles, stepping into the shadows. "Well, Beatrice, you better get back to your bunk now. They will probably make their rounds soon."

She's right. Gabe's shift will end, and someone else will take over. Someone who won't let me get away with not being where I'm supposed to be.

"Thank you for your help…um…I don't know your name either, come to think of it. I've only ever heard you called 'The Widow.' Why is that?"

She laughs bitterly and that whimsical look returns to her eyes. "Ah, my Beatrice, I'll tell you. As it was then and is now, you cannot marry Citizens when you live in the Institution. This is an infraction, but one I was willing to break to be with my love, Cameron. They found out soon after, and he was taken to the gallows for breaking a high law. I was so heartbroken then, that everyone came to know me as the Widow. That is all I wish to be called, to forever remind our government and the Institution of what they stole away from me."

"I am sorry." It's all I can think of to say.

"Don't be sorry, just be smart. Don't let my mistakes become your own." She moves her hand, gesturing for me to go. "Now hurry before you get caught."

I don't have anything else to say to her. But when I leave, I take a new wealth of information with me. One, beware the Dreamcatchers. Two, do not tell the Keeper about the strange Visions. Three, do not let the Institution take away what I love.

It's the last one that haunts me the most.

CHAPTER SIX

The glass shooter clinks against a smaller, purple and gray marble, knocking it clear out of the circle. At the Institution, we play for keeps, so Mae reaches over and grabs the swirled marble and drops it into her black velvet pouch.

"I wanted that one." She shakes the pouch with a smile as big as her face and all the marbles click together.

I roll my eyes, since there are about three marbles that look just like it still sitting in the circle. She's trying to flirt with Brandon again, but of course, he's not paying attention. Brandon never pays attention. This is why he hasn't earned his raven's wings yet. While he has Visions, he doesn't quite mind them, so when it comes time to report, he gets all the details confused and the Vision ends up being pointless. Just like Mae's flirting. But it's fun to watch. And in a way, I can connect to Mae. She understands the desire to keep someone close.

I imagine if I had sisters, they would be like Connie and Mae. They are the closest thing to family that I will ever have, so I confide in them and trust them to keep my secrets safe. Well, most of my secrets. I don't tell them everything.

Gabe sits next to me, and between Mae and Brandon, Connie nibbles on a snack.

It's her turn, so Constance puts whatever she is eating down and picks up her shooter. Holding it in front of her thumb and pointer finger, she tilts her wrist and angles it just right to send the larger marble rolling toward the smaller ones. A bunch of them *clack* and *tink* together, but none of them make it outside the chalk circle.

"Darn it." Constance swears and picks up her snack again.

When I look at Gabe, he is already looking at me and my heart beats a bit faster. I didn't tell him about my visit with the Widow yet, and I still haven't decided if I am going to. Keeping it to myself these past three days has been hard, but I fear bringing Gabe into it. He's all I have on my side right now, and the only one who knows about the strange Visions. Even without me saying, we both know to keep them secret.

"It's your turn, Gabe." I remind him, since he's still looking at me.

"Oh yeah. I only have three marbles left in there anyway."

"Well, stop sucking and maybe you'll do a little better," Brandon cuts in with a laugh.

Gabe doesn't rise to the taunt. He flicks his marble into the circle and knocks out an amber one with gold flecks inside.

"Aww, that was my favorite," Connie mumbles through whatever is in her mouth, crumbs flying everywhere.

I laugh and half lean against Mae when Gabe whispers something in my ear. "What's going on?"

I sit up again and let the others take their turns shooting marbles. They aren't paying much attention to us, not even when I pull at Gabe's shirt and nod my head toward the window on the far side of the room. "We can talk there."

We both stand, and before the others have a chance to complain, I say, "I need to talk to Gabe. We forfeit."

"Then you forfeit your marbles, too!" Constance blurts, eager to have her amber one back from Gabe.

Gabe rolls the marble in her direction, then walks to the window. I follow him, and behind me, I can hear Mae, Connie, and Brandon continuing the game without us.

When we are alone, I speak to Gabe in a hushed whisper, careful to not let anyone overhear us. The last thing I need is to be quarantined. To have them take away what I love.

"Gabe, I can't say too much."

"Why not? I thought I was your best friend." Immediately, he is turned off by my aloofness. I can hear it in the way he clips his words.

"You are, and that hasn't changed. And it won't." I nervously cast a glance around the room. "It's just…a lot is at stake, is all. More than you know."

"Then let me know." Gabe follows my gaze. "I won't tell anyone else."

I hesitate. Should I tell him? Will he keep it secret? And if someone finds out, what will happen to Gabe? But if I don't tell him, he will probably hold it against me…and I can't lose him.

"Here, I will let you know something in exchange." Gabe barters with me, which only heightens my intrigue. What can he possibly say that has the same weight as what he wants me to tell him?

"I had another Vision. But this time, you were in it." Gabe brushes his hair back out of his eyes, and I can see the struggle in his gaze as he tries to recall the details. This is often a problem with those whose Visions have yet to mature fully—they forget them soon after, like a dream. This is why the Keeper documents Visions as soon as they happen.

"Me?" I put a hand to my chest. "A Vision about me?"

"Yes. It was you standing in the middle of a ring of Dreamcatchers. Armed Dreamcatchers. They were all pointing their weapons at you, like the firing squad at Paradigm's execution. I don't know if they were going to kill you, though." Gabe pauses. "There was one in particular who stood out." He looks away. "But I don't remember much about that one. I just can't remember."

I think about the Vision and what it might mean. It could be anything. Will I be captured by the Dreamcatchers?

"Maybe it's not really important," I reply.

"I hope it's not, Beatrice. I don't want anything to happen to you, and surely not at the hands of the Dreamcatchers." Gabe leans his elbow against the wall, resting his head on the palm of his hand. "So, what do you have to say to top that?" He smiles his usual smile, and for that moment, everything is back to normal.

"I visited the Widow the other night."

"You *what*?"

"She told me that I have to keep my Visions to myself and make sure the Keeper doesn't hear of them. So you can't tell anyone about anything that you know, Gabe."

Gabe searches my face, his violet eyes round with concern. "I won't, Bea. But…why?"

"Because too much is at stake."

He frowns. "You aren't telling me everything."

With a sigh, I stare into his eyes, wishing I could let him know. I want to grab him and tell him about the Dreamcatchers, and how the Widow was removed from the Institution. I want to tell him that we are all in danger if I don't figure out what the Dreamcatcher wants from me.

But I can't.

Nothing comes out. Gabe turns away from me and stares out the window into the courtyard below.

I do the same, eying the carefully manicured shrubbery and the songbirds that flitter back and forth, their warbling echoing off the walls. They are so alive in a city that seems so dead.

"I'm sorry, Gabe."

"I don't understand how you can keep something like this from me." Gabe doesn't look at me when he talks, and it bothers me.

"I'm doing it to protect you." I reach out and brush my fingers against his. This draws his attention back to me, probably because I've never touched Gabe like that before, but it seems like the right time to do so. It paralyzes us both, and we are left staring at each other. Words should be spoken here. Something should be done, but nothing happens. We just stare.

Finally, Gabe relents. "Whatever." He pulls his hand away from mine and walks away, leaving me standing by the window.

A shadow of a helicopter passes by, drawing my attention to the outside. Fury creeps up my arms and through my body, especially when I see in the reflection of the window that Gabe has not only walked away from me, but has walked right out of the room as well. Damn him. I wish he'd just understand that I'm doing this to protect him, but he is stubborn.

"What was that about?" Connie calls out, and I turn to see her watching the others as they make their moves with their marbles.

Heading back in their direction, I stop next to the circle, towering above it like the Institution towering over the City. My shadow engulfs all the glass pieces as they *click* and *clack*, pushing and repelling one another around the floor. "He's feeling a little grumpy today. You know how Gabe is when he doesn't get his way."

Mae giggles, plucking up a marble or two that she's won. "He's a brat when he doesn't get his way, isn't he?"

Brandon grins at Mae, ignoring that she has just taken over two of his favorite marbles.

Mae shoots me a look, telling me without words not to point out that she's the new victor of Brandon's favorite marbles.

"Exactly." I sit down and grab my pouch of marbles, looking at Brandon and Connie. "So, whose turn is it?"

"Well, Mae just went, so I guess that makes it Brandon's turn." Connie leans on the palms of her hands. "Do you think Gabe will come back? He didn't finish the game, and his marbles are all over the place."

"I think we should just take them if we win them. Fair game, right?" Brandon picks up his shooter and aims it toward the gathering of glass in the middle of the circle. Squinting, he examines the field, then sits up. "Who took my red and cyan marbles?"

"You said we forfeited anyway. So what's it matter? Just take the marbles." I don't really care that much. I still have a few of my favorites left in my pouch.

Mae innocently smiles, which of course pinpoints her as the culprit. Shrugging, my slender and too-small friend makes a vague gesture toward the other marbles on the floor. "Fair game, right? I won them."

I didn't know Brandon could turn into the color of an apple. "What? I wasn't even paying attention!"

"She won them fair and square." I speak with authority. Brandon seems to settle down instead of erupting like a little volcano. His coloring returns to normal, no longer the deep crimson that made him fruit-like. "Anyway, it's your turn, Brandon."

Brandon begrudgingly shoots his marble across the circle and it hits absolutely nothing. This is the last straw for our otherwise sensitive friend. "I don't want to play any more." He scoops his marbles out of the circle and shoves them in his green velvet pouch marked with a golden "B."

"Don't be a sore loser, Brandon." I roll my eyes, but he's not paying attention. Once the marbles are collected, he storms out of the room in a Gabe-like manner. "What is with boys today?"

"What is with them every day? I can never figure them out. And you know what? It's like they are all the same, throwing their little temper tantrums and storming off." Connie starts to pick her marbles up, collecting each glass piece until only mine and Mae's are left on the floor. "I guess that's the end of our game, though."

"Maybe they are just made like that," Mae hypothesizes, and in my head I think about Gabe and Brandon going through an assembly line as they are put together, their temper tantrums and all.

"Maybe. I don't see how they ever think any girl is going to like them if they act like that." I look back up at Mae and Connie and grin. "Boys will be boys."

We all fall into a fit of giggles that are much too girly, and reserved for when we are alone. Mae and I start to pick our marbles up at the same time. I look over my shoulder at the door, wondering where the boys have gone. Probably back to their bunks where they can sulk in private. Should I have followed Gabe? Is that what he wanted me to do? "Oh well."

"So, what's up between you and Gabe anyway, Beatrice? You two seem to be getting closer…well, with the exception of whatever just happened," Mae says.

I don't know where to start with that question. What *is* up with me and Gabe? "I don't know, really. One moment he wants to be close, and then the next minute he acts like this. And all because I won't tell him everything that's going on in my life. I mean…that's my choice, right?"

"Right." Mae finishes packing up her marbles and lets the bag fall beside her with a *plop*. "But he's probably just frustrated because he cares for you and maybe he feels helpless when he doesn't know everything that is happening."

"Well, he'll have to get used to it. He can't always know every little thing that I'm going through. I have some things that I'd rather keep to myself. Just as I'm sure you both have your own secrets that you wouldn't want to blab about. You know how it can be in the Institution; once something gets out, every Seer on every floor knows it within the day. That's why I trust you two. I *know* you wouldn't go yapping behind my back." I hold up one of my favorite marbles, a mother-of-pearl one with ivory swirls in the middle. It's rare, made of stone and not of glass, and I seldom play it for fear that someone else will win it. "With my Visions lately, it's impossible for me to tell you guys everything. I wish I could, really, I do."

Connie pats my shoulder. "We understand, Bea."

"But Gabe doesn't." My words are pouty, too much so.

"He will, though. Just let him calm down, and I'm sure he'll come around. Everyone always comes around!" Mae squeaks in her too-happy way, then leans over and gives me a hug, arms wrapped around my neck. "It'll be fine. I think it would take more than this for him not to like you anymore."

Connie smirks and ducks her head to catch my attention. "Like? I think it's much more than 'like' by now."

I blush. I'm not going to get into this conversation, so I quickly put an end to it before it turns into anything more. "I guess we should go back to our rooms and get ready for the next Training Games. We're going to get that Rachelle one way or another, and I could use some rest before we do."

The other two follow me out of the Recreation Room and down the long, dim hallways with the occasional flickering light. The whole way back to my bunk I wonder if I'm making the right choice in leaving Gabe to run away without chasing him. He's so confusing, I just don't know what to think anymore.

Then again, I hardly know what to think about most things these days.

CHAPTER SEVEN

The Institution is eerily quiet. I decide to walk the halls. Swinging my legs over the side of my bunk, my bare feet press flat against the black, laminate floor. Everything about the Institution is cold. My chest tightens, as if something is about to happen. I feel it squeezing around my heart like two hands desperately trying to hold on. Even the smell doesn't quite seem right. It is stale, not the purified air that is normally blown through the vents. It reminds me of the odor of a freezer–the flat scent of coldness.

My door slides open and the hall is dark. A few fluorescent lights flicker on and off down the long corridor. No one is monitoring the halls like they should be. Everything seems dead.

I continue down the hall, careful not to make any noise as I walk. The lights flicker and dim to an even dingier contrast as I make my way to wherever it is I am being pulled. With each step, my feet slowly press into the ground, then peel off it, heel to toe. I don't know where I am going but I do know I have to get there, and soon.

Suddenly, I am in the Meeting Room, a vast area created to hold the mass of Seers who live in the Institution. We usually gather here for assemblies and ceremonies. The room is large with black catwalks along the perimeter, hitched onto the walls. At the front, a large stage remains empty, with the podium ominously in the center. It is as if someone should be standing there, as the room feels full, like everyone has already gathered to the meeting, ready to listen to the speaker on deck. When I take a few more steps into the room, I notice that all of the Seers are indeed here.

But they are all dead.

Piles of stacked bodies litter the floor and all of their faces look horrified, frozen in an expression of absolute fear. Their vacant eyes are open, trained on me.

Why are they looking at me? Watching me? I feel guilty and scared all at once, as if I did something to cause this.

It is then I See a dense, looming fog encircling the Meeting Room, as if protecting, or maybe claiming, the hundreds of bodies. A tendril of the blackness stretches out toward me and the tightness in my chest returns. This time, though, the hands that squeeze my heart clutch harder, and I wonder if hearts can pop.

I have no choice but to run, because that's what my body tells me to do. I scramble for the doors, but they don't automatically slide open when I get close, as they normally do. I am trapped, and the arm of fog is getting closer. When I close my eyes to try and will myself out of the situation, I See the eyes of the dead, staring at me in contempt. Is this how I will die too? What did I do wrong?

⟡

The Keeper types on her holopad as I relay the last of my Vision. Just like every other time, she does not look happy. When I get to the end of my story, she looks up, as if expecting more. "And?"

"That is all, My Keeper. It stopped there."

"You do not know if it caught you?"

"No." I think it is for the better that I don't know if it did or didn't. I don't want to know, actually. I don't want to picture myself thrown together with the other, stiff corpses. A chill crawls up my spine. "I don't."

It doesn't occur to me until now that Gabe and the others were probably in those piles of bodies. I also realize that Gabe has not come to see me as he usually does after I have a Vision. Maybe this time, he just didn't know I had one. Usually as soon as the Keeper comes down my hall, the gossip starts about what Vision I might have had now. And as soon as Gabe gets the gossip, he's here. But not this time, and I desperately want him to be.

The Keeper stares at me in suspicion. "So it reached out for you, but it did not catch you?"

"I don't know if it did or not, My Keeper. The Vision ended there."

"And the corpses…you said they were all looking at you?"

"Yes, and they all looked scared. Petrified would probably be a better word for it, since their faces were all stuck like that. Mouths opened, eyes wide. Pale."

"People who are no longer living are usually pale, Seer Beatrice." The Keeper deadpans, not bothering to look up from her holopad. "Do you have any idea why your Visions have suddenly changed? Suddenly, they have become more…" She struggles to find a word for it. "Inconsistent. Unfinished."

"I feel like they are warnings, My Keeper. Just like how I saw the Dreamcatchers coming to the City, now I am seeing this. Something will happen here. I don't know what…but I know something will happen."

The Keeper's eyes find mine. "What you're saying is very serious,

Seer Beatrice."

"I know, My Keeper."

Her gaze shifts as she types, her brows slanted downward in concern. "We will have to up the security…and the training. Whatever this threat is, we must be prepared to defend against it. I'll send out word to the City's Watch and the news circuit and hopefully the Citizens will…"

"There weren't any Citizens, My Keeper. Just Seers. Hundreds of pairs of eyes. Looking at me, as if…" And that is when it hits me. "As if I should have warned them."

"And you have." The Keeper closes her datapad and stares back at me. "You better hurry to lunch, then. We are finished here." She says this more like a mother to a child, and it takes me back. I've never heard her speak in such a way before. In fact, I'd thought she was wholly incapable of it.

"Thank you."

She continues to watch me, her eyes searching my face in suspicion. That unsettling tightness in my chest starts to return. The maternal slip of the Keeper disappears. With a turn on her heel, she leaves.

I look at the clock. I have ten minutes to get to the cafeteria and get my lunch before a new day of training begins. My stomach grumbles, urging me to get going, despite the fact that I have no desire to eat. Not after that Vision.

After scrambling into my jumpsuit, I throw my hair up into a messy ponytail and check myself in the mirror. My eyes still glow, surrounded by the tattoo of the black and grey wings that marks me as a full Seer. I brush a few strands of night-black hair out of my face, then start out of my room at a jog in hopes of reaching the cafeteria in time.

When I get there, the line for food has died down. I rush through with my tray, collecting whatever cold sandwich and vegetables they throw on my plate, then book it to our usual table. Brandon, Connie, Mae and Gabe are deep in discussion about the upcoming Training Games, their trays mostly empty. I plop down next to Gabe, breathless.

"I heard Team C beat out Team D, and that they are going to face Team B now. Do you think they'll win?" Mae idly pushes some peas across her plate with her fork.

"Nah. With how Team B is doing? I mean, *we* couldn't even beat them. What makes you think Team C could?" Brandon replies, but looks at me when I join them. "You're late."

"She had a Vision." Connie notices the luminescence of my violet eyes, pointing at my face. She leans forward, elbows on the table, and whispers, "What was it about?" And then, to cap off her conversation with Brandon, "Team B didn't beat us. Rachelle did. There's a difference."

"Don't bother asking about her Vision. She won't tell you," Gabe snipes from across the table without bothering to look up.

I narrow my eyes, but direct my response to Connie. I won't rise to Gabe's childish and snarky remarks, but he's obviously still sore about our discussion the other day. "It was new. Everyone in the Institution was dead. There were piles of bodies everywhere, and they were all looking at me. All those eyes. On me. It was…eerie." Now Gabe looks up. I meet his gaze and continue. "A black smoke or fog surrounded them, and it tried to reach out and get me."

"Did it?" Mae is drawn to the conversation like a moth to light.

I shrug. "Don't know. The Vision ended." My stomach reminds me to actually eat the food in front of me, so I bite into my sandwich while the others all lapse into silence, thinking about the Vision.

"Were we dead too?" Gabe strikes at the heart of the matter. With Gabe, it was either now or never.

I speak with my mouth half full. "I assume so. Everyone was dead. Everyone but me. But if you are asking if I saw you guys specifically, no, I didn't." Swallowing, I look to the others. "I don't know what it could mean, but the Keeper said we will be going on high alert. She said we have to prepare."

"Prepare for what?" Brandon pushes his tray away.

"Not sure. But whatever it is, it can't be good." I manage to get another bite in before the buzzer sounds. Lunch is over. I stand up with a groan. "I didn't even get to finish." I decide to bring the sandwich with me, chomping into it as we walk along.

As the group of us approaches the trash cans to dump and stack our trays, I see Rachelle heading in our direction. Ever since her little stunt in the arena, she's been cockier and looks down at everyone, as if we are beneath her. Other Seers part the way for her, some even whisper behind her back. When she gets to where I am, she positions herself between me and the trash cans.

The thing about Rachelle is, as much as you try to hate her, she has a natural charm that consumes her being. It's annoying. From her pretty blonde hair, delicate features and perfect stature, most find themselves drawn to her. Most everyone but me.

"What do you want, Rachelle?"

"I want to let you know that I'm not done with you yet."

"And?" I'm not impressed.

"That's all!" she squeaks merrily, turns, and leaves.

"She's so *strange*." Mae dumps everything off her tray and into the trash cans. "Who cares if she's not done with you yet? Who does she think she is anyway?"

Who *does* she think she is? I don't know. She's threatened by me though, in much the same way as the Keeper, I've noticed.

"Let's go before we are late for training." I change the subject, stacking my tray with the others. My stomach still protests for food, but in the clamor of the cafeteria, no one can hear.

Just like nobody can hear the rush of questions left over from my Vision that swirl together inside my mind.

◇

Gabe and I meet up after training to go to history class together. I immediately feel better when he's by me, and as we walk to class, I sometimes let my hand brush against his and pretend it's a mistake. At some point, he grabs my hand and holds it, entwining my fingers with his, and we walk this way until we get to our destination, shielded by the crowds of students heading to the same class we are. Maybe he isn't mad at me anymore. Or at least, it seems that way. Reluctantly, I let go of Gabe and we blend into the sea of other Seers.

This is one of the last courses we have to take for the year, alongside our survival course. The classroom is packed with other Seers our age, including Brandon and Connie who are already seated up front. Gabe chooses a couple of seats a row behind them so we can sit in a group. When he sits, he nudges the back of Connie's chair with his foot and grins.

"Hey Gabe, Bea. Ready for tonight's lecture?" Connie asks.

"Yes, actually. With everything that's going on, I'd like to know a bit more about the lead-up." I am excited about tonight. Though we've been taught about the emergence of the Seers and Dreamcatchers before, today we're going to go a bit more in depth about our creation. Until this point, we've always been told that we're born with a "gift" and that was the end to the conversation, but not the end of the actual explanation. There's more that we don't know, more that we'll find out tonight.

The Instructor enters the room, wrapped in his robe with the black satin sash that marks his station as a teacher. His name is Instructor Daniel and he's not that much older than we are. He most likely chose to become a teacher after his Seer training, since we all get to pick an occupation when the Keeper thinks we are ready to leave our lessons. Recently, he replaced an Instructor who passed away from old age over the summer. Most of us enjoy his classes because he's the young, cool teacher who lets us go on and on about certain topics, even if it means he won't ever reach the end of his lesson.

"If we can all settle down, I'd like to get this class started as soon as possible." Daniel steps behind a long desk with a black top and starts to unpack his books from a hemp satchel slung around his shoulder. The books are all bound in leather and are rare to find these days. Most books are kept on our digipads, as paper is pretty scarce and inefficient.

I scoot my desk closer to Gabe's and smile, and of course, when he smiles back, it's handsome and perfect. It makes my ability to actually concentrate on the class a little bit harder.

With a flick of a switch, the lights in the classroom dim, and the projector warms up to a bright glow. On the screen, the words "History of the Seer" spin in circles around a central axis, rotating endlessly. Daniel stands in the light of the projection, and his head contorts the words on the screen. "Welcome to history class. Tonight is one of your most important lessons. It is a confidential class, one that requires you to sign a statement promising that what you hear will not be repeated outside of the classroom. It will be assumed that others either share the same information you do, or they do not. Nothing here is repeated." Daniel's gaze slides over the other students in the room. There are about twenty of us in total, and when I turn to look around, everyone is wearing the same, grave expression. No one told us we'd have to sign a waiver today, and the gravity of this lesson hadn't seemed so heavy until now.

On our digipads, a screen with the contract flickers to life, and the line where we are supposed to sign our name pulsates, waiting for us to put the pen to the screen. Daniel waits as well, and one-by-one we pick up our styluses and scribble our names on the screen.

I stare down at my name and bite on my lower lip. "Did you know we had to do this?" I whisper the words to Gabe, glancing sideways at him as he finishes signing his name too.

"Nope, but I guess we don't really have a choice, do we? I don't know about you, Bea—" Gabe puts his stylus down and looks up at me. "But I want to pass this class and never have to take another one again. Don't you?"

I smile at him. "Yes. I do."

Daniel waits until the last signature registers, and only then does he begin the class. "Good. I am glad we are all on board today."

We don't have a choice.

"So, we are going to start with the creation of the Seers. How did we come to be? How come our abilities are so different from one another?" Daniel looks at me when he says this, but I pretend not to notice. Everyone sitting here knows that my Visions are almost clearer than those of the Keeper herself. They very well could be, since no one ever talks about her Visions anyway.

"Thousands of years ago, Seers existed among society. They were given the gift of prophecy from the ancient gods, or, as we know it, the Maker. Most were described as being blind, others as speaking in riddles and nothing more, but the one thing they did have in common was that they were oft respected and revered for their Sight.

"But as history wore on, the Seers were spoken of less and less, and eventually they disappeared out of the stories and recollections altogether. Those who claimed they had the Sight were mocked and abused as being false and nothing but entertainers at best. Some, the rare who actually possessed the gift, were used for profit, and those who had the money to purchase the Seers' services were the only ones who could benefit from their Sight." Daniel paused here and clicked a button on the small remote that he carried in his hand. Images of the evolution of Seers flipped over the screen, from women with long hair who sat on high, golden stools, to old men with wrinkled, blind eyes who were kept in shackles, penned up in side-show trailers.

"And then the world was left without Seers altogether. Terrible things happened, wars destroyed whole cities, and mankind was reduced to almost nothing. That is when the Institution decided that it needed to recreate the gift of Sight once more. If people could See into the future, then they could prevent the possibility of great battles annihilating what was left of man."

The screen flickers again, and this time a very old picture of the Institution pops up, rising high above the City, with suited people walking in and out of its rotating doors. Nowadays, it's very rare for people to come and go from the Institution, since there really isn't a time when Seers would venture into the City, or Citizens into the Institution. I lean forward in my seat, squinting to make out the details of the photograph. Flowers and shrubbery used to be planted around the building, and flower boxes were placed in almost every window, supporting hanging blossoms that dripped down the sides.

It looks beautiful, nothing like the industrial, stern structure that we have now.

Daniel continues with his lesson, entrapping each of us in his every word. "And so they made a serum that was secretly placed in the City's drinking water. This serum was tested for many years in the safety of the Institution, and it was said that it would search the genes of the Citizens and find only those who had the original mutation of the Sight, eventually restoring the ability to them. It could take just once, or it could take generations, the Institution did not know for sure."

Another student raises her hand, and with a nod from Daniel she stands up and asks her question. "How long ago was this, then?"

The Instructor points at her, smiling. "Good question. This was about four generations ago. So, it is still new and fresh in our history, but it's not something we like to…linger on."

"Why?" I ask, curious as to why we keep this a secret.

"Well, because the serum didn't only bring out our ability, but it also amplified that of the Dreamcatcher. Essentially, we manufactured our own enemy, a kind of people who possess certain Seer-like abilities, but can only look back in time and not forward."

"So we made up our own enemy?" another student calls out, her tone a bit incredulous.

"We sure did. Dreamcatchers function a bit differently as well, each having their own sort of niche. They need Citizens to recharge and heal themselves. They must have Citizens in order to thrive. They are their strength and their weakness." Daniel clicks a button and pictures of The City start to scroll across the screen.

Now Gabe speaks up. "So what happened to the serum? If everyone started to freak out about the Dreamcatchers?"

"The serum eventually had to be discontinued, as the Keeper

ruled it too dangerous if it was also bringing about the Dreamcatchers. They were becoming much too powerful, their mutations changing even more every day. Their power to See into the past and know one's intentions started to shift into much, much more."

He paused the pictures on the Institution, a newer photo, one that reflected the state of the grim building the way it looked now, with its shadowy exterior and tinted windows. Sleek and refined, the architecture was vastly different than the faded brick row homes and stores of the City. "A device called the Beacon was created for the rare event that the effects of the serum need to be reversed. It also destroys any matter that comes into its light, turning the object to dust, or so they say. We know very little about the Beacon, as its particulars are kept under wraps. Even the oldest Seers have no idea what the extent of its power is, and as an Instructor, I'm left in the dark as to what else I can say about it. I'm not even exactly sure where it is kept. Or if it still exists."

The class is eerily quiet as we are left to digest the information just given to us. It's the tip of the iceberg, as there's probably so much more to the story than we are allowed to know. I raise my eyebrows when Gabe looks at me, and with a shrug of my shoulder I let him know that I'm as shocked and confused as he is.

"I know it is a lot to process. It is. It's hard to think about the Dreamcatchers coming from the same source that has given us our abilities. It's hard to comprehend what the serum truly did, and why we need a weapon in case it was a mistake ever putting it in the drinking water. I sincerely hope, despite the recent Visions of an impending attack—" Daniel looks at me when he says this. "—that we never have to see the Beacon in action."

A boy who sits a few seats to the left of me muses aloud, "I never knew about any of this stuff. It's all so…so…amazing."

Instructor Daniel flicks the lights back on and the projector turns off, stealing away the image of the Institution in the process. "We have a lot that goes into our history, ladies and gentlemen. Some you will learn as you continue your education here at the Institution, but there's much of it that you won't ever be able to find out. We must trust in our Keeper that it is best this way, for sometimes too much knowledge is a dangerous thing."

Gabe laughs and whispers, "Then they shouldn't make us sit in class all day long."

Brandon, Connie and I giggle along with the sentiment, and I peek up at the Instructor to see if he heard. Luckily, Daniel is busy answering a question from another student, and we are in the clear. The class dissipates into their own conversations, little groups and discussions forming about what we just learned.

"Well, it seems we learn something new about the Institution every day, don't we?" Connie picks her multi-pocketed book bag off the ground and slips her digipad into it.

"This place certainly has its secrets." I chew on my lip, the words bringing about an uneasy feeling, like a premonition of things to come, without an actual Vision to accompany it. "Too many secrets."

CHAPTER EIGHT

I don't remember my parents at all, but sometimes I dream about them. I know they are dreams and not Visions because I never wake with my eyes glowing, or the headache that usually follows. The people and events in my Visions usually feel strange and disconnected. But when I wake up from a dream about my parents, I feel as if I know them, as if I've always known them, as if they are disappointed in me.

In one dream, I'm about to take part in the Seeing Ceremony. I am ready to officially act in my role as a Seer, but I am young. Too young. Usually, you do not get to this point until eleven or twelve years of age, but in my dream, I am maybe three, and I feel so lost and abandoned on the stage, standing in front of a hundred strangers. They are all wearing white, faces void of any emotion or indication that they care for me even a little bit. In the middle of the crowd, the only two people in color are my mother and my father.

They look totally different than I do. Instead of jet black hair, my mother has curly ringlets of gold, and my father's head is bald, reflecting the glimmering overhead lights. Mother is wearing a polka-dot dress, red with white dots and a high collar with buttons that stop just under the chin. It's classic and beautiful on her, and no one else looks as radiant as she does. My father is wearing a red suit, one that looks far too expensive for a Seeing Ceremony, but maybe he wanted to look his best while watching his daughter earn her raven's wings.

I realize, though, that I am the only person on the stage, and I suddenly feel very alone. I begin to cry for my parents. They don't react, and instead keep staring at me as if I am a complete stranger. How can I know who they are, but they do not know I am their daughter, waiting for them to come and get me, waiting for them to hold me and hug me and assure me that the rest of my life is going to be okay? I can do this. I can handle the pressure of being one of the greatest Seers the Institution has ever had. I can handle the pressure that comes along with informing the City if the next day will be safe or not.

But they aren't coming to hold me, and I'm left on the stage, little fists balled up to my teary eyes, crying. Out in the crowd, my parents' color starts to fade away. My mother's dress is going from a howling red to a faded, dull grey. Eventually, she blends in with everyone else, along with my father. She seems distant now, and there's some sort of recognition for me in her eyes, like she truly knows me and my pain, but it soon fades. They both disappear within the sea of white, and I can no longer discern them from the others. My parents are gone, and I am alone.

But when I turn to run off the stage, I am different. I am grown-up, and a grown-up Gabe steps out to block my way. He holds out his arms to embrace me, and I don't feel so alone anymore.

⬦

A month later, Brandon finally earns his wings. After his successfully reporting full consecutive Visions without any confusion, the Keeper deemed it time for him to join the Seeing Ceremony, along with a few others who have been waiting for their day to come. The Ceremony is today, and I am excited to have a day off from our brutal training.

From my closet, I pull out a flowing gown. It is white and plain, with only a long, ribboned bow to tie in the back. Everyone wears white on the day of a Seeing Ceremony, instead of our day-to-day black and grey jumpsuits and robes. It is a time of celebration, to acknowledge one another and the gift that we've been given. To be happy to be what we are. I think of my dream parents in red, bold against the stark white of the crowd. I think of my mother who seemed to know me, but suddenly didn't anymore.

I decide to leave my hair down, which is rare. There's too much of it, to be honest. And it's too thick for its own good. I sometimes debate wanting to cut it all off, to keep it short and by my ears, but Mae and Connie always tell me how jealous they are of my long hair, and for whatever reason, I listen to them when they insist on not cutting it.

The black tresses tumble down almost to my waist, and I drag some of it behind my ears to keep it out of my face. When I look in the mirror, I can hardly believe the girl standing there is me. I look radiant, like a light in the darkness. What will Gabe think when he sees me in my gown? Will he even care?

Sometimes, I wish we were allowed makeup like the Citizens. I think I'd look pretty with some lipstick or blush, but the Keeper has banned cosmetics, reminding us always that we are not here to be vain, we are here to See and protect the people. She is the only one to wear make-up, and usually only does so for important ceremonies.

Someone knocks on my door and I snap out of staring at my reflection. I push a button and the door slides open, revealing Mae and Connie dressed in their white gowns.

"Isn't this exciting?" Mae spins in a circle and the skirts of her dress open up around her like a blossoming flower.

Connie reaches out and touches some of my hair. "You look so pretty with your hair down, Bea."

"Thanks." I smile at her compliment and am filled with hope that Gabe will think the same. "Are you both ready?"

"Just waiting on you. Gabe's down the hall. He said he'd meet us at the hub." Connie lets the hair drop back into place.

I follow them to where Gabe is. Everyone in the halls is dressed in white, the girls in their gowns, and the boys in their ceremonial robes. Gabe stands, staring down another corridor, his right arm folded over his chest, grabbing the other arm.

"Gabe! We got her!" Mae is a bit on the hyper side today, and her voice easily rises above the others. She nudges me and grins. "Go get 'em."

Connie has some cinnamon candies with her, and she starts to pop them in her mouth. The spicy scent wafts in the air as she chews into them, one-by-one.

Gabe fleetingly looks at Mae when she calls to him, but his eyes are immediately drawn to me. When he sees that I've noticed his stare, he glances away, and a blush quickly follows. I pretend I didn't see it, but I feel the same blush warm my stomach from the inside, and I glance away too.

"Let's go, or we are going to be late. Brandon will never forgive us." Gabe speaks to no one in particular and starts walking. We follow him, Mae half skipping, Connie chewing on her candy, and me hoping Gabe will look at me like that again.

The closer we get to the Meeting Room, the larger the crowd becomes. We funnel through the doors, and the anxiety of my Vision comes rushing back, seizing me. I stop a moment and the people behind me crash into my frozen form. A few swear at me, which draws Connie's attention.

"Are you coming, Bea? Let's go! We want to get a good place to stand." Connie pulls my hand and drags me into the room. I have no choice but to follow.

We push and shove our way to the front of the standing area. Huge screens have been set up so everyone can see the proceedings, even if they can't see the stage. I find I am not the only one looking around, though. Everyone takes note of the armored and machine gun carrying Watchmen who are stationed on the catwalks and the second floor landing. Their guns are held close to their chests, at ease, but every one of them is on alert.

"What is all this for?" Mae's previous sunny nature is dampened, and the brightness that warmed her features begins to fade.

"It's because of Beatrice," Gabe notes flatly. The truth stings me, and I feel it in my bones. It is because of me; it has to be.

"Because of Beatrice?"

"Please don't say that too loudly." I notice a few glances shot in my direction from the people around me. Some even back away, perhaps afraid that they'll be shot if the Watchmen have to open fire.

Mae repeats in a whisper, "Because of Bea?"

"Yes. Remember her last Vision?" Gabe continues, despite my request to keep it quiet. Others are listening, though they pretend not to. "The Keeper probably called the Watchmen here, just in case. After all, we are all gathered in one place...just like we were in her Vision."

With a mouthful of candy, Connie adds, "But we were all dead in her Vision."

A pause.

Gabe points to the Watchmen. "And that is why they are here. To keep that from happening."

If the other Seers didn't know about my Vision before, they certainly will now. Like ripples of water, they begin to whisper to one another and the story spreads outward until everyone looks a bit panicked.

"Great, Gabe," I mutter, but before I can say anything more, the Keeper steps out onto the stage and to her podium. She is also dressed in white, and her hair has been intricately curled and pinned up. Her gown is so long it drags on the floor behind her, looking as if her feet aren't touching the ground when she walks. The effect almost makes her look pretty.

Then there is her raven, a stark contrast against her white gown. The black bird caws loudly and stretches his wings out to an impressive span. Pushing off her shoulder, he flies to a wooden perch that has been set up by the edge of the stage.

"Welcome, everyone, to the Seeing Ceremony." When the Keeper speaks, she uses her arms and gestures in long, graceful motions. She reminds me of a giant bird when she does this, especially in her flowing skirts, which continue to settle about her, like ruffled feathers returning to their natural state.

"Today we are here to mark Seer Brandon, Seer Lacey, and Seer Emelia as full Seers. They have earned their wings after their diligent dedication and intense studies. In keeping with our Code, they've successfully reported their Visions to me, their Keeper, and I've deemed the clarity of those Visions to be acceptable."

On the large projection screen, I watch as the camera zooms in on Brandon's chubby cheeks as they pull back into a wide smile. He's scanning the crowd for us, but we are so buried in the thick of it all, he'll probably never succeed in finding us.

When I look around, people are still staring at me. They continue to whisper, and very few of them actually pay attention to the Ceremony. Those who aren't looking at me stare up at the Watchmen pacing back and forth with their machine guns.

The Keeper probably knows there is a distraction, because she clears her throat in an attempt to draw attention back to the proceedings. "Seers, I wish for you all to take one another's hands as we pray together and give thanks to the Maker for the gift of our Sight. We'll pray for the continued clarity of Seer Brandon, Seer Lacey, and Seer Emelia's Visions, and we will pray that we all remain protected from the threat of the Dreamcatchers."

My fingers brush against someone else's fingers, and after they intertwine with mine, I look up to find Gabe knowingly staring down at me. He bows his head and prays, whispering the words loudly enough so I can hear them. It's not until he's halfway through his prayer that I realize he's not praying at all, but is speaking to me. "Listen, I don't know what is going on…but if you need my help, I am here for you. Just as long as you stop lying to me."

Covered by hundreds of other whispers, I continue our conversation by "praying" in return. "I am not lying to you, Gabe."

"Then what are you doing?"

I stare into his violet eyes. "I told you. I'm protecting you."

The prayers around us taper to an end. Gabe and I look back to the stage, where the Keeper is motioning for the tattoo artists to come out and set up their stations. Around us, caterers pull sheets off long tables that are lined up around the perimeter of the arena floor. They reveal different kinds of pastries, cakes, and bowls of multi-colored punch, a pleasant distraction from the presence of the Watchmen who continue to be on guard.

"While our Seers are enduring the application of their tattoos, please feel free to visit the refreshment tables." The Keeper makes one of those birdlike sweeping motions toward them.

Usually, there would be a rush for the tables at this point, but no one is moving right away. People are still staring at me.

Gabe is still holding my hand. He tugs it, encouraging me to head toward the food. "Maybe the others will follow."

"It doesn't look like it. You shouldn't have said anything." I can't help but to be a little spiteful. Now I'm not only the Seer who predicted the invasion of the Dreamcatchers, but I'm also the Seer who predicted everyone else's deaths.

"They deserve to know the truth." Gabe politely nudges people out of his way as he heads toward the pastries and other goodies. Mae and Connie follow after, gabbing to each other.

"But it's not the truth. We don't know what the truth is yet, Gabe."

"But you saw it."

"And not everything I See turns out to be true!" I stop walking, forcing Gabe to come to a stop with me.

He frowns and lets go of my hand. "Most of what you See comes true. Most of it. That is why you are so important to the Institution, and we are all nothing."

"That's not entirely correct—"

"It is! Look around! The Watch is here because of what you saw. But if I saw the same thing, the Keeper wouldn't even have acted on it. She'd just chalk it up to another fuzzy Vision. She'd put it on her list of 'Maybes' and leave it at that. But if you told her that tomorrow we'd all turn into fish, she'd fill the arena up with water in preparation." Gabe's speech has caught the attention of many others, including the Keeper. From the stage, I can see her watching us, and even though she can't hear what is being said, she can see the way the others are anxiously crowding around Gabe and me.

"Keep it down," I hiss, my gaze flickering to the others. By the time Gabe is through, they will hate me. I don't understand why he insists on continuing, why he would put me in this position. Gabe is supposed to be my friend, he's supposed to care for me, not put me out there in front of everyone. And I do mean everyone, because by the end of the day, the whole arena will have heard of this conversation.

He does listen, though, at least as far as quieting down goes. His violet eyes find mine, and I detect a hint of sadness in the way that he stares at me. "You can't deny it."

"I don't know what is going to happen. I don't know what my Vision meant, and I don't know what will happen...and if the Keeper wants to act on everything that I say to her, that is her choice. But please stop making this my problem. I can't control what I See, and I can't control what the Keeper wants to do with it." When I look back at the table, Connie has already picked up about ten pastries, with one shoved into her mouth. I want to smile, but the weight of everyone staring in my direction prevents me from doing so.

"Fair enough." Gabe follows my gaze to the tables. "Come on, let's eat."

We push our way through the crowd, and eventually people begin to break off and go their separate ways. I look to the stage where Brandon clutches the sides of his chair and grits his teeth while the artist tattoos the raven's wings on his face. The Keeper is still standing there and watching me. A chill runs up my spine and sends shivers through my body.

"Do you think he'll pass out?" Mae's voice breaks into my thoughts. She's holding a small plate with a half-eaten chocolate glazed donut on it. Because Mae is so tiny, it looks like her dress is swallowing her up. She's practically swimming in it.

"Nah." Connie grins and points at Brandon. "He's doing great. Look at him."

We all look at the same time. Brandon is still where he was before, eyes squinting shut, then releasing. The tattoo artist is probably telling him to stop squinting, but just as soon as Brandon does, he goes right back to it.

We laugh, or at least the others do. I make a noise that is akin to laughter, but it's forced and obvious.

"What's wrong?" Mae puts her little hand on my arm. Her touch is warm, her skin so soft. You'd never think that she is one of the best fighters we have on Team A. But she's small and crafty. I'm glad she's on my team.

"Nothing. Just some business that happened out on the floor. No one is going to let it go." I don't mean to be accusatory, but I do shoot a glance to Gabe, who hasn't bothered to touch any of the food yet. Then again, neither have I.

"Maybe if you tried to let it go, it wouldn't bother you so much, Bea." Mae's advice, though offered nicely, seems like something Gabe would say. I frown at her. She frowns back, though it's more confused than angry.

"She's right." Gabe nudges me, elbow to elbow. "Just let it go. We're supposed to be celebrating."

I lift my chin, gesturing to the others who have chosen to remain behind on the floor, talking in their groups and shooting sidelong glances in my direction. "They aren't celebrating. They're talking about us."

"So let them talk, Bea." Connie forces a plate with a piece of chocolate cake on it toward my middle. I have no choice but to take it, or risk getting the icing on my gown. "Eat up."

I carefully pick up the piece of cake and take a bite. It's not often the Institution gives us anything so rich and delicious, and I sincerely try to enjoy it. As I chew, though, I notice the Keeper approaching the microphone. On the projectors, the cameras have zoomed in on her face, which is stern and sharp.

"Something is wrong," I note, and after one more bite of savory cake, I ditch the plate on the table.

"What?" Gabe looks up at the screen, hair falling in front of his eyes. "Oh."

The Keeper taps on the microphone, and the muffled noise loudly echoes through the room, catching everyone's attention. We quiet as we are trained to do when the Keeper is present, and once the room is silent, she stands up straight and begins to speak.

"As our new, full Seers are finishing their tattoos, the Institution has a very important announcement to make. To some, it might be upsetting, but we've entered a new era in our fight against the Dreamcatchers."

There hasn't been an actual fight just yet. That's the first thought that comes to my mind. We've only been preparing to fight. But to say we've been fighting all the time makes the message that much more urgent. It makes it more real, more now.

"Our training exercises will change." The Keeper looks at all of us, speaking in a tone that one would use when trying to inspire their troops before they go out into battle. "There will be no more room for the weak. A great threat has been detected, and I am sure you've noticed that we've upped our security as a precaution."

Again, eyes are on me. This time, I don't bother to look.

"In order to stay prepared, we will be introducing live rounds to the training games."

The collective breathing in the room stops.

Did I hear her correctly?

"We will be using Citizen convicts as our targets, and they will be armed." The Keeper pauses as the tension in the air becomes crisper and more taut. "We have, up until this point, kept our Seers under protection for the good of the City. But what good is it if we are protecting Seers who aren't strong enough to protect in return? You need to be able to take a life. To kill. To protect the Citizens."

"Is she serious?" Connie whispers, a waver in her words.

"It is a new day! We are at war, and now, more than ever, we need to be strong! We will begin to use live rounds tomorrow. Get a good night's rest, and remember, it is for the good of the City." The microphone clicks off and the Meeting Room is silent.

The wave of whispers starts somewhere in the back, and by the time it reaches us, everyone is talking. Connie is freaking out and has reduced herself to tears. Mae is trying to keep Connie calm with reassuring pats on the back. Gabe reaches for my hand and when he finds it, he holds it without saying a word about anything.

CHAPTER NINE

With nothing else on my mind but the upcoming Training Games and our new mandate to use live rounds, I find it hard to believe that Mae is so excited about our journey off our bunk floor.

Mae, Connie, and I are packed into an elevator that speeds down its shaft, passing floor after floor at a high speed that makes my stomach feel like it is in my throat.

"So, has Gabe stopped being ornery?" Connie leans against the metal walls that box us in.

"Somewhat, I guess. It's definitely better than it was before." I shrug a shoulder, not quite content with my observation. "But who knows? I was pretty angry with him after that whole thing at the Ceremony. Maybe he's annoyed with me again."

Connie picks at a scratch on her arm. "Boys forget pretty quickly."

"Yeah. Brandon forgets every day that I like him." Mae laughs and playfully pushes my arm. "Sometimes, their skulls are so thick that nothing gets to their brains."

I grin and nudge Mae back. "Maybe you're right."

"Ooh! I can hear them already!" Mae suddenly squeals as the elevator slows and comes to a stop.

Today is our turn to visit the lower levels of the Institution, where the young Seers are kept. It is a requirement for all girls over the age of fifteen to help at least once a month in the children's wards. We don't interact much with the young Seers, as there's such a gap between what they know and what we know, and sometimes it becomes frustrating when communicating. It's not one of my favorite things to do, but today is important because when Mae, Connie and I are done with our visit, we need to come up with a report on how the younger Seers can be better integrated with the rest of the Institution.

The doors slide open and the three of us step out and just barely miss being run over by a gaggle of Seer children who run full speed down the hallway and turn a corner, laughing and screaming. It's far too noisy for my liking, and I cast one of the Caretakers a sympathetic glance. In return, the Caretaker bows her head. "Seer Beatrice."

Maker, how I hate how they all know me.

I nod and ask over my shoulder, "So, where are we going to go?"

"I want to visit the nursery," Mae blurts before Connie can get anything out.

"The nursery seems fine." Connie shrugs without much conviction either way.

"Fine. We'll go there, even if I don't understand why you are so obsessed with the nursery, Mae." I start down the hall in the direction of the highly-guarded nursery. Watchmen have been placed down the perimeter of the hallway, about every twenty feet or so. I feel like the infants are better protected than any of us in the Institution, and

I suppose it makes sense when they are so helpless…and useless.

"Because they are just so cute! I wish that I could have a baby of my own when I grow up." Mae's words lilt at the end.

"That's just stupid to think about. It'll never happen. You know we can't have babies. Only the Keeper has babies, until she has a girl, and even then, no one has any idea who the baby is until she is told herself." Connie proudly puffs her chest up. "For all you two know, I could be the next Keeper."

I laugh at the notion. Connie would be the worst Keeper, only focused on when her next snack would be, or the next game of marbles. Nothing would ever get done in the Institution. "Okay, Connie."

Connie frowns. "What? Don't you think I could be the Keeper?"

"I think the conversation is kind of ridiculous myself. The Keeper isn't going anywhere any time soon. It's not like she's that old or something," I say. But who knows? Seers don't live all too long. Most Seers lose their sanity and expire somewhere near their sixties because of the strain on their minds. The Keeper is thought to live longer than the rest because her powers are more controlled, but no one has ever really been clear about that. We know little about the deaths of Keepers in the past, as it doesn't seem to be information that the Institution gives out willingly.

"Yeah, she's not old." We get to the main doors of the nursery and are stopped by the Watchmen. Mae waves. "Hello! We're here to see the little babies!"

The Watchmen take out their identification devices and each one of us has to confirm our IDs with a fingerprint and retina scan. I place my thumb on the datapad's screen and watch as a blue line runs down the length of it and bends over the shape of my thumb. A beep signals that it is done, and the Watchman holds the device up to scan my eyes next. When both precautions are done, my name and picture flicker to life on the datapad, identifying me as "Seer Beatrice, Bunk 34A."

Connie and Mae undergo the same routine, and while I wait, I peek into the hallway beyond, spotting only more guards, their guns, and bright halogen lights. I think about Mae's wish for a baby of her own, and I can't quite understand where a thought like that would come from. Seers don't have children—we can't. Each of us is sterilized in infancy to protect us.

In history class, we learned that when Seers were first created, no one thought reproduction might be a problem. Fairly quickly everyone realized that most Seer's offspring never lived past the age of ten. The children's gift of Sight would go horribly wrong, and their Visions would break them down, filling them with pain and destroying a part of their minds in the process. This happened to everyone's offspring except for the Keeper's. Once it was realized, the Keeper decided that no Seer should be born into such conditions, except for a child of her own—one who could bear the advanced gift.

But no one ever knows who that child is until the child is told herself, as Connie mentioned. Sometimes, people have their guesses based off how advanced someone's Visions can actually be, and I'm more than aware that there are many who have their bets hedged on me, though I can't stand for an instant of thinking that the Keeper might be my mother. The woman doesn't seem to have a heart of her own, let alone a part of it to give to a child.

Mae and Connie pass security, and the Watchmen step aside to let us continue into the nursery. We pass a couple of staffing rooms, filled with chattering Caretakers who are on their breaks. They fall silent as we walk by, but then go right back to talking once we are past them. I smirk and look back at the other girls. "I wonder what they are talking about?"

"Probably how cute the babies are!" Mae beams and claps her hands together twice. "We're almost there!"

We pass by a section of the ward that is mostly quiet. The Receiving Room. This is where the Seer babies are brought after they are delivered in the City's hospitals and their violet eyes are noticed, the sign of their gift.

Then they are brought here, into a new family, their new home: the Institution.

I shudder, the silence creeping through my body like a parasite.

In that same history class, we learned what happens to the Dreamcatcher babies when they are born. They are also born with violet eyes, but they lose the color in a few days. After that, they are quite simply snuffed out, like a little flickering candle flame that never had the chance to burn. Sometimes, it even takes a couple of years before they're identified as Dreamcatchers, years of bonding, memories and love shared between parent and child before the Watchmen come and put an end to it. And anyone caught harboring one of these children is subject to the pain of death. For their whole family. The consequences are severe, and no one has ever tested it that I have heard of. There are rumors, though, of an underground group of Citizens with Seer or Dreamcatcher babies that they have kept or, in the case of the Dreamcatchers, smuggled out of the City and to Aura.

But those are just rumors.

Finally, we reach the nursery doors, and the two Watchmen who flank them step aside to let us through. Inside, there are about three rows of ten infants, each swaddled in their own cradles. They vary in age, some of them newer than others, some of them close to their first year, soon to be transferred out into the children's wards.

Mae rushes over to the newer ones, who are at the front of the lines, and she bounces on her toes, waiting for a Caretaker to come over and help her. "Can I hold this one?" She asks this as if the child is more like a pet, and it occurs to me that to Mae that is what these babies are—pets.

"So, for our report, what do you suggest that we write about?" Connie gets right to the point, which is fine with me. The sooner we can figure out what to write, the sooner we can get out of here.

"What was the assignment again?" Mae asks as the Caretaker places the infant into her arms. Mae cradles the baby with extreme care, then turns and walks over to us as if she were walking on a tightrope without a safety net under it.

Connie pulls a folded up paper out of her robes and unwrinkles it. "The assignment says that we must think of one way we can improve a part of the children's wards that would not only benefit the children but the Institution as a whole."

"Hmm. That sounds a little rough." Mae looks up at the other caretakers to see what they are doing with their babies, and then tries to emulate them by bouncing the tiny bundle in her arms. "Maybe if they let us take care of the babies in our bunks!"

"*No!*" I blurt almost immediately, imagining how it would be if we had a baby crammed into our small, personal space along with us. A crying, wriggling little baby that we had to care for all on our own? "That's a horrible idea."

"Something tells me that you don't really like babies, do you, Bea?" Mae grins.

I smirk in return. "It's not the babies I don't like, it's the idea of being up all night caring for one. You *do* know that they cry all night, right?"

Mae looks to a Caretaker to confirm this, and the one that overhears nods her head. "It's true. They do. But, if you love them so much, Scer Mae, you can always ask to become a Caretaker."

"True!" Mae coos down at her baby. "Wouldn't you like that, little, bitty Seer baby?"

"I think this place is a madhouse, to be honest. I think the children should be in classes sooner, so they can learn more. We do a lot of our learning at the end of our schooling. It feels like we find things out all at one time," Connie interjects and sits down, avoiding the opportunity to interact with the babies at all.

I walk over to one of the cradles and peek down inside at the sleeping baby contained in it and wonder how it can sleep so soundly with the other babies crying. "So, you think that their learning should start earlier?"

"Yep. Like, with history stuff, I suppose. At least the things that they'd be able to understand. We deserve to know more."

"I like that idea," Mae agrees after she's done cooing at the baby in her arms.

"Okay. So, we came up with something to write about." I say this hoping that Mae will get the hint that Connie and I want to get out of here.

Thankfully, she does pick it up, and Mae puts the baby back into its cradle. "Okay, okay. Well, I guess we can get out of here and start our projects, then. Maybe we can even get it done before the Training Games tonight."

"Maybe." I smile at Mae and then to Connie. "Though, I wouldn't mind going back and playing some marbles first."

Connie and Mae laugh and we turn to get off this floor and back to the sanity of the quieter levels, the ones without the dozens of wailing Seer children. When we reach the lift again, the three of us step in, and I push the button for the doors to close. Just before I do, though, a dark-haired little girl stops in front of the elevator and stares up at us with her glowing, violet eyes. I smile at her, but the girl doesn't smile back.

She's Seeing.

The doors start to shut, but I strike out and wave my hand in front of the sensor, and they jerk back open. By the time the doors are open again, the girl's Vision is over, and her eyes dim to a more subtle glow. She looks frightened, her face reading of horror and things she cannot unSee.

"What do you think she saw?" Mae asks, as if the girl isn't standing right there in front of her.

"I don't know, but we could ask her." I watch as the girl puts her hands to her head, holding it and shaking it as if trying to erase the images from her mind.

"But we aren't supposed to ask before the Keeper gets here." Connie reminds us of the rule that we both already know. I knew it before I suggested we ask; I just don't care.

"She's obviously upset. There's no harm in trying to calm her down." I step out of the elevator, then crouch down in front of the child and try to take one of her hands. How do the Caretakers do this? It seems so awkward interacting with something so small and so innocent. "What's wrong?"

I can feel the girl trembling through her fingers, and when she looks at me, it is like she's looking through me, as if I were made of glass and she could see everything under my skin. "I Saw horrible things."

"What sort of horrible things?" I ask.

Even at her age, she hesitates. She knows I am not who she is supposed to be telling this to. Surely, the Keeper is somewhere on her way, though. Surely she knows that someone down on this level has had a Vision. Somehow, she always knows these things. "The City. It was burning. There were flames that reached way up into the sky, disappearing into the clouds which were black and thick and grey." She pauses. "Maybe it was smoke and not clouds."

"Maybe." The Vision worries me, but not all too much. She's so young, and her Visions are still inaccurate. They can't be trusted any more than the next under-developed Vision can be. "Was that all you saw?"

"There were burning people too. Their arms…they were flailing their arms, and it looked like they were screaming, but nothing was coming out of their mouths." The girl's eyes fill with tears, her resolve breaking down.

That is how the Keeper finds us as she steps out of the lift and between Connie and Mae. "What is going on here?" She puts a hand on her hip, cradling the digipad against her side with her other arm. The raven on her shoulders spreads its wings and folds them back again, making small honking noises as it moves closer to the Keeper's neck.

Now we have to explain ourselves. Connie and Mae look at me expectantly. Of course, since it was my idea to speak to the little girl, it's my responsibility to explain myself to the Keeper.

When I look up at the Keeper, though, I can already tell I'm in trouble. "She was upset."

"And?" The Keeper waits.

Say something substantial, Beatrice, I tell myself. "And I asked her what was wrong, and she told me about her Vision." I realize when I say this that it will probably get the little girl in trouble, and immediately I amend my excuse. "After I told her to tell me, that is. She wasn't going to otherwise."

"So you asked someone about their Vision before I could ask them myself?" The Keeper's questions come one after the other, almost as if she wasn't listening to my replies at all.

"Yes, My Keeper." My gaze shifts to Connie and Mae. The latter is biting on her lower lip, worrying on it until I can see a piece of skin peel off with the scraping of her teeth. Connie looks terrified, as if I were standing in front of a firing squad myself, waiting for my end to come.

"You know this is a violation of our rules, Seer Beatrice?"

The little girl continues to tremble. I haven't let go of her hand yet. I feel as if there's this connection between us now as we both witness the wrath of the Keeper. I wonder if it's ever been done before, and a rebellious little piece of me rejoices in maybe being the first.

"Yes, My Keeper…but I thought, at the time, that it was the best for the girl." I look to the child. "She is so scared."

"Isabelle." The Keeper pulls the datapad out, addressing the child. "Tell me about your Vision."

Is that it? My reprimand is over? The question must read on my face, because Connie shrugs her shoulder, and Mae shakes her head 'no,' heading me off at the next question, which would be if I should try and leave or not. I stay put.

The child, Isabelle, retells her story about the Vision, and this time, when she's done, I let go of her hand and stand up straight once more. The Keeper makes her notes on her datapad and when she's done she nods her head, gesturing down the hallway. "Very well, Isabelle. Please return to your activities."

Isabelle gives us all one long last look before turning down the hallway, walking as if she were in a daze with her hands on her head.

"Now, Seers Beatrice, Constance, and Mae." The Keeper turns

to regard us all as one group. "Might I ask your business on this floor? Aside from breaking policy and risking spending time in solitary confinement?"

Connie locks up, as she usually does when put into a confrontational situation, and it's Mae who answers for us. "We were preparing for our research paper about how to better the young Seers and somehow incorporate them more into the Institution."

The Keeper nods her head, but doesn't look impressed. "And tell me, does that report entail prying into other's Visions before I can properly inventory and study them myself?"

"No, My Keeper," Mae responds in a tiny, mouse voice.

"And now tell me, have any of you been trained in the art of deciphering and inventorying Visions?" She fixes us all with a disapproving look.

"No, My Keeper." Mae's voice is even softer this time.

"So when Seer Beatrice decided it would be a good idea to counsel a girl about the extent of her Vision, neither of you thought it would be a good idea to stop her?" This question is directed to Connie and Mae, both of whom shake their heads and lower their eyes to avoid the Keeper's stare.

"So you are all equally responsible for Seer Beatrice's transgression." The Keeper says this as if it is something that has already been decided. And it has been. She takes out her datapad and makes a few more notes. Notes about us, most likely.

"Seer Beatrice, I am not impressed. You are interfering with the duties of the Keeper—a very serious offense." She puts her datapad away when she's done making her notes, resting it back on her hip. "I think it is time for some disciplinary action. For the three of you, not just Seer Beatrice."

"Disciplinary action?" Connie whispers.

"Yes. You three will spend the rest of the day scrubbing the Arena's floors for the Training Games. They are very dirty, and it's been a long time since someone has really given them a good washing."

This doesn't seem so bad to me. It's better than solitary confinement, which I've heard is unbearable. I can scrub some floors, as long as it means the Keeper will leave me alone.

Which I know she won't.

"Yes, My Keeper." I'm the only person who remembers to speak in this moment.

"And I will be keeping an eye on you, Seer Beatrice. You have a great responsibility to this Institution, and I don't want you distracted from this fact. Shape up, or I will have to do something more...permanent." On that note, the Keeper walks off down the hallway, and all the children stop their running around just as soon as they see her coming.

Permanent.

I don't know what this means, but I remember the words of the Widow, and I renew the promise to myself to not let Gabe out of my sight.

CHAPTER TEN

"Beatrice."

I am at the border. It is quiet, and the guard towers loom overhead. The electric fence surges with energy, the low hum bouncing back and forth, stretching between each link. I don't know why I am here. I only know that the closer I get, the louder the voice becomes. Inside, I feel as if I am close to discovering something I shouldn't know.

Once I reach the fence, I stand in the shadow of the night— hoping the guard won't see me. There isn't anywhere else to go. I start to panic, limbs tensing, because it's only a matter of time before the spotlight sweeps across, exposing me.

"Beatrice."

The voice echoes from my right. I walk in that direction. My feet fall quietly on the ground, and I am careful not to make any more noise as I continue to slink through the darkness. When I reach the end of one of the sections of fence, I notice there's a hole, and there might be enough space for me to crawl under the chain links.

"Beatrice."

I have no choice. I need to figure out who or what is calling my name. I need to know what has been haunting my dreams, my Visions, and even my waking thoughts when I am clear-headed, lucid. Maybe he'll know what to do about this situation, the live rounds at the Training Games, the threat of the impending invasion, and the sudden seriousness of it all.

Kneeling on the dirt, I shed my black robes in a pile by my feet. I can't risk getting my clothes stuck on the barbed wire of the fence, though it's also a risk leaving behind evidence of my being here.

I shimmy under the wire, my stomach and legs dragging in the dust, and then snake my way out to the other side. Carefully, I reach through the fence and tug my robes under. Despite the grime that covers the garment, I slip it around my form, wrapping myself up in its familiar comfort.

I now stand in a land of unknowns; no one I know has been outside of the City before. Somewhere in the back of my mind, I remember this is just a Vision. Or maybe it's a dream? I can't tell the difference until I wake up, and I can't wake up because he's still calling me through the darkness.

"Beatrice."

For some reason, I feel the need to run. I need to get to where he is. An urgency surges through my body, and my fingertips pulse with the sudden rush of energy. We learned in one of our classes that the human body has two reactions: to fight or to run. I wonder why my body is choosing to do the latter. There is nobody to fight here, so what am I running from?

I race through the shadowy brush, my feet sometimes snagging on what feel like vines or the raised roots of trees. Except there aren't any trees. It's just flat, open land with a rolling mist that covers everything like a fluffy blanket. A faint light filters through the fog, but I can't see where the glow is coming from. The sky is too dark and cloudy, so it *certainly isn't the moon.*

I continue to run, and when I don't think I can run anymore, that's when I see him.

A young man, around my age, with stark blond hair, the fairest skin, and startling blue eyes. He wears plain robes of white with long sleeves that hide his arms and hands, and the trim is red, maybe satin. He's watching me, and I stop walking.

"Beatrice." His voice sounds so much softer, so much less demanding, but it's still alluring. Entrancing.

"Who are you?" I can't take my eyes off of him. Inside my chest, my heart beats too quickly. I'm afraid he can hear it just as clearly as I hear him now.

He smiles. It's a handsome smile, one that makes me hesitate. In one of our preparedness classes, our instructor told us that the things we should not trust are the things we want to trust the most. For example, the most poisonous of flowers tend to be the most beautiful. The deadliest of animals tend to be the ones who are most interesting.

"My name is Echo."

"Why do you keep calling me?"

"I must save you, and you must save me."

"Save us from what?"

His smile fades, replaced by a sorrow and seriousness that doesn't meld with his features. He looks at the ground. "From each other."

"I don't understand."

Echo looks up, his eyes seeing through me. "You will. The invasion is coming, Beatrice. The plague has begun, and the Dreamcatchers need Citizens." He reaches to touch me, but he must think better of it, because he immediately withdraws his hand. "I need to protect you. The invasion is coming…the plague has started…"

◇

The piercing, electronic beeping of my alarm jars me out of my sleep. The first thing I do is grab the small mirror from my nightstand and peer into it. My eyes are not glowing. I did not have a Vision.

Echo was just a dream.

Still, the dream was so clear—like my Visions—that I'm left in a state of confusion. Do I report this, or not? Do I tell someone, or keep it to myself? Then I remember what the Widow told me, about dreams that are like Visions and Visions that are like dreams. I've been caught by a Dreamcatcher—there is no other explanation— but how is he getting to me?

I decide to keep the dream to myself. It's easy enough to do when every time I close my eyes, I see Echo staring at me, telling me that we have to save ourselves from each other. What did I look like when I stared back at him, dumbfounded and lost? Why did he place his hope of being saved in me, anyway? Why did anyone?

I will drive myself crazy if I stay here, thinking of all the *whys* and *what ifs*, so I swing my legs over the side of my bunk and stretch my arms up over my head. Today is the first day of the new Training Games, and there's a lot more that should be on my mind, like the fact that I could die. And for what? To take part in this stupid game that is supposed to prepare us for a fight against a people who somehow pop into our dreams without warning? How is a gun supposed to stop them anyway?

Everything is starting to unravel into a pool of nonsense. And standing in the middle of the pool is Echo, handsome and tall, pleading with me to save him. Save us.

I shake my head and force myself to get ready. Team A is first on the schedule. We are first into the arena, the first to use the live rounds…probably the first to kill, or die. As I slip my combat suit on and pull the zipper up to just under my chin, someone knocks at my door. I idly slap the release button and the door slides open, revealing Gabe, suited up and ready to go.

"Running behind today, are we?" Gabriel lacks all the conviction that he used with me the previous day. It is as if we've never gotten into a fight at all, and I immediately find myself wanting to tell him all about Echo. I want to pour out every detail to Gabe so that I don't have to bear it all on my own. But I can't. Something inside of me tells me not to, as if Echo were there, countering my every decision in regard to him.

"Yeah. I set my alarm a little later because I couldn't fall asleep last night."

Gabe drags his hair out of his face and it falls right back in place, some of it hanging over his eyes. It's my favorite part of Gabe, that *I don't care how I look* facade. "I don't think you were the only one. Everyone is nervous about today."

"With good reason." I shove a foot into my combat boot and tug the laces until they are tight.

"I still can't believe she's doing this. Making us kill Citizen prisoners with live rounds. It doesn't seem right."

"It isn't right, Gabe." How could it be right? Even if they are convicts, sentenced to the rest of their lives in prison for violating laws of any degree, they still didn't deserve to be prey.

"I know." Gabe leans against the black lacquer dresser. "But, in a way, I wonder if we just don't understand it right now. The Keeper knows what's best, right? I mean, she's seen what the Dreamcatchers can do."

"Has she?" Now dressed, I nod toward the door, signaling that we should go. "I just hope she's right. It would suck to lose you." I realize what I've just said and quickly blurt, "Let's go. We'll be late."

Gabe doesn't move at first, at least I don't hear his footsteps behind me. When I peek over my shoulder, he just shakes his head with a smirk and follows after. "It'd suck to lose you too, Bea."

We are late, but we aren't the only ones. As Gabe and I double-time to the arena, others lag behind, hesitant and unwilling to make much more of an effort to get there on time. I can hear some of them whisper as we pass, but it isn't about us. The tension packs in the air so tightly that I'm starting to think I can't breathe. When I look at Gabe, I notice his chest rising and falling quickly, like he just finished jogging a mile. Maybe he can feel it too.

As we round the last corner, I notice that the two teams have already lined up. Team A and Team B are both holding their new weapons, standard black machine guns. We will be working together to kill the convicts, but working against one another in terms of game points. There's still a rivalry, a want to do better than the other team. To *be* better. Team A has been holding their own for weeks now, but Rachelle and the rest of Team B have slowly been creeping up on us and are near to besting our statistics. I can't let that happen. I'm not giving Rachelle an inch.

Gabe and I fall into line behind the last person in Team A. Elan is a small boy with protruding ears who is skilled at sneaking through shadows and popping up when least expected. He's one of the younger Seers at eleven years old, and pretty much keeps to himself most of the time. Today is no different.

One of the attendant Seers shoves a machine gun at me and one at Gabe. I take my weapon cautiously and let it hang by my side. I choose not to give it the respect it deserves. I won't let it rule over my emotions and cloud my judgment once the arena doors open. I notice others who are pale and stark-faced already, and realize that these are the people who will probably fall first. I can't be one of them. I need to stay alert, if not for my sake, then for Gabe's sake, because I refuse to let him fall either.

The Keeper's voice pulsates over the arena speakers, which also face outward into the lobby where we are all gathered. Gabe nudges me in the side and nods toward Rachelle, who stands stiffly, eyes distant and glowing.

"She had a Vision," he whispers while examining his gun. "Hopefully, it will keep her distracted, and she won't pull any stunts this time around."

I don't pay too much attention to Rachelle. I instead notice Connie shoving a shortbread cookie into her mouth before pulling her helmet over her head.

"Hey! I saved it from lunch. Why let it go to waste?" Connie smiles after finishing her snack.

I roll my eyes and nod her way, and Gabe catches sight of the crumbs tumbling out of her helmet and all over the front of her jumpsuit. He laughs, and it breaks some of the tension that is consuming us all.

"Next time, bring us all some cookies, huh?" I jest, but it's half-hearted with the reality of what is to come.

"Welcome to the first advanced round of Training Games!" the Keeper announces, her voice rising above all others. Though we can't see her, I can imagine the woman sitting in front of a microphone, watching us on multiple flatscreen holovisions, studying our various expressions of fear and uncertainty. Detached from the emotion, where she wants to be.

"Today surely will be a challenge for you, as you are the first teams to enter the arena and use live rounds. You will be the first to fall, the first to conquer, and the first to show us that we will not be helpless and unprepared when at last we have to face the onslaught of Dreamcatchers. You will shoot to kill, as you would our enemy."

An image of Echo flickers through my mind. I see him standing, dressed in all white, with his platinum hair and piercing blue eyes. In his hands, he also holds an ominous black machine gun, though his stance is more confident and stiff. It's not an image that comes and goes either, but instead it lingers, even when I close my eyes to try and will it away.

"You will also be the first to fall, and the weak will be quickly weeded out from the others. I have no need for Seers who can't hold their own." The Keeper pauses for a moment. Then, she continues to speak. "It'll be a difficult day for us all, but in the end we must remember that we are doing this to protect the City and its Citizens from a horrible fate. Without us, they will be helpless, and it is our duty as Seers to guard and serve them. If it means I have to lose a few of you to make sure that we are the strongest we can be, then that is what will happen. We are a large Institution, and there are many of us to defend the City."

In other words, some of us are replaceable.

Out of the corner of my eye, I see Gabe shake his head. The intercom clicks off and we are left in silence. Soon after, the red light above the arena door starts to circulate, and the bright halogen bulbs flicker off, leaving us in the dark with rotating strobes of crimson.

Our team begins to march through the doors. We have three minutes to enter the arena and set up our positions. I look at Gabe again, wondering if I will see him when our time is up.

"We need to plan this out. I'm not going to have us be the first to die out here," I relay to Team A through the intercoms in our helmets. "This is serious. It's no longer about being zapped until we are unconscious. Once we are down in these Games, we are down to stay. Forever."

I let the gravity of the word "forever" seep into the minds of the others. I want them to hear the word over and over again in their minds as they run through the simulated streets, hunting while being hunted.

"Let's try and stay together. Find a partner and cover each other. Walk back to back so that one is looking in front and the other is looking behind. Look, listen, and communicate." I glance up at the arena doors, then at Gabe.

The siren begins to wail. There's no more time for talking. The convicts are released. Their doors open and they flee with weapons in hand, right into the holo city.

The Games have begun.

As both teams filter into the arena, we are amazed by what we see. The space has been transformed into the City's streets, and there are holo projections of Citizens walking around. They don't move out of our way or even look at us, but wander about as if we aren't there at all.

Just as soon as the three minutes are up and both teams have completely set up in the arena, the heavy doors locking behind us, a shot rings out. The first shot.

The first death.

Someone on my team is screaming. As I try to find the source of the manic shouting, I notice globs of deep-purple blood on my sleeve. I hear something hit the ground. Gabe stops walking, and I stumble into him. Only then do I realize that he has stopped to avoid walking in the puddle of blood that is pooling by his feet. But it's not his blood.

No, it belongs to the girl who now lies flat on the ground, her limbs sprawled every which way. Some members of Team A huddle around her, and I squint to get a better look. There is too much blood for her to be alive. And then I realize…

"Connie," I whisper and turn with my gun raised to see who did this.

Rachelle stands with her gun trained on the lot of us. "It came from that way. You should have been paying attention."

I narrow my eyes at Rachelle and her failure to protect her fellow Seers. "You mean you saw them and you didn't even bother to shoot at them?"

"She's not on my team. She's not my problem." And Rachelle sprints off.

I want to go after her and wring her neck until it snaps, but there's blood gathering by my feet, blood that once ran through my friend…my friend who used to be alive. Leaning down, I push my fingers to her wrist to check for a pulse, but shots zoom by over my head, and Gabe grabs me by the back of my jumpsuit and starts to drag me off. "Come on, Beatrice! They are still out there!"

Team A scatters down the streets, heading in any direction, most of them paired together as I suggested. I try and follow Gabe, but he turns a corner too soon, and a mousy, dirty girl pops out from an alleyway and opens fire at me. I stumble backward and duck behind a Dumpster. Hiking the gun up into a good position to shoot, I wait for her to come by, but she never does.

Somewhere in the distance, more shots echo through the streets. Is that Gabe? I can't catch my breath. Neither can Connie. Poor Connie…the game had hardly even started and she's already gone. What will Mae think? Or Brandon? What do I even think? I'm paralyzed here behind this Dumpster, and I don't want to move.

Someone pulls my jumpsuit from behind, and I fall backward

on my butt. I twist around and point my gun in that direction, and notice just before pulling the trigger that it's the boy with the ears, Elan. He puts his palms up in surrender, gun hanging around his neck, and when he realizes that I won't shoot, he gestures down the side street for me to follow.

I have no idea where he is taking me, but I also have no idea what I am going to do sitting behind a Dumpster, so I follow him. He is moving fast so I break into a jog in order to catch up. As we run, building fronts turn into blurs, and I don't pay attention to whether they correlate with the real streets of the City or not. If so, I could maybe take him to the Widow's home, and we could hide out there, but that's assuming that these doors even open into the buildings at all.

Elan instead leads me into the Central Park and our feet fall unheard on the thick grass. He grabs my hand and pulls me toward a small creek that cuts through the middle of the park. Just like at the real Central Park, multiple bridges span different parts of the stream, all made of beautiful masonry with figures of lions' heads and victorious women.

He picks the bridge with the cover over it, which seems an all too obvious place to hide. He lifts a finger to his lips to "shush" me and we both climb under the small space between the creek bed and the supporting structure of the bridge. My gun pokes me in my side as I wedge in and try to catch my breath.

"We can stay here," he suggests, and I can hear him wheezing. It's then I realize that he is bleeding. "Stupid Keeper and her stupid ideas."

"You've been hit!" I pull at his jumpsuit to try and get a better look at how bad it might be. There's a lot of blood, but not as much as there was around Connie. "When?"

"When we all started to run. Someone caught me with a shot, I guess." He lifts a hand and we both stare at his red fingers. Had this been the normal Training Games, Elan would be suffering from only a shock…not something so real. "This is stupid. Sometimes, this place makes no sense."

"I don't think we can hide here for too long." It's then that I realize that I have no idea how long this game will be. Usually, games end once one of the teams is eliminated. Would it still be that way now? Would we have to kill all the convicts for the game to end? Or will they have to eliminate all of us? I can't hide here, not with Gabe out there somewhere. "We should move."

"But I can't." Elan sounds so small now, and I can't help but feel bad.

"But you have to. Come on." I don't give him time to rest, and I tug on his arm until he realizes that we really aren't staying there. He groans, and we make a run for it. Because the park is open and mostly flat, it is a dangerous place to be. Anyone could shoot at us from anywhere.

Elan whimpers and makes all sorts of pathetic noises as I hightail it back toward the City. Spats of gunfire illuminate the streets, lighting up the faces of buildings for brief spasms of time. It kind of looks like a deadly light show, or like fireworks that never made it off the ground. Shadows run down streets and into the small spaces between buildings, but I can't tell if they are convicts or Seers.

We finally make it to an unnamed street. I pull Elan along with more urgency, and we turn and disappear between the buildings. Sprawled in the middle of the street is someone from Team B. Her helmet is cracked, and blood is running from somewhere around her neck, matting her hair together into ugly clumps. Around her are dispatched bodies of convicts, just as lifeless.

Elan makes another noise before pulling up his helmet and retching all over the asphalt.

"Come on." I continue to run. He is just going to have to pull himself together.

I want to find Gabe since I have no idea if he is still alive. I have no idea if anyone is still alive, because for all I know, it could be down to just me and Elan, and we are keeping the games from ending.

But as we move around a storefront, Rachelle and two other members of Team B point their guns into our chests.

"I should kill you," she growls, her violet eyes narrowed. "You're the reason all this stupidity is happening."

"You should." I look into her eyes, which no longer glow.

"And I would. If I didn't have a Vision."

"What does your Vision have to do with me?" I step in front of Elan, hoping that in the dark, none of them can see that he is bleeding.

"Everything. Just wait until the Keeper sees you." Rachelle laughs, her gaze flickering to Elan. "But this one wasn't in my Vision at all." Her hips move and she points her gun at the boy with the sticky-out ears.

"The object of this training session isn't to shoot each other, you moron." Before I can go on, Elan kicks Rachelle in the leg and she drops her gun in surprise. The other two lackeys behind her look at each other, shocked that someone would strike out against Rachelle.

"You little brat," she calls out and reaches for her gun. I wouldn't put it past Rachelle to retaliate, so I kick the gun out of her grasp.

The lights of the arena flicker on.

"This game is over." The Keeper's voice bounces off the City walls, but I can hardly hear it over Rachelle.

Medics rush in wearing white with red crosses on their backs. They disappear down the alleyways, fanning out in every direction. Elan whimpers behind me, and his leg hasn't stopped bleeding.

Rachelle is still cursing on the ground, holding her knee in her hands. A medic eventually gets to us, surveys the scene and radios over his radio for two stretchers and some body bags.

I see Gabe running toward us, gun in hand. He doesn't look hurt, though there are some stains on his jumpsuit. His hair is shaggy and damp from sweat, matted to his face around his temples and above his brow.

"Gabe, thank the Maker." I step around Rachelle as two newly-arrived medics load her up on a stretcher. Another set of medics tries to get Elan up on his own stretcher, but he insists that he's not hurt that much. Mae and Brandon pull off their helmets and stand by us, quiet. Mournful.

Gabe takes me by my arms and looks me over, genuinely concerned. "Are you hurt?"

"No, but Rachelle is."

He looks back at Rachelle as she's hauled away. "How'd that happen?"

"Elan kicked her for being an idiot. She could have saved Connie, Gabe." I pull my helmet off and brush my fingers through my hair.

Gabe smirks, though it's not his typical smirk. It's heavy, filled with the weight of what we had just gone through.

"She pointed her gun at Elan. Said something about how he wasn't in her Vision. In fact, she said something about how I *was* in her Vision, and she couldn't wait until the Keeper saw me." I still don't know what this means, and judging by Gabe's confused look, he hasn't any idea either.

"Will she be okay?" Gabe asks.

"Who cares?" I look back up at Gabe and see he is frowning. "What matters is that you weren't killed. Or Brandon or Mae."

"Elan shouldn't have held back. She practically killed Connie."

"And if he didn't hold back, we would be no better than her, Gabe. It's better this way. Let her live with what she's done. What she could have done." I have no sympathy for her. She let our friend die.

The stretchers are wheeled off. Other medics load the two bodies into their black bags and leave without saying a word.

"Let's get to the debriefing." I turn on my heel and start out of the arena, with Gabe following behind me. I try to concentrate on the lecture to come, but my thoughts are everywhere and anywhere at once.

CHAPTER ELEVEN

Echo is back. This time, he sits under a tree with wiry limbs that stretch outward, umbrellaing over him. He still wears all white, his clothing a stark contrast to the deep brown tree trunk behind him.

I walk toward him through a field of tall grass. I don't even know how I got here, but I know when I reach him, I am where I need to be.

"Is that what you needed to save me from? The Training Games? Did you know they were going to do that?" The sky above us is an eerie light purple, the color of my eyes. The clouds move too quickly, racing across the horizon, trying to get to where they are supposed to go.

Echo looks up at me and smiles. He lifts a hand, gesturing for me to sit beside him under the tree. "That is just a little part of it, Beatrice."

I sit cross-legged and run my hands down my robe to flatten it out. "So why won't you tell me the whole of it?"

"Because I can't."

Looking to his hands, I wonder if he could seize me here and kill me like they do the Citizens. But his hands seem so soft and gentle, incapable of doing anything so violent and senseless.

"*You're afraid of me.*" *Echo notices my stare, then reaches out and lifts my chin with a bent finger. I don't immediately die, so he must be safe.*

I also don't move away from him. "I'm afraid of what you can do."

"And what do you mean by that?"

"I mean…" What do I mean by that? I mean everything that we've been told about the Dreamcatchers. I mean that they are on their way to kill us all and take over the City, and that I've seen it in my Visions. I mean that Echo is the enemy, and that he's not supposed to be in my dreams, but here he is, having a conversation with me under a creepy tree.

Echo's finger drops and he looks away and over the long grass. "I know what you mean."

"How…how are you even in my dreams, Echo? Do you know I could be run out of the Institution for this if anyone found out? They might even kill me now with all of the new rules."

"Then they can't find out." Echo plucks a blade of grass out of the dirt and twists it between his fingers.

"But why are you here?"

"I told you why already. I'm here to save you, and you are here to save me."

I am growing tired of these cryptic responses. I grab Echo by his arms and shake him as I speak. "Echo! Now is not the time for riddles and puzzles! My friend is dead, and so are six other Seers, and none of us know why we are being put through this. The Keeper tells us it is our duty, and we have to be prepared, but you know what?" I stop shaking him, exasperated.

Echo doesn't even flinch at what I've done or said. "What?"

"We don't even know what we are. We don't know what we are

preparing for past the invasion of the Dreamcatchers. Our only mission in life is to protect the Citizens, and that is all we know."

"It's because you are not supposed to know, Beatrice."

"Well, I want to know, and I want to know how you know and I don't."

Echo smiles an easy smile then flicks the balled-up blade of grass off one of his knees. "Because I am the Dreamcatcher. I know what's in your mind and the minds of many others. It's because we can know this that we are dangerous to your Keeper. It's because we do not hide our past or try to pretend that it never happened." He points a finger at my chest. "But you, you are the Seer. You know what will happen tomorrow and the days after. And that is how you are dangerous to us."

"Us? Dangerous?" I laugh at this as I think of lazy Brandon and too-talkative Mae. "We're hardly that."

"Are you?" Echo pushes back some of his hair when it falls in his eyes. "How many Seers did you say died today?"

"Seven."

"And how many convicts did the Seers kill?"

I pause. "I don't know…maybe around twenty?"

Echo only nods his head and goes back to staring across the never-ending field. The number is my answer. We are dangerous. The Keeper has turned us into weapons, ready to shoot and kill at her command.

"Beatrice. In a short while, the Dreamcatchers will come. This you already know. We will come because we are running out of Citizens. The plague is spreading and killing all of us, and we have no way to heal." He pauses, bringing his blue eyes to stare directly into mine. "But what you don't know is that I will be one of them, and I'll be forced to kill you, just as you are being forced to kill us." He doesn't *look at me anymore. He's looking far away at something I can't see.*

"And?"

"And you will have to find me, Beatrice. You'll have to find me and save me, just as I will have to find you and save you before we kill each other in this war. I will take you away from here. Take you with me."

I shake my head, not understanding. "What do you mean? How will you save me and yet be trying to kill me?"

"Exactly what I said, Beatrice. We will have to save each other before we kill each other. I don't know why, and I don't know when or where, but I know it will have to happen." Echo stops looking off into nothingness and stares at me instead. "We'll set each other free. You won't be a Seer anymore, bound to an unknown service governed by the Keeper, and I won't be bound to the service of the Dreamcatchers anymore."

"Free." I don't quite understand what it means to be free. I live a life that other Seers have lived before me. This is simply how things are when you are born with this gift. There is no being "free." Do even the Citizens know freedom? They too are corralled behind barbed-wire fences and watchtowers, tucked away under a faulty dome with the promise that they are protected. And for what reason? What are they trying to keep us from? Or rather, what are they trying to keep from us?

Echo reaches out and touches my lips after I speak the word. He smiles, and the air between us becomes tense. Before I can say anything else, he stands up. "I must go."

And then I'm awake.

◇

The debriefing for the Training Games happens today. They

postponed for a day due to the accumulated shock shared among everyone in the Institution. Yesterday, by the end of the games, we lost eight Seers. One more of them died in the infirmary, bled out on the table. Thankfully, it wasn't Elan, but he has problems of a whole different sort.

They've put him in a holding cell, a quarantine room, if you will. But, it isn't because he is being quarantined from anything at all. Rather, it's because he won't function. Elan won't talk, he won't eat, he won't sleep. And his eyes? They keep glowing, as if he's in a constant Vision, but has yet to snap out of it. No one has seen anything like it before, and to keep us from witnessing any more, they've swept him under the rug.

We are in the Meeting Room. The stage is empty so far. I sit next to Gabe, and beside Gabe, there is an empty chair. Mae and Brandon came up with the idea to keep the chair empty to honor Connie's memory. Brandon and Mae sit on the opposite side of it, staring ahead at the stage like everyone else. All I can think about is Connie, and the lack of her presence in our lives now. And why? All because we have to fight in these stupid Training Games? Killing convicts who were told that if they survived they would be set free? But this is just the rumor. And I don't like it. I put my hand on Gabe's, glad that I don't have to leave a chair empty for him as well.

If it weren't for the nagging grief that tugs at my heart, I'd find it mildly amusing that we all look like zombies. But, I also know that as soon as this meeting starts, it will turn all too serious.

I turn and look behind me, and back a few rows I spot Rachelle, sitting there with her leg bandaged and crutches leaned up against the poor person sitting next to her. She doesn't look very well, but I don't care. Had Rachelle bothered to even try firing back at the convicts that she saw aiming at Connie, then maybe Connie would still be alive now. If she even just *tried*. All she had to do was *try*.

For some reason, I think about what Echo said. I think about his touch against my lips and how in that meadow with the strange tree, we were both alone and free. It was peaceful, and there wasn't any grieving or anger.

Free. I still can't figure out the concept of this word and how it applies to me. But being herded like sheep into this pasture of a Meeting Room, I'm beginning to learn what the concept *doesn't* mean.

I bar the thought from my mind, slightly guilty that I am thinking about Echo when Gabe is sitting right next to me. He still has no idea about my dreams, and I still don't have any idea how to tell him about them. If I even can. For my own safety it would be better if I don't say anything, but it's hard to keep everything to myself. Especially something like this.

The speakers vibrate as the microphone turns on, and the sound draws the attention of everyone in the Meeting Room. Mae leans over and whispers something to Brandon, and whatever is said makes him giggle before he puts a hand over his mouth to stop the embarrassing sounds from spilling out. A few people look in their direction, but it isn't long before they are focused on the stage once more.

The Keeper steps out, dressed in red, flowing robes—a new color for her. A daunting one that is probably worn to remind us all of blood and war. Her hair is pulled up into a neat twist that belies her age. She looks severe, as always, and stands rigid behind the microphone.

"Seers. Yesterday was the first day of our new Training Games. They went well, but not well enough. As you all know, we lost eight Seers yesterday, and this is eight too many." The Keeper's violet eyes sweep over the crowd as she pauses to let the number sink in. Eight people. Connie is one of them.

"I suspect that it will only get worse before it gets better. You will be more scared and hesitant. You will shoot at shadows and sometimes they won't be shadows at all. But the point of this is... you will get better."

Gabe harrumphs and blows his bangs from over his eyes. He needs a haircut, and will probably be ordered to get one soon enough, even if I like his hair when it's a bit long. "Easy for her to say. She's not the one doing it."

"I know that it is easy for me to say. But I am also the Keeper, and I can See things that not even you can See." It is as if she is talking to only Gabe, though she is looking at all of us.

"I'm sure you can," Gabe mutters.

"Shh." I slap Gabe's knee to get him to shut up. Talking like that could get you in trouble for treason against the Institution, and everyone is already on high alert. Now, after the Dreamcatchers started to sneak into the City, it only takes one jittery person to report you before you're in trouble. And "trouble" nowadays meant your life. The Keeper is not taking any chances. To her, the threat is better off dead.

Gabe reluctantly stops talking and continues to listen to the Keeper. She lists the names of those who have fallen, and it becomes uncomfortably quiet. I shift in my seat, remembering how Connie died, remembering the sound of her lifeless body as it crumpled onto the arena floor. She didn't deserve that. Not for something we aren't even sure of yet.

"The Games will continue tomorrow. For today, you will have a break to meet with your teams and strategize. Remember, Seers, the Dreamcatchers can be anywhere. They could be here with us right now, in fact. We must always be prepared and ready to fight them."

Just when I think she is going to dismiss us, the Keeper takes the microphone out of the stand and steps to the front of the stage. "Now. Onto another important matter." Her voice drops an octave lower into a serious and firm tone. "A Vision has been reported that is of some concern. It specifically focused on a particular Seer who is seated amongst us, but it wasn't clear enough to pinpoint exactly who that person is."

At this, everyone looks at one another, already suspicious. I lean over to whisper to Gabe. "I bet this has to do with what Rachelle said."

"What did she say?" Gabriel's attention flutters away from the Keeper and to me instead.

"She said she had a Vision, and that I was in it and that she couldn't wait until the Keeper saw me." I still have no idea what she meant by what she said. But maybe the Keeper already does.

Gabe purses his mouth in concern. I can't quite bring myself to stop looking at his mouth, but somehow, I do.

The Keeper continued. "In the Vision, the Seer was Seen speaking to a Dreamcatcher. He or she was in league with the enemy, plotting alongside them. Again, we do not know the absolute validity of this, as the Vision was not clear, as most of your Visions aren't. But, this overall concern is still present: someone here will betray us."

Gasps of surprise roll over the audience. Everyone scrutinizes the person next to them, wary and cautious. I can feel the collective tension in the air pull into a taught film that settles over us all. The Keeper has managed to catch us in her net like defenseless butterflies.

Mae leans over and looks down the line of chairs to where

Gabe and I sit. "Do you hear this?"

"I think everyone does, Mae." Gabe is grumpy and crosses his arms over his chest.

Mae frowns. "Right."

"Stay alert, Seers. Always stay alert, and report anything suspicious to the Watch or myself." The Keeper puts her closed left hand over the violet eye emblem sewn onto the right breast of her robe. We all return the salute, which also serves as our dismissal.

Gabe pushes back his chair and rises. "Now we're all going to be judging everyone. I think she does this stuff on purpose."

"Why would she do it on purpose?" I ask. Brandon and Mae follow behind us as we filter out of the row.

"I don't know. I just have a feeling."

I have the same feeling, but I don't vocalize it. When I look around, I notice the other Seers whispering and casting nervous glances at one another.

"I think she's just trying to warn us, is all." Mae is always optimistic. I don't know how she manages it. No matter what happens, she'll find the good in it, despite how disastrous it might be. It's why I enjoy her company and think of her as a sister. No day goes by where she'll let any of us mope and pout for too long.

"Yeah, maybe she is trying to warn us." Brandon agrees with Mae, as expected. Maybe he's finally catching on to the fact that she likes him.

"Think what you will, but I don't agree." Gabe ends the conversation and follows behind me as I push through the crowd to get to the exit doors. The Watch is still standing on the catwalks, their guns at the ready. Their stares are blank, concentrated on details that are too small to see.

I recall the black fog, the piles of corpses, and my heart begins to race. This is why I don't like to go to the Meeting Room anymore. I know something horrible will happen here. I just don't know when. It is as Echo says. He can see our intentions, and I can See the future…but sometimes the future isn't clear enough. And I wish it were.

Just as we get outside, two black-robed officials step in my way. Gabe tries to push forward and in front of me, but I put out my hand to stop him before anything can turn confrontational.

"The Keeper wishes to see you, Seer Beatrice." The woman official wears her hood over her head, shrouding her blonde hair, some of which manages to escape and almost fall in her eyes.

The male official doesn't wear his hood, and he is bald, reflecting the fluorescent lights that hum overhead. He is the one who reaches out and grabs me by my arm. Immediately, Gabe reacts, shoving him away.

"What are you doing?" He pushes the man a step back.

"You will not touch me again, Seer Gabriel, unless you wish to find yourself in a holding cell." The bald-headed man is strangely calm. He reminds me of a different type of person altogether, not like the other Seers in the Institution.

Gabe reminds me of a scared cat with its arched back and hair on end. "Who are you anyway?"

"Yeah. Why should I follow you? You could be one of the Dreamcatchers that the Keeper warned us about." I am not moving and plant myself where I stand. It's a subtle act of defiance. They could be Dreamcatchers, after all, and this one of their traps.

Behind me, I hear the heavy footfalls of combat boots. I turn and see two members of the Watch close in around Mae and Brandon. Their guns are trained on Gabe and me.

"Because you do not have a choice, Seer Beatrice." The woman's eyes bore into mine and make me feel uncomfortable. "Now please, come peacefully before you make my partner upset."

The shiny-head man cracks his knuckles one at a time. The pops of air releasing from between his bones are sickening to listen to, and I want to go, if only to make him stop.

"I'd like to bring Gabe with me, then." My words are spoken between clenched teeth as knuckles continue to be cracked.

The two officials look at each other and the woman, who seems to be making all the decisions, nods her head. "Very well. Bring him along."

Gabe is rigid with annoyance when he moves beside me as I'm tugged down the hallway. It's not necessary for them to pull me along at all—I will follow willingly—but it's not worth arguing about either. I'm more concerned about what is going to happen to us. Or to me.

CHAPTER TWELVE

The Keeper's office is cold and uninviting. It's a large, open space, one side of which is a big, tinted-glass window with a view to the skyscrapers just outside the Institution. We are the heart of the City, the largest and tallest building, though I've never been on more than a handful of floors.

Everything in the Keeper's office is either black or red. The desk's surface is wide and shiny and sitting just behind it, her reflection mirrored off the tabletop, is the Keeper. She also follows the color code of the office, her black robe trimmed with a thin line of red satin. This place will drive me crazy because there is nothing original to it. It's so bleak.

The bald man unhands me as soon as we are inside the doors. Gabe pushes him aside so he can stand beside me, his arms crossed over his chest, though he's hardly as imposing as the Keeper's icy stare. Why does she look so angry with me anyway? What did I do?

"You may leave." The Keeper nods to the officials, who thump their hands on their chest in salute before turning and marching away. The door slides shut behind them, silencing their footfalls. The raven sits on his perch in the corner of the room. I feel like it is constantly watching me, just like the Keeper.

"You asked to see me, Keeper?" I don't mention Gabe. The officials had begrudgingly let him follow, though they seemed more concerned about making sure I arrived to the Keeper.

"I did. And since Seer Gabriel is also here, you may both have a seat."

Simultaneously, the both of us pull black, plastic chairs situated in front of the desk. When we sit, the backs of the chairs extend past our heads, maybe even a good half a foot higher. We must look so small in these seats, but I always manage to feel small in the Keeper's presence, tall chairs or not.

"A Vision has been reported this morning, and it beckons caution." The Keeper always manages to speak in riddles. With her pinched lips and hollowed cheeks, she also always looks severe, too severe to beat around the bush. It annoys me that she can't just say what is on her mind. Instead, she'll tease the curiosity out of us.

For some reason, I feel like her enemy right now, and I don't want to give her the pleasure of my curiosity. Gabe also doesn't inquire any further. He probably feels the same way that I do.

"It was Seer Rachelle's Vision, and her Visions have always been clear. Not as clear as yours, mind you, but clearer than most." The Keeper pauses and the raven noisily flaps its wings. "She saw you, Seer Beatrice, leading a revolution. You marched a single line of all the Seers out the front door and into the City."

I subtly roll my eyes. "Of course Seer Rachelle would say something like that, Keeper. She hates me."

"Hate does not dictate our Visions, though." The Keeper steeples her fingers in front of her, her soft, bubbly fingertips pressed against one another.

"No, but she could very well be lying."

"No one lies to the Keeper, Seer Beatrice. To suggest as much is a heavy charge."

Gabe sucks in a breath and bites on his lower lip. *Don't talk, Gabe, you will only make it worse.*

"Yes, it is." I leave it at that. I don't want to face off with the Keeper. Maker only knows what she could do to me. To Gabe. To any of us. Everyone is suspicious of one another. No one is safe from anyone. Especially not from the Keeper.

She seems pleased that I do not argue with her belief that no one would lie to her. Does that mean that she knows that I have been lying to her? That I've not been reporting my dreams? Does she know about Echo? Can she see it in my eyes? Can she See it in her own Visions?

"You are too valuable to us to be put aside, Seer Beatrice. You are a leader, it is true, but not of any revolution. You are a leader of your fellow class of Seers. You will be a leader of your own unit when we must go out into the City and fight. You'll be a leader and much, much more."

It occurs to me, as the Keeper continues to drone on about my role in the Institution, that Rachelle is probably making up everything she can in order to get me shoved out of the spotlight. No one has ever lied to the Keeper, though. Rachelle would have to be bold. Seriously bold.

"…and this is why I need to assign bodyguards to you. For your own safety. It will only be at first, and then we will be monitoring you through the surveillance systems set up throughout the Institution."

I blink. "What?" Maybe I should have been listening.

Gabe stiffens in his seat and leans forward, hands sliding over the edges of the armrests. "She needs bodyguards because someone made up some Vision about her leading a revolution? I am sorry, Keeper, but even I can see through this. Bea…Seer Beatrice has only ever been an asset to everything that we've done."

"Enough, Seer Gabriel. It is my ruling. The bodyguards will be assigned by the end of the day. They will report to duty before lights out."

I don't even know what to say. My mouth opens and closes like a fish out of water, but nothing comes out. I am to be monitored? Watched like some criminal?

"It will be temporary, until we can figure some things out." The Keeper's violet eyes shift to where I sit. She presses her mouth together until her lips form a line. "Know, Seer Beatrice, that I do not like doing this any more than you like it having to happen. But, we are in fragile times, and I cannot ignore the Visions of others. Not even when they are most likely not as clear as yours. Not now."

"I understand." The words are forced. I don't understand, not at all. Rachelle has gotten away with another something, and again we have to suffer for it.

"Very well. You are dismissed." The Keeper stands first, her hands folded in front of her, as if in meditation.

Gabe and I stand after she does, and together we turn and leave the office. The doors retract into the walls, opening out into the hallway, where the officials no longer stand. As soon as the doors shut behind us, we wordlessly turn and march away. Our boots fall onto the black laminate floor tiles as we retreat without actually running. I have a million things that I want to say, but it isn't safe to say anything now. Gabe takes my hand and holds it as he walks me back to my bunk, where I'll inevitably fall asleep with too much on my mind.

◇

We've been walking across this field for far too long. My feet ache, my head hurts, and I am pretty sure we are never going to get to where Echo wants to take me. His homeland is forever away, or at least it feels that way judging by the blisters that are starting to form on the soles of my feet.

"Tell me, when we get to Aura, what are we going to do?" I still haven't figured out why we are out here. One minute, we are running away from the City, and in the next moment, we are trudging across miles of flat terrain, trying to get to Echo's homeland before anyone can get to us. Every few steps, I look over my shoulder, expecting someone to materialize out of the golden grass, which grows more golden the farther away from the City we get. The blades sway back and forth, and in the distance, it looks as if they are licking the blue of the sky, like tiny paintbrushes repainting the world. Fortunately, I never spot even a hint of anyone out here except for us, and Echo continues to travel along before I get a chance to stand still.

"You will find out when we get there." This isn't said unkindly, and Echo smiles over his shoulder, letting me know that he's not trying to be rude by the statement. "It's best if we keep what you know to a minimum for now, Beatrice. There's only so much I can let you know in your dream, because this is not a Vision. This is a 'maybe' and not a 'what will be.' In this dream, I just want to take you to my home."

It's an innocent request at the surface. I smile and nod my head. "Okay then. So, you want to take me to Aura…but I can't know what we are going to do when we get there?" I shrug a shoulder and it brushes my jaw line. "Fair enough." I tilt my head and look at the sky as grey clouds roll in and threaten to block out the sun. It's been so long since I've felt the full radiance of the sun on my skin, and when the overcast steals away the warmth of the rays, I look down at my arms and realize I'm turning a slight shade of red. "What is this?"

"It's sunburn. We've been out in the sun too long. Your skin can turn red from the light." Echo follows my gaze to the storm clouds. "We should find somewhere safe where we can hide, though. When it rains out here, it is brutal."

"Are we almost to Aura?"

Echo turns, surveying the land that looks the same no matter which way he faces. "Almost, yes. But it's not close enough to reach before the rain comes." When he looks to me, he points over my shoulder. "There."

I glance and note one, tall evergreen tree with heavy boughs dragged down by gravity, tips pointing toward the ground. This tree was not there before, not when I originally faced that way. And now, suddenly, it is there, beckoning for us to go to it before the sky opens up and lets the rain pour down.

Echo grabs my hand and we run for shelter, making it to the tree just in time. Echo pulls back a branch and we both slip underneath, my boots crushing the tiny, dried pine needles that make a bed inside the tree. Just as soon as we are safe, the rain comes, and the sound of the droplets hitting the branches is almost deafening.

Echo slips out of his robes and spreads it across the needles so I have somewhere clean to sit. Under the robes, he wears a sleeveless tunic with a folded collar and golden buttons. His arms are well muscled, but not too much. His white pants are creased and perfectly pressed, with crimson seams that run down the sides of his legs. A golden chain is tied around his waist like a belt, looped on the side so that two sections hang down lower than the others.

I am staring. I know I am staring at him, but I can't look away.

He is so handsome in his Dreamcatcher robes, but is even more so without them. I don't want to look away, but when he smiles at my blatant show of admiration, I blush and finally avert my eyes.

Acting as if nothing happened, Echo sits beside me, pulling his knees up to his chest. "The rain is heavy out here. The force of its falling is almost the same as being hit by tiny, little rocks. It's good we found this tree."

"You made this tree up. It wasn't here before." I want him to know that I'm not oblivious to what he can do. If he wanted, he could probably have made Aura much closer so that we didn't have to walk all this way. Why he is making us endure the journey, I don't know. There could be absolutely no reason at all, and I'd probably be okay with that at the end of the day. As long as I could continue to be by his side.

What am I thinking? I want to be by Gabe's side. Is Echo controlling my decisions too? Maybe, to a fault, he is…but I also remember protesting to return to the City, and him distinctly saying that we could not.

"Why can't I go back home?"

"Because we need you in Aura."

"But you haven't told me why."

Echo twists one of the buttons on his lapel, his lips pressing together into a thin line. I watch his mouth and my mind wanders as I think about what it would be like to kiss him. I shake my head. I can't think about him like that for now. He's kidnapped me for all I know.

"I told you that I can't tell you some things, Beatrice. This…this is just a dream. And you will wake up from it, and you'll not know truth from fiction." Echo drops his fingers from the button and turns his head to look at me. "I hope, though, that you don't forget how you feel with me."

I'm dumbstruck by his comment. "How I feel with you?"

He nods and reaches out, brushing his fingers down my cheek. The rain is still annoyingly loud, and I can barely make out his words.

I know how I feel with him. I feel like I never want to leave my beautiful dreams. I don't want to wake up and lose him all over again. I feel like I'm betraying Gabe, but am I really betraying him when all of this is in my head? Does it matter that somewhere out there, Echo the Dreamcatcher is waiting for me? Soon, we will be at war, and we'll probably never see each other face to face anyway. So, can't I be allowed my dreams?

When Echo leans in to kiss me, I gravitate to him until our lips brush against each other. There's no immediate kiss; at first it's just lips touching lips. But then Echo tilts his chin up, and I follow the motion in opposite, completely melding our lips together. When he breathes in, I exhale, and when he exhales, I take in his breath, eyes closing.

The rain stops abruptly. Echo grabs my wrist, his mouth never leaving mine. He holds me as if I'm about to slip away from him, and I know why. My dream is ending, and so is our moment. It will fade away into nothing, and Echo will be lost to me again. Why can't I keep them both? Why can't they both be mine?

Echo breaks the kiss. "Because you can only have one of us, Beatrice. And you'll lose one of us as well."

Before I can ask him how he knew what I was thinking, Echo is gone, and I wake, still feeling his fingers pressed into and around my wrist.

CHAPTER THIRTEEN

Every February 16th, the City takes part in Citizens' Day, a day of remembrance for when the Seers vowed to protect the Citizens for the rest of time. Despite the rising tensions, the Keeper insists that we continue the tradition without any interruptions. It is a risk bringing all of us outside, gathering us with the Citizens, and hoping that the Dreamcatchers don't make their appearance today. But just in case, under my robes, I strap on a pistol loaded with beacon bullets, the only kind that can truly incapacitate the Dreamcatchers. They are made from the light of the Beacon, a technology only known to us. With one hit, a Dreamcatcher is no longer able to use Citizens to revive himself. These bullets are only given to Seers— and we protect them, because what can kill the Dreamcatchers can kill us. We can't risk the weapon falling into the wrong hands.

Until now.

I leave my bunk only to be met by my bodyguards, who don't seem to be all too serious today. They chat about something or another as they tail behind me, and I don't even bother to listen.

Brandon, Mae and Gabe meet me down in the Gathering

Room, where we'll receive the same speech we always get this time of the year, just as the Citizens who are now gathered in the Central Park are receiving their speech as well. Theirs goes something a little differently than ours. It speaks about how without the Seers, they would be exposed to the perils of the broken world, the harsh environment, and most of all, the Dreamcatchers, who would enslave them all and use them as chattel. I believe most of their speech speaks the truth, though I also wonder if they could have just found a way to make it on their own, without ever having turned to the Seers for protection in the first place.

We sit in a line, and I traditionally take my spot next to Gabe, who is quick to smile at me and scoot over a little bit. "Hey, Bea." His eyes are glowing, which doesn't happen often for Gabe. While he has received his raven's wings, there's a part of me that wonders how he ever reached that point when his Visions are so infrequent.

"You had a Vision," I casually note, though he and I both know that it's obvious and doesn't need pointing out.

Gabe shifts himself in his seat to face me. "I did, and it was a bit disturbing to tell the truth." The mention of anything being disturbing grabs the attention of the others, and Brandon and Mae all lean in to hear what Gabe has to say.

"Are you going to tell about it?" Mae chirps, her hands folded together like a child waiting for her Caretaker to read her a bedtime story.

"I guess I can. It's already been reported, and the Keeper didn't give me any instruction to keep it to myself." Gabe hesitates a moment, his gaze flickering to me. The way he looks at me makes me shiver, and I quickly look away.

"Well?" Mae asks.

"I don't know. It was of this man. He was my age with blonde hair…blue eyes. He kept staring at me, like I was looking in a mirror or something, and all I could do was stare at him, and all he could do was stare back at me." Gabe's words send a chill down my spine as I immediately remember Echo from my own Visions and dreams. Has he found a way into Gabe's mind as well? Or is this all just a creepy coincidence?

"Eventually, I tried to speak to him, but nothing made sense when it came out of my mouth. He seemed to get angry and walked away from me, leaving me behind, staring into a blank mirror where nothing stared back."

"It sounds like one of your clearer Visions," Brandon notes almost jealously.

"I guess it was clear," Gabe replies. "It didn't make any sense, though."

"Well, the Keeper is the one who is supposed to make sense out of them, not us," Brandon adds. He wouldn't do any extra work if he had to anyway.

"What do you think, Bea?" Gabe asks me directly, and I don't know what to think because all I can think of is Echo.

"Well…I don't know. Maybe it has something to do with your identity?" I hazard a guess that has nothing to do with the fact that the same Dreamcatcher who caught me might have caught Gabe.

"That's what the Keeper suggested. Something about an identity crisis, and how all boys my age go through one…and that we will go through one later when we grow up and have to figure out who we are." Gabe's lips shrink into a confused frown. "How many times do we have to figure out who we are anyway?"

The microphone crackles, startling us all to attention. The lights on the stage brighten, illuminating the Keeper when she comes out in her red robes and stands before the congregation of Seers. Her raven screeches loudly from her shoulder and preens itself idly, as if it were not a part of a huge presentation. With her arms spread out to us, the Keeper stares blankly at the sea of faces and begins the celebrations with no extra fanfare.

"Greetings, Seers. Today marks Citizens' Day, when we remember the sacrifices that we made for those in the City, and we thank them for their roles in our lives. When we are done with our reflection, you will have the chance to co-mingle with the Citizens and take part of the festivities, but this year, it will be a little more monitored because of the Dreamcatcher threat."

We watch the same presentation every year, and every year it seems so strange and far away from me. How did we get to this place? The Keeper turns and activates a holoscreen that projects a picture of pre-War Earth, with all of its greens and blues and white swirly clouds. I've never seen a white cloud myself—after the War the atmosphere was contaminated, clouds no longer formed like they used to. "This was our earth as our ancestors knew it. A mass mostly made of water that formed large pools called *oceans*." She clicks a button on the remote she holds in her hand, and the picture zooms in on a part of pre-War Earth once called Italy. There are flickering images of ancient ruins, people in floppy sun hats and sunglasses milling about the Coliseum with trees that look like scattered umbrellas.

"People were content, then. They went on vacations, boarding airplanes that took them from pre-War America to pre-War Europe. They co-mingled, and for the most part, everything was at peace."

Another click. Some people beside me whisper to each other about imagining the Earth if it was still like that. I try to imagine a world where we could travel and see other places and people, but it's hard to grasp onto any thought at once. I can't even think of a world outside of the City. It's almost impossible to even dream up.

This image was much different. A darkened, grey and dead earth spins on its axis, the bodies of water no longer recognizable from the masses of land. One is a dirty green, the other a dirty gray that seem to blend into each other like a camouflage pattern. With another click, the image zooms in on post-War America, the East Coast, where the City was formed just in the middle of north and south. There is nothing around in any other direction, not on the East Coast, at least, and I am reminded of how very alone we really are here.

"Here we are now. A thriving City in a dead land. We've built ourselves up from nothing, and we've decided to never let such destruction happen to us again. Instead of giving into fate, our scientists decided to bring back a gift given to the people by the Maker a long time ago: the gift of Sight. And those who had it were then expected to use it to protect the Sightless, the Citizens, in order to guide them and keep them from doing any more harm to our broken Earth."

I swallow and look sideways to Gabe, who is staring contently at the images, having seen them a hundred times before. Still, the expression of fascination on his face suggests he's never watched this presentation, and I smile at how Gabe can turn anything old into something brand new and brilliant.

"Isn't it amazing?" he whispers to me, catching my gaze.

Caught off guard, I nod my head and then look back to the images as the Keeper keeps flipping through them. The crowd is transfixed on the photos of destruction. There are images of the War, of many dead people in piles, littered around the earth, skin burnt, land burnt, everything burnt and infected with enough radiation to raze a planet. The photographer must have been brave to risk radiation poisoning to document the horrible acts of mass destruction that ripped our planet apart, piece by broken piece. No doubt he died, and as I think up this person in my mind, I grieve for him, too, and hope that at least his death wasn't slow and agonizing but quick and painless. I wonder if anyone else is thinking of him.

Then, there are images of the rebuilding. First the colonies living in shelters built in the underground subway systems. Then the colonies that found the courage to build up again and brave the world that they were left with. I always find it fascinating that the earth could have gone from having nothing to supporting tiny sprouts of life that took a chance and started anew.

When I look around at the Seers gathered here, I realize how amazing it is that we'd survive something so brutal and unforgiving. I catch the gaze of another Seer who is about the same age as me, Analise. Though we aren't close, she smiles a sad smile, as if commiserating, then goes back to watching the presentation. This is a survival that we can all appreciate, and a loss we can all mourn.

"Somehow, out of all of this, here we are today." The Keeper's words break through my thoughts, and I blink my attention back to her. "We must protect what little we have left. We are the Seers of the future, and had we been there before the War, maybe we could have avoided the mayhem altogether. But instead, mankind fought with one another until there was no one left to fight, and no fighting left to be done." The Keeper's violet eyes seem to meet with each pair of eyes in front of her, and she pauses for a long moment, allowing for the gravity of the past to settle in.

"When you go out there today, I want you to remember how much it is that you do for the Citizens, and how much they depend on us. You are their protectors, each and every one of you. You are the machine of Visions that keeps us alert and ready to defeat whatever comes at us next. They are the people who have borne you, who have made you possible. We want to thank them just as much as they thank us. For this reason, every year, you are awarded a small stipend for this day only. It will go directly into the City's economy, supporting all of the Citizen families. Spend it wisely."

The Keeper disappears behind a curtain to the left of the stage, the microphone clicking off. There's mounting applause and cheering, a rush of excitement that soon we will be able to speak with and stand side-by-side with actual Citizens. Most of the time, they seem so far away from us, as if they exist entirely on their own, and soon our worlds will be combined into one.

Mae claps her hands, jumping to her feet with the excitement. Brandon rolls his eyes and juts a thumb out toward her, and the rest of us laugh at how she carries on.

"I hope they have those fried hot dogs that they did last year. Those were to die for," Brandon wishes aloud, his only goal in life being to eat as much food as he can when he possibly can.

Gabe stands up and stretches his arms up over his head, lifting the hem of his robes from the floor about an inch. "Wanna stick together?" he asks me, and of course, I have to agree. Why wouldn't I want to stay with Gabe? Firstly, there will be a large clash of people when we get outside, and secondly, to spend any time with Gabe, free from the Institution, seems like a small celebration within itself. If we're lucky, the Keeper's guards won't find us and split us up.

"Yeah. I'd like that." I file in behind Gabe as the Gathering Room starts to empty out into the streets. In one mass, the Seers make their way to the Central Park, where tents and tables have been set up to sell all sorts of foods and different wares. Mae and Brandon head off in one direction—toward the food—with Mae chattering all the while.

There's a plethora of Watchmen who stand guard, large machine guns in their hands, eyes scanning everything and anything that moves. The threat of the Dreamcatchers is even more prevalent now than before, since one could easily slip into the crowd and blend in with the Citizens and Seers. It makes me wonder what the Watchmen are looking for, exactly. How do they know who is a Dreamcatcher and who isn't?

And then it occurs to me that they don't.

Gabe reaches and finds my hand so that we don't get separated, and I take it and hold it tightly, even when the crowds do let up, and I don't really need to hold onto it anymore. When I look behind me, I notice the two bodyguards trailing a distance behind. At least they are giving me my space.

"Where do you want to go first?" Gabe looks down at me, waiting for me to make the call.

"I guess we can go over to the vendors and see what they're selling. I always like getting something from them to put in my bunk. We never get to do it at any other time of the year, you know?"

Gabe nods his head and changes his direction so that we are headed for the market instead. "What did you get last time?"

"A pretty sequined shawl. I'll never be able to wear it, but it looks nice on the wall." I laugh pathetically, wondering when I would wear it, even if I could. There aren't many times when we are dressed up in anything aside from our robes and our jumpsuits, and the one time we are—the Ceremony—we are required to wear special outfits for that, too.

"I'm going to get something for you this time," Gabe vows.

"You don't have to do that. Their stuff is expensive anyway. I probably don't even have enough— "

Gabe shakes his head and tugs on my hand. "I said that I'm

going to get something for you. There's nothing you can do about it, Bea. You can complain all your little heart pleases." He grins down at me and shrugs his shoulders. "But it's not going to help, you know. I'm still gonna do it."

"If you insist." I roll my eyes at him, but in truth, I've never had anyone get me anything before. Not like this.

We approach the market and it's already flooded with curious Seers, all perusing the different stands filled with wares such as clothing, shoes, trinkets, jewelry and more. There's a particular stand that sells tiny, crochet animals that seems to be the most popular, even drawing in the heartless ones like Rachelle, who is holding up a teeny pink turtle with big, beady eyes.

Gabe doesn't stop there and instead keeps going toward a table that has different pieces of jewelry set up on it. I hesitate mid-step, and Gabe stops and looks back at me to see what's wrong. "You okay?"

"Yeah. But what could you possibly buy from there?" He picks up walking again and we don't stop until we're at the table. Behind it sits a young woman with long, lavender-blonde hair. She offers us a nervous smile. Everything is awkward at this part of the celebration, since Seers don't really know how to talk to Citizens, and Citizens don't really know how to talk to Seers. She stands up, perhaps out of respect for our stations, and then motions to her collection of silver bottle cap jewelry. Some of the caps, gathered from soda cans and beer bottles, have been decorated with glitter and charms. Others have been flattened out to form rings and bracelets or even necklace pendants. I am amazed with how this woman took something so ordinary and dull and turned it into something so pretty and unique.

"Hello. I'm Beatrice and this is Gabriel." I introduce us semi-formally, dropping the titles of "Seer" out of our names as not to make the gap between us any wider.

"You can just call us 'Bea' and 'Gabe' though." Gabe grins at her the same way he grins at me, and it immediately puts me on edge. "These are pretty things you've got here."

The woman blushes. On her feet, she's taller than the both of us, with a long torso and a somewhat flat face. She's plain at best. Maybe that's why she turns plain things into beautiful ones, because she wants to do the same for herself. "Thank you," she says and lifts up one necklace in particular, a pressed bottle cap from a Pre-War Pepsi bottle, with gilded silver edges. The inside of the cap has been covered with a clear, plastic bubble, and under the bubble is the picture of a raven perched on the branch of a dead tree.

I'm immediately drawn to it. This woman had to have made a necklace like this specifically for a Seer to buy. I reach out and touch it, and the woman lays the necklace down in my hands. "My name is Gina."

"This is beautiful…" I compliment, forgetting about the way Gabe smiled at her. He smiles that way at everyone, really. It's just the way Gabe is.

"We want that one." Gabe interjects and hands the girl a wad of cash that he pulls out from the pockets of his robes.

"Wait. What?" The transaction is over before it even began, and Gina counts the money and then smiles at Gabe and me.

"It's all yours." She pulls out a little box to put the necklace in, but Gabe holds out a hand to stop her.

"We don't need that. Beatrice will wear it."

"I will?" I'm still confused.

"Yeah. It's pretty. It deserves to be on you."

I blush furiously, even more so than Gina did before, and though I want to object, Gabe already has the necklace in his hands and is fastening it around my neck. "Gabe, this is really not necessary. I mean…how much did you *give* her?"

"I don't know. And I don't really care either." Gabe finishes clasping the necklace and walks back around me to look it over.

I lift my hand to touch the cool piece of metal that rests at the hollow of my neck. A necklace. From Gabe. It's too special too quickly, and I blush again. "How's it look?"

"Beautiful." Gabe takes my hand again. "Of course."

We leave that stand and begin to meander down the rows, checking out the products the other vendors have to offer. Gabe's words linger in my mind. *Of course.* I shiver.

I stare at the ground as we walk, keeping one hand on the bottle cap around my neck. I immediately know that it is something that I'll never want to take off again. Something to cherish. Have I ever owned such a something in my life? Most of our stuff, including ourselves, belongs to the Institution.

I squeeze Gabe's hand harder. Even he belongs to something else.

Red robes come into view, and Gabe and I come to a sudden halt. The Keeper stands in front of us, her violet eyes peering from one of us to the other, then to the necklace around my neck.

"My Keeper," we both say in unison and respectfully bow our heads.

The Keeper doesn't respond right away. I feel like her eyes are peeling me apart, looking into my insides, trying to figure me out. There's a smoldering anger that burns deep within the violet orbs, and as I lift my head to stare up at her, I can see it way back there inside her mind. No one knows what's inside there. Whatever it is, it doesn't make her happy.

"I see that you've made your rounds of the market, Seers

Gabriel and Beatrice." The Keeper reaches out to examine the pendant around my neck, and I silently beg for her not to take it from me. Please don't. It's the only thing that Gabe has given to me that I can cherish and hold dear.

Her fingers close around the bottle cap.

Gabe, in confusion, asks quietly, "Is everything okay, My Keeper? I bought that for Beatrice from this girl named Gina down there." He idly gestures over her shoulder in the direction of dozens of vendors, any of which could have been Gina.

"I suppose so." The Keeper lets go of the pendant and folds her hands in front of herself, a peaceful posture, one that smothers the flames in her eyes. "I am glad that we are enjoying ourselves. Seer Beatrice has been working very hard to protect these Citizens, and it's good that they get to see her."

"See me?" This is news to me. How do they even know who I am? I peer around now with new eyes, and I notice that there are, in fact, people who are watching me. Pointing at me. It makes me nervous, and I tear my gaze away from them to look back at the Keeper. "How do they know me?"

"They've heard stories, I'm sure. Not everything is kept a secret at the Institution, Seer Beatrice. Despite our best efforts, there's always something that gets out. And news of a girl who has potentially saved the whole City from a Dreamcatcher attack?" The Keeper doesn't smile, but if she ever smiled, I would think that one would be perfect now. "Well, that is something to talk about."

"Hear that, Bea? You're a celebrity." Gabe must have momentarily forgotten that the Keeper is standing in front of us, and he's right back to his normal, light-hearted self. I shoot him a look to remind him not to be silly in front of the Keeper, but he doesn't notice it and only continues, "Maybe you can sign some autographs?"

The Keeper puts an end to it. "She'll do nothing of the sort."

Gabe becomes quiet once more.

"I am taking Seer Beatrice back inside. A Vision was just reported before the festivities. It suggests that a female Seer will be attacked, and while the Vision wasn't clear enough to determine who, exactly, will be attacked, I can't take any chances." The Keeper only looks at me when she says this, and then she pulls her hood up over her dark black hair and leaves with her retinue of guards, who had scattered into the crowd to allow for some privacy.

Just when I think she's walking away for good, she turns and adds, "And Seer Gabriel is to report to his bunk immediately upon his return. You two have had enough of each other for the day."

"What?" Gabe blurts, but the Keeper is already gone.

I sigh, knowing it's no use arguing with her and instead take Gabe's hand again. "Let's just enjoy the walk home together, okay?"

"I don't see what her big deal is with me spending time with you. First the secrets, and now I can't spend any time with you?" Gabe's irritation seeps into his every word. I understand his frustration, since I have no idea why the Keeper insists we stay apart either. I want to know so I can soothe Gabe and promise that it won't be for long...but I have no idea how long she's going to do this.

We walk back to the Institution and say nothing the whole way there. I come up with many reasons why the Keeper wouldn't want me near Gabe, but none of them make any sense. Maybe she thinks he's a Dreamcatcher? Maybe he's in league with the enemy? Maybe he's under investigation for something she doesn't want me dragged into?

Maybe, maybe, maybe, but there aren't any definites. All that's definite right now is the fact that when our walk is over, Gabe will be away from me, and I'll be alone in my room again, with only a bottle cap to keep me company and to fill the space that is left when Gabe is gone.

At least she let me keep the necklace.

CHAPTER FOURTEEN

Blood runs down the gutters. It flows like rainwater, except rainwater is innocent and pure. Rainwater gives life, and blood is the evidence of life sifting out of the living.

I am standing on a bridge, gun cradled under my armpit, combat jumpsuit soiled and stained with the grime of the City. The screams of innocent people reverberate from everywhere around me, and I don't know which way to run. Everyone needs to be saved, and yet, I cannot save everyone. But somehow, the weight of it is on me, and it's a heavy, suffocating weight. One I don't want to carry, never wanted to carry, and yet I must.

The rap-tap-tap of a gun sounds somewhere from my right, and soon after, the yelling and screaming starts all over again. Citizens dart from the shadows of one alley and into another, their footfalls slapping hard in the puddles of blood.

I twitch my gun in that direction, but when I notice that they are just Citizens, I lower it once more. I could be wrong, though. They could be Dreamcatchers. I won't know until it is too late, and so I've taken to not shooting anyone, for fear it will be a Citizen and not a

Dreamcatcher at all. That would make me a murderer, not a savior. And I'm to be a savior. At least, that is what was told to me.

I hear someone walking up behind me, and I twirl around, my sights aimed on whatever approaches. Again, though, I resort to pointing my gun downward and aiming at nothing. Standing in front of me is a little boy wearing tattered clothes of ugly brown. He holds a destroyed and mangled teddy bear in his hand, and it dangles by his side lifelessly. His cheeks are smudged with dirt, and his knees are scraped and bleeding.

He is so young.

The boy reaches his arms out toward me like the toddler Seers do when they want to be picked up. He must be around seven or eight years old, a little too old to be asking for comfort in this way. Something inside of me urges me to run to him, to lift him up, to hug him and hold him and tell him it will be okay. It will be okay, right?

But before I have the chance to even entertain the notion of doing this, a woman appears behind him. His mother, maybe? Where the boy is dressed in rags, this woman wears a beautiful salmon-colored skirt with a white blouse, neither of which is stained. She has a very motherly appearance about her, with full, dark curls that frame her face, and beautiful sea-green eyes that sparkle even without the light.

She reaches for the boy and takes him by the hand.

And then it happens.

The boy's pupils dilate and become wide and empty. His little mouth opens to gasp, but his chest doesn't rise as it should when your lungs fill with air. The teddy bear drops onto the pavement, one of its tiny paws stretched out into the gutter blood.

The boy slackens, and then hangs in the woman's hand like the bear he once held.

The woman smiles at me. She's smiling at me.

And I can't move.

⬦

It is crowded this time when the Keeper comes to collect the details of my Vision. My two night guards, who are at least ten times bigger than I am, with guns that look ten times bigger than mine, cram into the small bunk space with the Keeper.

When I finish relaying the details to the Keeper, she looks at me for a long moment. "These Visions are very interesting, Seer Beatrice. They seem to be shifting dramatically from one thing to the next. One day they are obscure with hidden meanings, and today, for example, they are clear, with a very clear message."

"What do you think that message is?" I ask, since I certainly didn't think about it myself. I look at the guards, and they stare back at me. Already, I hate them.

The Keeper stands, her new red robes with the black satin lining falling down to the ground, sweeping around her feet. "That message is exactly what you saw, Seer Beatrice. A boy will die today from being Caught."

I blink. "Can't we save him?"

"We have no idea when during the day it is going to happen, and I don't have the resources to set my Seers out into the streets to canvas for a little boy who could show up at any time, anywhere. I'm sorry, but it's not something we can do." She turns and leaves me with a ton of unanswered questions about a Vision the Keeper claims is very clear.

Shooing the guards out, I tidy myself up then leave to go find the others in the Recreation Room. The walk down to the room is a long one, since all I can think about is that boy's falling body, and his teddy bear in a pool of blood. If only my Vision were clearer, then I could See where and when this would happen, and I could save him.

Mae and Brandon sit in front of the television as the news reporter reports on a story that is irritating Brandon. "Come on, she's said this at least ten times by now."

Gabe is seated on the couch, also watching the TV, so I join him, but I also keep an eye on the Keeper's guards by the doors. They bother me.

"This is the City News reporting a devastating incident that happened on the west side today. Around five in the morning, a Watch unit entered a row home on 25th street. Tipped off by a Vision reported by one of the Institution's Seers, they found a whole family of four already dead inside the home."

"That's so terrible," Mae whispers with a hand to her mouth.

"Shh, keep listening. It gets better." Brandon gets up and sits closer to the TV, blocking half of it with his head.

"After this, the unit breached a family member's home, as the Seer reported someone close was the culprit. With testimony from neighbors that Mr. McCue hardly comes out of his house and seems rather strange, the City decided it necessary to bring him in for questioning. Some even report that they've seen him engage in Dreamcatcher-like activity. We can only hope that our City will take care of this swiftly in order to prevent more deaths. This is Karen Little reporting for City News. Back to you, Mike."

I shift in my seat, recalling the Vision I reported this morning. In this case, mine was not the Vision that tipped off the authorities to move in on this house, it was another.

"Didn't Seer Amanda report that Vision?" Gabe asks, picking some dirt out from under his fingernails.

Brandon finally turns from the TV, like it is some big chore. "That's what I heard."

"I heard," Mae chips in, pushing herself up off the floor, "that Amanda had some problems with people outside of the Institution. Something about family that she found out existed…"

"Family?" I repeat the word strangely, as none of us have families. It seems like such a foreign concept to me. How could someone figure out where her family is? And on top of that, what sort of problems could you have with them if you couldn't go and see them in the first place? "I don't understand."

"Me either. But if that is the case, she could have just made up the Vision to get back at them. I mean…the reporter said that Mr. McCue was known to do some 'Dreamcatcher-like activity.' What does that even mean?" Gabe looks at me when he says this, as if I have any idea what it is that Dreamcatchers do, aside from what we've been taught.

"It all sounds strange to me. Arresting people based off of second-hand suspicion." I pick up the remote and turn the TV off just as they are showing a video of the operation. As the camera zooms in on the struggling Mr. McCue, the screen goes black.

"Me too. How long is it going to be before everyone starts to point fingers at one another?" Mae sounds so young when she says this. Somehow, everything she manages to say comes out sounding naïve and pure. She's younger than me by only a few years, but yet she seems like she's ten and not mature enough to understand that it won't be long at all until everyone is pointing fingers.

It has already started to happen.

"I had another Vision this morning," I confess, since again, Gabe did not come around as he normally does when the Keeper is called to bunk 34A.

This draws his attention, though, and he stops picking at his fingernails long enough to lift his violet eyes to me. "Oh?"

I nod my head and glance to Brandon and Mae. "Yes. I think it disturbed the Keeper, even."

"How so? What was it about, Beatrice?" Mae sits on the arm of the sofa where Gabe and I are seated. "Something bad?" There is worry in her words, probably because most of what I See actually does happen in some form or another…and soon.

"It was about the City. There…there was blood running through the streets…people screaming, running. Escaping." I look down at my hands when I say this, blankly staring at them. "I was standing on a bridge holding a gun, and when I turned, there was this ratty little boy just…just standing there with a teddy bear in his hand."

"What was he doing?" Brandon swivels around where he sits on the floor. "Just standing around?"

"Yes. And staring at me. He was all dirty, too. Then he held his arms out for me, and before I could take him, a woman appeared. A Dreamcatcher. She grabbed the boy by his hand and killed him. He just hung there limply, and she smiled the whole while. And I?" I pause here, pursing my lips together in anger. "I did absolutely nothing to stop it."

The three of them silently stare at me. I realize now that I am anxiously wringing my fingers together. Gabe puts his larger hand over mine and squeezes. "It's okay. You probably didn't know, right? Usually we do not know who the Dreamcatchers are until it is too late."

Mae perks up and bobs her head, black pigtails flopping on either side of it. "Yeah! You didn't know. There was no way you could have known."

"Sounded like she was just gonna do it anyway. I mean, how are you gonna shoot her with a kid standing in the way in the first place?" Brandon's deep baritone voice is almost soothing. And for once, what he says isn't something completely stupid.

"That's true, Bea. Not like you could have shot her even if you wanted to." Gabe squeezes my hands again, then lets go and puts both of his hands behind his head, stretching out lazily. "It does sound pretty grim, though. What did the Keeper say?"

"She told me that there wasn't anything we could do to save the boy. She just took her notes and left. I thought maybe she'd be concerned to hear that the City would be in such a state...but it is as if she already knew this was going to happen somehow." I thoughtfully run a hand through my hair, tugging on the tresses that get stuck between my fingers. "Maybe through her own Visions?"

"She is the Keeper. She probably does already know a lot of things that we don't know, or that we See later." Mae shrugs her shoulders and stands back up, bouncing on her heels. Her cheerfulness is refreshing, and though she looks like she is going to leave, I wish she would stay for that reason alone. "I have to head off to the shooting range for target practice. Those guns are too heavy for me, and I don't want to get caught by anyone else's bullets before I can fire my own."

Her words make me sick to my stomach.

"Remember to hold tightly when the gun jerks back. Your aim will be better." Gabe tosses the helpful information out there then his questions return to me. "So why do you think that boy was reaching for you? And why were you just standing on a bridge doing nothing?"

"I have no idea. But I felt so heavy. Burdened. And I knew I had to save everyone, but I couldn't move. It was like I was stuck there, transfixed. I don't know how else to say that even though I wanted to move in my Vision, I couldn't. Something kept me where I was. Something wanted me to witness this poor little boy's death."

"Huh," Gabe huffs.

"What?"

"Nothing, I mean…it just seems strange, is all. Your Visions are becoming clearer…but more unclear as you get them. Haven't you been realizing that? I mean, the stuff that you say happens usually happens, but then there's all this other stuff that feels like some sort of a puzzle. Or a game."

I think on that for a little bit. It is true, and I have realized it more now than ever. It's like my Visions are trying to tell me something without actually telling me anything. And why would that happen? Why wouldn't they just show me like they usually do?

And then I remember: Echo.

What if Echo is the one who is messing up my Visions? Can he even do that? Or what if my Visions know about Echo? Do Visions know? Can they learn?

"Interesting," I finally say. What more can I say, really? It's not as if I can let Gabe know about Echo. I can't tell him that maybe that's why my Visions have been so clear and unclear. I can't tell anyone.

"It is. Maybe it's something you should talk to the Keeper about?" Brandon's suggestion brings Gabe and I to look at each other. I toss a glance over my shoulder at the two guards who stand by the doors of the room, watching me. Always watching me.

Gabe and I don't have to say anything to each other to know that talking to the Keeper about any of this is probably not a good idea. Not with her being so suspicious of me of late.

"Maybe," is all Gabe says. But in this case, "maybe" is more of a "that is never going to happen."

Brandon grabs the remote and turns the television back on to watch the same breach footage over and over again.

I catch a glimpse of a scene where Mr. McCue is being dragged away and into the back of an unmarked, shiny black van. To the right of the picture, there's a view of a bridge that spans a busy street. I squint and tilt my head, getting up from the sofa. "Do you see that?"

Brandon peers closer at the TV. "See what?"

"That." I push my finger against the glass. The whole tip of it nearly covers the very tiny and blurred image. I move it out of the way so Gabe and Brandon can get a closer look.

"It's just a kid," Brandon comments.

Gabe kneels on the floor in front of the TV and looks closer. "It's a boy."

"On a bridge," I note.

A moment later, another figure appears. She wears a salmon-colored skirt and edges up behind him. No one on the scene is paying attention to what is happening yards away. No one sees when she reaches out and touches the boy.

"There! Right there!" I blurt in panic. The guards by the door are alerted to my yelling and push off the wall in unison. They start to cross the room as I tap my finger against the TV screen over and over again.

But no one on the street sees when the boy becomes slack with the woman's touch and then collapses, disappearing from our view. No one sees when she seems to be staring right at the camera, smiling.

No one sees it.

No one but us. And it's too late.

CHAPTER FIFTEEN

The skyline is bright with lights that all look the same color and contrast. They glitter in the stark silence that is only interrupted by the occasional wailing Watch sirens. Up here on the roof, I'm alone. Well, as alone as I can be with two guards following me around. Because it is the middle of the night, though, they prop themselves against the door that leads back down into the Institution and only half pay attention to me as I stand by the ledge, glancing over the City.

The memory of my Vision and what we saw on the television continues to flutter through my mind. Every time I remember the boy dropping down on the bridge, my heart sinks deeper into my chest, so far I'm sure it is sitting somewhere by my stomach. I could have done something to help him, right? I could have gone out there to look for him. I could have done *something* to help him. But I didn't. None of us did. All we did was sit there and watch him perish like he was some fictional character in a television show.

I wrap my arms around my chest, hugging myself against the brisk night wind. With the Keeper depending on the Visions of others, acting on them, believing in them…maybe she will stop paying attention to me. And of course, there's always the option of just hiding my Visions from her altogether—but then I risk her Seeing this herself. And no one has ever faced the punishment of deceiving the Keeper. Nobody has ever tried.

The door clicks open and the two guards are suddenly awake again. Out of the shadow of the stairwell Gabe emerges, dressed in his black robes, just as I am. He nods to my two spies and without waiting for any sort of permission or approval from them, he approaches me. "You know, I don't like when I go to your bunk past curfew and you aren't in there. Makes me think something's wrong." He stares out at the lights, just as I had been doing. "How'd you manage to escape up here anyway?"

I laugh, rubbing my arms with my hands to keep warm. "I walked out. Figured if I was going to get in trouble for it, I would have right away, thanks to these guys." Idly, I wave a hand back toward the guards, who have predictably gone back to half-watching what I am doing. "I don't think the Keeper cares if I spend my night on the roof."

"You never know." Gabe runs a hand over his head, his eyes still directed toward the City lights. "I feel like things are about to change for the worse. I can just…sense it. Maybe it doesn't help that my own Visions, as sparse and brief as they are, are always of something so shadowy and unknown."

"I think things have already changed for the worse, Gabe."

"How so?"

I hook some of my hair back behind an ear and move toward the ledge of the building. The Institution stands taller than any other building in the City. We are the center. We are the most important. We jut up from a sea of dark and grimy buildings that never seem to get clean, no matter how often it might rain. "I've been thinking a lot about the boy on the bridge. You know, if I didn't have that Vision, none of us would have seen it."

"And? We can't See everything all at once, Beatrice. No matter how hard we try."

"No, we can't. But I *Saw* this before it happened, and…and then it *did* happen. And it just seems so wrong that I knew that boy was going to die before he actually did, and there was nothing I could do about it." My chest tightens again as the images replay in my head. I close my eyes, trying to will them out of my mind. "And what if that is how it is going to be for the whole war? That all we can do is See these things happening, but none of us can actually stop it?"

Gabe doesn't answer.

"Isn't that what is going to happen? None of us have actually tried to *stop* the war. We are all just *preparing* for it. Why are we even letting the invasion happen in the first place if we know it is coming?"

"Maybe it's something we can't stop." Gabe sits down on the ledge of the building and stretches his legs out in front of him.

This isn't good enough for me. "And how do we know? Have we even tried?"

Gabe stares at me, his violet eyes pooling with the light from the City. "Come here."

I sit beside him and he puts an arm around my middle and scoots me closer to him. It's affectionate in a way that Gabe usually isn't, and I am suddenly reminded of my heart in my stomach.

"I don't think it is something we should talk about in this company." Gabe nods in the direction of the sleepy guards. "Or at all, really. Not unless we want to find ourselves on the gallows along with the others who are being taken away and questioned. And I really, really don't want anything to happen to you."

I sigh, knowing he is right. What possessed me to say any of that aloud anyway? "I don't want anything to happen to you either, Gabe."

"I know. And I know how you feel, so you don't have to tell me, as I feel the same way. We are fighting on the same team, Bea. And…" His words taper off as he looks up into the night sky, perforated with tiny, glowing stars.

"And what?"

"…I feel like you are keeping more from me than I want to know."

It is my turn to be silent. When Gabe looks at me, I look down into my lap, unable to meet his gaze. I'm not good at lying to Gabe, and I know he can see right through me, especially now. I don't want us to fight again. I don't want to try and convince him again that as much as I want to tell him, I can't. I can't give up Echo. Not even to Gabe.

Gabe's arm snakes from around me when I don't reply. He runs a hand over his head again, a nervous gesture. "And, I am just going to assume, as much as it pisses me off, that you have a good reason for this…just as we have a good reason for not speaking about what the Institution could be doing and what they *should* be doing." He reaches out and lifts my chin with a crooked pointer finger, urging me to look back up at him. "I don't want to lose you, Beatrice. And it's getting easier every day for us to lose each other. Especially with the Keeper so against us."

"I understand," I whisper, staring into his violet gaze.

"So promise me that you won't do anything that would make it easier to do so."

I can't promise this. I can't promise it because I don't know. And

Gabe knows this. Why would he ask me such a thing when he knows very well that I can't promise it to him anyway?

Maybe to see if I'll lie.

So, I don't. "I can't. I will try, Gabe, you know I will try…but we don't know what is in store for us. We don't know what the Dreamcatchers will do. We don't know whose Vision will be the next one scrutinized. We don't know what new rules will be forced upon us, and we don't know what the next step in the Training Games is, if there is one. We could all be fighting on the streets tomorrow for all we know." I grab one of Gabe's hands and squeeze it, desperately wanting him to understand that right now, no one is safe. Not me. Not him. Not Mae or Brandon. Nobody. "I can promise you that I'll do what I can to protect myself and to protect you and hopefully, when this is all over, we'll be on this roof again talking about how silly all of this was."

Gabe returns the squeeze, and in the next moment he leans forward, closes his eyes and presses his lips against mine in a fierce kiss. I'm paralyzed with the unknown, and instinct urges me to return the kiss, which I do, despite the fact that until this point, I've never once been kissed before. Not in real life. When the thought occurs to me that someone will steal Gabe away just because of this moment, I push him away with a sudden force.

Gabe's eyes flicker back open, startled. "Beatrice?"

I stand, robes falling around my form. "I have to go." When I look at the guards, they both have their eyes closed, dozing against the wall. They saw nothing. But that's not to say that no one else did. I'm sure the Keeper has her eye on us somehow. I swallow the fear back down somewhere into my middle and rush for the stairs.

"Bea?" Gabe calls, his voice tugging on me like a hook caught in some fish's mouth. But I can't turn back. I need to get off this roof.

I need to get back to my bunk, and I need to stay away from Gabe. At least until everything is settled again. I can't lose Gabe. He's the only constant I have.

The door flings open and bangs against the wall, waking the guards. They both jump and are quick to follow after me as I run down the many stairs back to level thirty-four. I'm moving so quickly, but somehow manage not to trip on my robe and fall down the rest of the flights. When I get to the black door with the large "34" printed on it, it slides open to let me pass.

I round the corner of the dimly lit hall and jet back to my room faster than the guards can keep up with me. Once I get there, I enter the code to open the doors and step inside. Slamming my hand on the button to lock them behind me, I slump against the wall and sink to the floor. The footsteps of the guards stop just outside, but neither of them bother to actually try and follow me into my bunk. They don't come in here anyway. Here, I am safe. Mostly.

Putting my fingers to my lips, I feel where Gabe's mouth was against mine and the butterflies awaken in my stomach. Why did I run away from him? Why couldn't I have stayed? It isn't Gabe I'm running from, though. It's the thought of losing him.

I put my ear against the door to listen for any other footfalls, any sign that Gabe might have chased me. Thankfully, though, I hear nothing except the murmuring of the guards outside. But maybe I wanted him to chase me, to go that far to get me back.

CHAPTER SIXTEEN

I watch Echo peel back the skin of an envy-green fruit that I've never seen before. Juice drips down his fingers as he separates the outside from the inside, and the fruit in the middle is a deep pink. It peels apart like an orange, but its fragrance is more flowery and less citrusy.

I'm starving, and my stomach growls. My legs hurt like we've been walking for hundreds of miles, and the arches of my feet are fallen and raw. Although the dream for me has just begun, it seems part of it has gone on without me being involved at all. "Where have we come from?"

Echo offers me a half-moon slice of the fruit and it rests in the palm of his hand, extended out toward me. I pluck it out and smell its strange essence. "We've been walking."

"From where?" Popping a piece of the fruit into my mouth, I purse my lips at its sour taste and fight the reaction to spit it right back out. That would be rude, though, and on top of that, I'm much too hungry to let any food go to waste. So, I suck the juice from the pulp, which lessens the sourness and brings out the floral flavor instead.

"From the City. I am taking you to my home." Echo chews on

a piece of the fruit and makes no face. He must be used to its rather strange taste. The juice runs down his hands and arms and somewhere under the white robe with the red satin trim that he wears.

I can't take my eyes off him as he eats. He mistakes this for wanting another piece, which he readily offers me without a touch of hesitation. I take it from him, and though I am not a fan of the fruit, I eat it all the same to sate the growling in my stomach. "Where are we?"

"In the field."

"Where?"

Echo licks the juice off his fingers to clean them. "The field. Between the City and Aura. It's pretty big. We've been walking all day."

I look behind me, but the City is not there. Does Gabe know where I am? Does anyone know where I am? How did I get out of the City anyway? I open my mouth to ask all of these questions, but before I can get any of them out, Echo begins to speak once more.

"We will be there soon. Just over these moors is the wall that surrounds the outskirts of Aura. Once we are inside of the walls, we will be safe."

"Safe? From what?" I forget about my other questions for now. What do I have to be safe from out here? I take another glance around, but all I can see are miles and miles of tall, golden-colored stalks of grass. Sometimes, a shadow of a bird dances across the amber field, but I can never look up in time to actually see it.

"The Rogues."

"And where do the Rogues come from?"

Echo finishes the rest of the fruit and tosses the rind somewhere into the tall grass. "They are people who could not make it to the City in time, after the war, and were turned away. They live somewhere out here, waiting to rob or kidnap those who come through. It's rare, though, that anyone comes through on foot. We have airships that take us where we need to go, and there are special warships that are used to leave Aura, but that is rare too."

This is all interesting to me. I've not heard much about the home of the Dreamcatchers. The Keeper seems to only fill in some of the picture as far as our history is concerned. There are blank spaces throughout the retelling of the City's past, parts that don't quite make sense.

Just like it doesn't make sense how I got to be out here with Echo. Or why we are running away from the City at all. But I do realize that with him I feel safe, and the apprehension that is building deep down in my core doesn't seem as overwhelming as it could be. Echo is my calm. In this dream, he is what grounds me. The whole world could be going to hell, and I'd probably never notice if Echo was by my side.

It makes me not want to leave him in the same way that I don't want to leave Gabe. But here we are, Echo and me, in the field of golden grass. There is no wind. Everything is quiet. I reach out and touch Echo's face, wiping a drip of fruit juice from his chin, and I want to be here forever, frozen in time, distant and free.

◇

The paranoia doesn't get any better as the weeks go on. The City is in a panic, and today the Seers are being deployed. I stand in line with the other members of Team A who are all lined up before a gigantic bay door that leads outside. Though we can see the chaos from the Institution windows, perched high above the buildings surrounding us, it's hard to make out exactly what has been going on outside.

"Do you really think the Dreamcatchers are running around killing people?" Mae tugs on one of the straps that holds her gun close to her chest. She looks ridiculous, since her weapon is nearly half the size she is, which throws off her balance and makes her seem uncoordinated.

Brandon brushes his scraggly hair out of his eyes, but the breeze from the vents pushes it back into his face and his efforts are immediately futile. "Probably. Did you see that one clip where this man was running down the street, grabbing people by their hands, infiltrating their minds? They just dropped down to the ground, one-by-one, like dominoes."

"They don't even bother to hide in the shadows anymore. They are just out there, in the open. And anyone could be one of them." Mae stops fiddling with her straps and turns to stare at me when I don't respond. "Bea?"

Something about this doesn't feel right. That's all I can keep thinking as I watch the others suit up and prepare to deploy. What are we going to change by going out there? No one even told us what we are to do, aside from shooting suspected Dreamcatchers. But even then, how are we supposed to know who is a Dreamcatcher and who isn't until it's too late?

"Sorry. I was running behind." Gabe's voice shatters my thoughts. He stops beside me, but doesn't say a word to me, nor does he look in my direction. "When are we heading out?"

"Five minutes," Mae chirps and holds up her wrist, which is wrapped in a silver watch with a violet face. It looks cartoonishly big on her little frame.

I stare at Gabe and the obvious way that he seems to be ignoring me then I dismiss it in favor of more important and dangerous thoughts. It is fine if he wants to ignore me now, just as long as we don't lose each other later in the mass chaos on the other side of those doors. "Five minutes." I echo Mae's words, violet eyes flickering to the rotating lights that suddenly come alive, casting their orange-red hue around the bay.

The Keeper appears on a catwalk to the left of us. She clears her throat and speaks loudly, with no need for a microphone. "Seers. Today, you are to set forth on your first, real mission. It has been many, many years since we've had to battle the Dreamcatchers in this fashion. They have somehow managed to breach the City and are dangerously close to threatening the security of the Institution."

"No one mentioned that before," Brandon mumbles.

"The truth is, Seers, if they come any closer, then our very existence is in peril. The Seers cannot be proficient once we are infiltrated. Our powers are connected to one another and once tapped, we will be threatened, exposed, and possibly defeated." The Keeper continues, arms raised in the air as if addressing a massive crowd, when in all reality there are about forty of us down here: Team A, Team B, and Team C.

I notice Rachelle leaning on a column as if all of this were some normal event. She picks the dirt out from under her nails and flicks it away, not even looking at the Keeper as she continues her speech. Rachelle looks as though she was already privy to this new information. As if someone already told her.

"We cannot allow this to happen. When you set out today, you will experience another side of your gift. You have learned how to harvest your Sight, you have learned how to physically combat those around you, and now you will learn how to seek out the Dreamcatchers." As if knowing we were all asking "How?" in our minds, the Keeper only pauses for an instant then answers all the unasked questions. "You will find, as you walk the streets, that you will be drawn to the somewhat painful aura of the Dreamcatchers. We, of course, had no way of teaching you this without bringing one of them into our midst. Perhaps, though, you might have felt it at the execution we had some time ago."

I try to think back to the day we saw Paradigm riddled with bullets. I remember how I couldn't look away, and the way that she was staring at me in return. I remember how my chest felt tight, squeezing until Paradigm fell to the ground, dead. A shudder crawls up my spine and goose bumps form on my arms.

"You must be careful. Just as soon as you feel the connection, they could be a mile away or they could be standing right next to you. Do not take any chances." The Keeper pauses, and the "s" sound reverberates through the bay. We are all quiet. We know what this means. Taking no chances means shooting and killing people who may not be Dreamcatchers at all. We will be adding to the chaos before we even begin to quell it.

"This isn't going to be pretty," Gabe remarks in a whisper to the group. I look over at him, but he is still pointedly staring in any direction but mine.

"Do we really have to…just shoot people? What if they aren't Dreamcatchers?" It finally clicks for Mae, and her eyes darken when she figures out the answer on her own.

"Then they are dead," Brandon answers.

A loud groan fills the bay as the massive doors unlock. All at once, the three teams take a step back away and stare nervously at the seam, which slowly begins to part. Our guns are loaded with beacon bullets, and we are as ready as we will ever be.

"I wish you luck, Seers. Eradicate as many Dreamcatchers as you can until you are ordered back to the Institution. Remember to stay alert! Don't take any chances." The Keeper pauses there as the doors finally open and the dim light from the outside fills the dark room. "Kill or be killed."

With those last words, our teams are ordered forward and before we even have a chance to think about what we are running into, we are all hustled out of the Institution and into the streets of the City. I cast a look over my shoulder and watch as the bay doors shut behind us, locking us out. A seed of panic begins to grow in me. I know this will not turn out to be something good. *Echo, isn't this when you are supposed to save me?*

Team C takes off to the left and hurries down a through street. They are quick to disappear, and quick to open fire. We hear the pat-pat-pat of their machine guns and the clinking of the shells as they hit the asphalt. Rachelle and Team B gung-ho it right into the center of the City, which I should have expected, being that all Rachelle cares about is bringing home glory.

Our team, Team A, is following Gabe today. "Listen! Despite what we have been told, I don't want you shooting up just anyone, you hear me? Look and listen. Observe. Feel. But don't just go out there killing anything that moves!" Gabe shouts at us, his dark hair falling in his face at the end of every punctuated sentence. Sweat beads on his brow and drips down the sides of his face. He's nervous. We are all nervous. I can even hear Mae's teeth chattering together in her head. "Do you understand, Team?"

The air resounds with a series of "Yes, sirs" and "Yeahs!" I don't shout anything. I'm too busy staring at Gabe and wondering if we'll make it back to the Institution alive so that I can apologize to him for running off after he kissed me.

Gabe turns and starts for President Street, one of the main roads that lead to a more populated area of the City. We march double-

time, and the mix of our boots hitting the ground, the screaming of
Dreamcatchers and Citizens alike, and the eerie calm of the streets
brings an uneasiness to our mission. I wonder if Gabe has a plan
as he keeps marching ahead, running by the occasional Citizen
gathered in a window, peering out into the disorder beyond. Does
he feel where he is going, or is he just running blindly into mayhem?

As we turn a corner, we nearly collide into each other as those
in front of us suddenly break the cadence in order to avoid stepping
on a crumpled body huddled in a street gutter. Half of the corpse's
head is blown off, and though I don't get a good look at it, I piece
together that it is probably a woman, since the body is rather small.

"Oh my goodness!" Mae puts a hand to her mouth to hold back
the reactionary retching.

"Keep moving!" Gabe reminds us through the com in our
helmets, and we are back to marching in two lines. When we near
the end of the street, he puts his hand up in a closed fist, signaling for
us to stop. He lowers his hand, and we crouch on the ground.

At first, I don't know why we've stopped. But then, I start to
feel it: a strange, tugging sensation that burns and feels empty at the
same time. I've felt it before, with Paradigm, but never with Echo.
Why haven't I felt this with Echo? I can tell we all feel it.

"They are near," Brandon whispers, his hand on the side of his
head. He holds it like he has a headache. My head is also beginning
to throb as the feeling becomes more intense.

"They must be getting closer." I peek up at Gabe to see what his
next move will be. All of us are holding our heads now, and though
it doesn't exactly hurt, the throbbing is a nuisance and I can't think
straight. Between my ears, it is hot and murky. I can hear Echo's
voice calling to me: *Beatrice, save me…*

His words physically hurt. I whimper, and Mae looks back at

me in concern. "Beatrice?"

I wave my hand to dismiss Mae's unease. Then I hear Gabe yelling, "There! That one!"

We look ahead, but all I see is a family standing in the picture window of their home, staring at us with wide eyes. There's a mother in her pale blue robe, a father with his arms around his wife, and two children in their pajamas. The others in Team A pull up their weapons, fumbling with them since we all let our guards down while holding our heads. Our sights are aimed at the family, but no one in particular. *Which one, Gabe?* We all must be thinking the same thing. The family might have stopped breathing by now, standing in the line of fire from a dozen machine guns.

"Which one?" another teammate finally yells, but it is too late.

From behind a sofa, a young girl darts out and grabs the other children by their wrists. Immediately, the boy and the girl beside her drop to the floor, dead. The child starts to laugh, until Gabe yells, "Fire!"

The mother and the father scream and jump out of the way as a few from our team fire a spray of bullets that shatters their picture window and riddles the Dreamcatcher girl's body. Her laughing stops abruptly and the girl falls to the ground in a puddle of her own blood, which now speckles the room with crimson.

"Cease fire!" Gabe shouts over the loud discharges of our weapons. When the firing stops, all we hear are the wracked sobs of the parents, who clamor over their two fallen children—even the Dreamcatcher. The headache goes away. Mae starts to vomit, spewing her guts up all over the pavement. One-by-one, we stand and turn away from the grieving parents. Every time Echo calls to me I feel a twist of pain in my chest. Eventually, though, his voice dissipates and I can only hear my own heavy breathing.

"Let's go." Gabe's words are muttered as he is forced to turn away from the scene and press on. We can't stand here and grieve too. We are sitting ducks if we dare.

I pat Mae's back and tug her gun up and into her hands. "Come on, Mae. It's not going to get any better."

"She was just a girl!" Mae cries, wiping spittle off her mouth.

"She was a Dreamcatcher who was a girl. She killed her own brother and sister." I nudge Mae forward as the team starts to march again. "She was the enemy."

Mae sniffles, and I watch as plump teardrops trail down her tanned cheeks. Doesn't the Keeper care about what Mae will become at the end of the day? Mae looks back at me, violet eyes dimming. "She was just a girl."

I don't argue with her. Mae only sees the good in people. Even if she just watched a Dreamcatcher's merciless killing, all Mae will concentrate on is the fact that the Dreamcatcher was a child, and is now no more. I let her cling to her goodness, because I wonder how it would be to only see the positive. When she looks out over the City and its barricades, does she see a different place?

We march down another street, toward the sounds of a major scuffle. Gabe puts a hand to his ear, where a small radio has been attached so he can keep in touch with the other team leaders. After an attentive pause, he turns back to us, but his gaze locks on mine. "The other two teams are in big trouble. They've come across a mass of Dreamcatchers who have taken over a row home south of here."

I jump at a loud explosion that goes off from that area, and smoke and flames are quick to rise into the air after the noise. Putting my hand up above my eyes to shield them from the brightness, I watch as the plumes of fire lick into the air like fingers wiggling at the sky.

"Come on!" Gabe doesn't give us any more information as we take off toward the looming disaster south of here. I can't let him get too far away from me. I can't lose him. So I dart down side streets with the rest of my team and keep an eye on Gabe and Mae, though Mae still looks pale and disoriented after our first kill. As we run to our target location, groups of Watchmen also book it to the scene.

The heat of the explosion stings my face. When we round the last block, we come upon a scene much more gruesome than the family in the picture window. A whole house is on fire, rapidly burning out of control. The brick walls encase the flames, giving them a safe place to grow and overwhelm the rest of the structure. Hunkered down on one side are Teams B and C, taking cover where they possibly can, behind Dumpsters, hiding in alleyways and inside other houses. They are shooting toward the fire, where I can barely make out about ten or eleven Citizens— No, Dreamcatchers. We've found our enemy.

"Get to cover! Get to cover!" Gabe grabs my arm and drags me with him before I have a chance to move. We shield ourselves behind a brick wall that encloses someone's front yard. I duck down to keep my head safe and check my gun to make sure it's ready to fire. Really, I need to catch my breath to make sure *I* am ready to fire.

"Grenade!" The shout goes up from more than one person, and Gabe throws himself over me, pushing me to the ground. The explosive goes off to the left of us, destroying the facade of the nearby house. Pieces of brick tumble from the sky like hail in a storm, and one catches Gabe's face, tearing the skin by his eye.

"Damn it!" He climbs off me and wipes the blood out of his eye, but as soon as it is brushed away, new blood pools in its place. "I can't see!"

"It's okay, Gabe. I got this." I push myself up and rest the barrel of my gun on the wall in front of me to keep it steady. Staring down the sight, I try to find a Dreamcatcher in all the smoke, fire, and mayhem, but I can see nothing but, well…smoke, fire and mayhem. "I can't see them anyway."

"*Feel* them, Bea." Gabe points somewhere off to the left, and though he can't see, when I turn my sight in that direction, I can make out the form of a man with a gun, shooting at our forces. *How did you do that?* I don't ask any questions aloud, though. Instead, I open fire. The first few rounds, I don't seem to hit him, but as soon as I start firing again, I catch the man in his shoulder with a beacon bullet and he drops his gun to the ground.

"Got him!" I chirp, waiting for Gabe's praise.

"Did you *kill* him?" Gabe already knows the answer to this, though. I know he does, because he shoves me back toward the wall, one hand over his eye. "Kill him."

The words sound so unfair to me. Though we've been training for this moment, I don't feel right knowingly murdering someone. I don't even know what is going on here. Sure, we are fighting off the Dreamcatchers before they can infiltrate the Institution, but why are they attacking anyway? Why do they want the Institution?

I don't think when I pull the trigger. I do see the man go down, though, and he doesn't get back up. He's dead. Gabe nods his head and wipes at his eye again. "Good!"

There's the praise, but I don't feel good about what I've done at all.

The Watch is also opening fire on the Dreamcatchers, and one-by-one they fall, followed by a shower of beacon bullets from one team or another, and the return fire eventually stops. A cheer goes up from one of the other teams, and eventually everyone is cheering.

Everyone but me. They could still be out there. We shouldn't be celebrating yet.

Gabe pats my back, and we both stand. The other Seers pop up as well, like the prairie dogs we've seen in our environment textbooks, peeking up from their burrows. I spot Rachelle standing on top of a pile of rubble, holding a Dreamcatcher's head up by the hair, his body a dead weight underneath him. She is proud of her trophy and lifts it high for everyone to see. We've become bloodthirsty and savage. The Keeper has turned us into well-oiled killing machines, and though I couldn't see it then, I clearly see it now.

"We did it, Bea," Gabe whispers and wraps an arm around my shoulders, pulling me close, seemingly forgetting about the fact that I ditched him on the rooftop.

I hug him in return, but not because I'm happy. "Yeah…we did it."

The blood by his eye doesn't stop running, and is getting everywhere. I pull away from Gabe before it can get on me, and I reach up to examine the cut. "You are going to need to get that sewn up, you know."

"What's another scar?" Gabe smirks lopsidedly. Despite the chaos, I can't help but be reminded about how ruggedly handsome he is, especially in his new role as a leader and soldier. "I heard you girls like scars anyway."

"Us girls?" I look up as a siren begins to wail, calling us back to the Institution. "I'll take a scar over you being dead, Gabe." I take his hand in mine and start back to the Institution, wary, confused, but still alive.

CHAPTER SEVENTEEN

Gabe lies on a cot in the infirmary while a nurse stitches together his cut. It's about two inches long, and too close to his actual eye. The stitches are the clear kind that disintegrates when the wound heals, minimizing any scarring. When the nurse is done with her work, I can hardly tell the suturing is in place, save for the raw, pink line that surrounds the cut.

My bodyguards have found me again, and stand out of the way by the door leading from the infirmary. They watch us closely, but thankfully they haven't tried to separate me from Gabe. Yet. And if they tried, I don't think I'd let them this time around. I almost lost Gabe. I'm not going to allow them to take me from him now.

"How's it look?" He asks me as he pushes himself up to sit. Surrounding him are rows of other cots, spanning out left and right. In about a dozen of them, other patients lie groaning and holding their middles, or their legs, or their arms. There are trails of spattered blood that lead to back rooms where more serious operations are taking place.

"I didn't know so many others got hurt," I absently note as a familiar girl from Team C starts to yell from her bed. The doctor pulls on her shoulder then pushes it back in a rough, jerking motion to pop it back into its socket.

"Yeah, but how about my eye?"

I look at Gabe and his eye. "It looks like an eye, Gabe."

"You know what I mean. How's the cut?"

"It looks fine." He always looks this way. More than fine. But I don't have it in me to say anything like that to him. Instead, I reach out and brush some of his hair out of his eyes. "You look fine."

The nurse pats Gabe on his leg and pushes her little supply tray out of the way. "Make sure you keep it clean with the anti-bacterial fluids I gave to you, Seer Gabriel."

"I will. Thank you, Nurse."

She walks away and into the infirmary's well-organized chaos, leaving both of us alone.

"Think the girls will like it?" Gabe tentatively touches the stitches and winces in pain. "It still hurts."

"That's because the stitches were just done, Gabe. And I don't know what the girls will like. Why do you care anyway?" I don't realize the defensiveness in my tone until the words play back in my head. Surely Gabe didn't miss it either.

"Because maybe I care about what other girls think?" Gabe challenges, swinging his legs around the side of the cot until his heels are back on the ground.

"Oh really?" I don't buy it for a second. Especially not after the kiss. The very thought of it brings a blush to my cheeks, and I duck my head to hide it. "Just make sure you keep it clean or your face will look all messed up. And no girl likes a messed up face."

"Very clever, Bea." Gabe rises and grabs the anti-bacterial solution from the tray. "Let's get out of here. There are too many people screaming and carrying on."

My attention is drawn to those who are wounded. I blindly follow behind Gabe, and my guards follow behind me, but I can't keep my eyes off the others. There's a Seer who can't be past twelve years old who cries on her cot with a bloodstain as big as a plate on her chest. A nurse passes by her and hits a button, which controls the IV stuck in the girl's arm. Her crying dies off and eventually stops altogether as the painkillers cloud the suffering.

"I didn't know so many others got hurt," I repeat, looking at Gabe as he beelines out of the infirmary. Perhaps it is bothering him as well.

"I heard there were fourteen in there. Three of them pretty critical. They were probably in the back."

"None from Team A?"

Gabe shakes his head, smiling proudly. "Not one. Well, not one but me. Then again, we did get to the fighting a bit late."

And if we got there sooner, would we have been able to prevent all those people being in the infirmary? I cast one more look over my shoulder as the doors close behind me and block out the sights and sounds of the other patients. My guards have become more restless, even as they follow, and they start to walk faster, gradually closing the space between us. "Well, I guess it's good that there were only fourteen people hurt. I'm not really sure what happened out there. I feel so…disoriented."

"What is there to understand? We had to help the Watch seek out the Dreamcatchers and kill them, and we did." Gabe stops in front of one of the lifts and slaps the up button.

"Why didn't they tell us we could do that before?"

"What do you mean?"

The doors to the lift open and fortunately no one else is inside.

Gabe grabs me and pulls me into the tight space. The doors shut behind us, leaving the guards behind, and the lift starts to shoot up the shaft to where our bunks are.

I slam my hand on the stop button and the elevator jams to a halt. Gabe almost tumbles over at the sudden stop and frowns. "What the hell, Bea?"

"You aren't listening to me, Gabe. We aren't on the same page here." I search the elevator, knowing it's probably bugged. They are following me, after all, and I'm sure that even now the Keeper has her sights on me. "We have to talk."

"Well, you have me trapped in here, so why don't we start talking?" Gabe folds his arms over his chest, his eyes stern and filled with annoyance. Still, he looks so handsome with the dirt and soot smeared on his face, and the cut by his eye. I can feel myself blushing again, and I quickly turn away and pull on the stop button so the lift starts to move once more.

"We will talk later."

Gabe continues to stare at me and drops his arms to his sides. "Fine, whatever Bea. After dinner, then. I'll meet you…somewhere."

"We'll figure it out." I frown because I know I am still blushing, and if Gabe isn't suddenly blind from his injury, he surely sees it too.

Our elevator stops at the bunk floor, and the doors slide open with a hiss. We step out at the same time and turn in opposite directions to where our assigned rooms are. Down the hall, the stairwell door slams open, nearly knocking out another Seer, and my two bodyguards stumble out and start to look for me.

"I'll come get you for dinner." Gabe starts to walk off. "You better be ready."

I watch him leave, or rather, I watch as he walks halfway down the hallway and some lingering female Seers follow him and gush about his dire wound. I roll my eyes and start for my room. "Stupid girls," I mutter to myself as my fingers rake against the walls, making an annoying screeching noise. The guards eventually catch up with me, and they are not very happy. One tries to lecture me about running off, but I ignore him and eventually he gives up.

When I get back to my room, finally alone with the door shut behind me, I'm filled with an overwhelming sense of relief. I sink into my bunk and start untying my boots, which fall to the ground with a clunk. Next, I strip out of my jumpsuit and throw that to the side. My room smells like smoke and sweat. Left in my white T-shirt, I curl beneath the covers and pull my pillow over my head. There has to be a reason why we've never been told about this Dreamcatcher sense before, these pounding headaches, and why they are just starting to kick in now.

As I think about it, exhaustion grips at my body, and I fade into sleep.

When I open my eyes, Echo stands over me. We are in my bunk and not in the field, and I shoot up into a sitting position, startled.

"What are you doing here?" I whisper in exclamation, though Echo seems unconcerned about his sudden appearance.

"What were you doing out there?" He asks me in return and sits beside me on the bed.

"I…we were ordered out there. To fight."

Echo sighs. "It is getting worse now, Beatrice. There will be more and more danger, and all the more reason for us to save each other."

"You keep saying this…but I don't understand how I am supposed to save you, Echo." I chew on my lower lip, peeling some skin from it in the process. "I don't even know where you are."

He laughs and reaches out to turn my face to look up at him. "I am right here, Beatrice."

I'm filled with that tingling, fluttering sensation as I stare into his eyes. I can't look away from him. I have no desire to. In fact, I don't want him to go. I want him to stay here with me, because with Echo, there's a sense of security that I don't feel the rest of the time when I am alone. Or with Gabe.

"You know what I mean. You aren't really…here. You are here." I tap my temple to indicate that he's only inside of my head, my dreams and nothing more.

"Am I?" Echo smiles at me like I'm a child who can't comprehend what he means. "I'm out there too. You just have to find me."

"And what about you? Will you be looking for me?"

"I will be hunting you and the other Seers." Echo's hand drops from my face, but his eyes never leave mine. "Like all of the other Dreamcatchers. I will be trying to find you and kill you. Destroy you and all of your kind, and then the Citizens will be ours."

I feel the blood drain from my face. The fluttering feeling immediately stops. "What?"

"Don't act as if this is a surprise, Beatrice. I am a Dreamcatcher. You are a Seer. We have been at war with one another for more years than we've been alive, and now the war is on your front step." Echo stands and moves to the window. He pushes the button that raises the blinds, and inch-by-inch the City is exposed in its full glory. The dingy afternoon sun tries to illuminate all of the buildings, and in some places the light reflects off the many windows, making it seem brighter than it actually is. Smoke still rises from the south, but is slowly dissipating so that it looks more like fog or exhaust than the aftermath of a bomb. "We are out there, waiting for the order to attack."

"This isn't your attack?" I walk over to stand beside him, pressing *one of my hands against the glass.*

"No. This is your *attack. You will know when we attack.*" Echo *puts his hand next to mine, and we both gaze out over the City.* "The *Dreamcatchers are desperate, Beatrice. Our people are dying of the plague in Aura, and we need the Citizens in order to live.*"

"That is madness, Echo. I am sure there are other ways to heal *yourselves…*"

"There aren't. This is the way it has to be. It's how we were made. *It's all we know.*" Echo *glances to our hands.* "I'm sorry it upsets you, *Beatrice.*"

"It upsets me that you cannot see how wrong this is."

"Is it wrong to want to save your own kind from becoming *extinct? You might be safe in your City here, but we are quickly fading into nothing back in Aura.*"

I think about what I would do if I had a chance to save the lives of thousands by taking the lives of others. It doesn't make sense to me, but I'm also not the one watching all of his people die. Would I kill a Citizen in order to save Mae? Or Brandon? Or even Gabe?

"It feels like a piece of the puzzle is missing, Echo. Like we only *know so much and someone is hiding the rest from us.*"

"I know. I've been trying to figure it out myself. Perhaps that's *how I came to be in your dreams. We heard that your Sight was strongest, and I thought to try and reach you and see what you knew. And now I know that you are so strong and brave…so smart.*" Echo *looks at my reflection on the window as he speaks to me.* "That is why *we have to save each other. My talents exceed my kind, and yours exceed yours. I need to free you from here, take you with me where you can flourish and help us.*"

"And where would we go? No one has been out of the City in *many years. I don't even know what is past the barricades.*" *I never really thought about it before, either. No one ever made it a goal to break free. We've been taught from a very young age that the City is all of the world we have to know. It is all there will ever be for us. It is hard to imagine a place that has never existed for me.*

Echo smiles. "You will see when we get there."

For the first time, I am impatient with him. "What do you mean by that? You can't have a plan and then not tell me how it ends."

"That's what life is, Beatrice. It is unknowing." His smile doesn't falter. It's as if distress cannot reach him. I admire the resilience and part of me envies it as well. "Besides, you are the Seer. You are supposed to be telling me what will happen...not the other way around."

Now, it's my turn to smile. How I can be smiling at a time like this, I don't know, but Echo's infectious demeanor is beginning to wrap its tendrils around me, embracing me in calmness, and I don't resist. Then Echo really does put his arms around me, drawing me close to him and guiding my head to rest on his chest. Unlike Gabe's startling kiss, this feels much more natural, like I belong in Echo's arms, and nothing could possibly come between us. And what could in my dreams?

"You haven't told anyone about me, have you?" Echo whispers in a soothing tone. His hand strokes my hair down to the middle of my back, over and over again.

"Of course not."

"Not even Gabe?"

Echo has never mentioned Gabe before. I pull back, curiously looking up at him. "No, not even Gabe. How do you know about him anyway?"

"He's in your dreams too, is he not?" Echo's fingers lace through my hair as he drags some of the black strands away from my face.

"Yes, but–"

"So, I know who he is. And that you feel for him. And that he kissed you." Echo's stark blue eyes lock on mine. Is he jealous? I can't read him through that guarding smile he wears at all the right times.

"Yes, he kissed me, but so what?"

"Do you love him?"

I realize now, despite the obvious tension growing between us because of Gabe, that Echo and I are still close together. I rest one of my hands on his chest and then lay my head down on my hand. "I don't know, Echo. What does this have to do with anything? We are in the middle of a war, and we have to figure out how to save each other from it…"

"And we have to figure out if you will be willing to leave Gabe behind in order to be saved."

This startles me. A pang of fear shakes me from the inside out, and I propel away from Echo, as if he was made of electricity and had physically shocked me. "What?"

Echo shakes his hair out of his eyes and turns back toward the window. "You don't honestly think we can save everyone, do you? We are responsible for each other. We have the connection."

"And why wouldn't I be able to take Gabe with me?" I snap and whatever bit of confidence and hope I had in Echo's plan slowly seeps out of me, like water through a cracked glass.

"He's not part of the plan."

"What plan?" I blurt at him, enraged at this point. "We don't have a plan! Even if we did, you are just going to exclude Gabe anyway? My best friend?"

Echo doesn't look at me unkindly. In fact, his gaze is sympathetic and understanding. I don't see a bit of jealousy anywhere in his eyes as I fight for Gabe's freedom as well. "I will try to think of a way,

Beatrice. Just know, that there may not be a way…and if that's the case, you are going to have to choose between staying with Gabe or running with me before the City is overcome."

"Stay here with Gabe, where I know where I am and who I am… or run off with you into the unknown, where I will have no clue who I am any longer…or what my purpose is."

Echo reaches out, turning my face so that I have nowhere else to look at but up at him. "Beatrice, you will always be you. Beautiful you." His thumb brushes across my lips, and he stoops down and kisses me, gentle and soft. It's not like Gabe's kiss, hungry and needy, but instead it's a patient, sure thing that happens between us, as if this moment was always supposed to happen, and we both knew it would happen right now, and there was nothing else to do about it but give in.

And I give in. I let him kiss me for as long as he wants, and I kiss him in return. His hand falls from the side of my face and trails down the curve of my neck before settling on my lower back, where he pulls me in a step closer.

Everything seems blurry as we stand there in each other's arms. I feel like a short-circuiting television, and ripples of static flicker through the darkness behind my closed eyes.

And then, it's over.

◇

"Teams A, B, and C report to the Debriefing Room immediately." The intercom screams, jarring me out of my dream. I put my fingers to my lips, where I can still feel Echo's kiss. I stand and fix my hair in the mirror, noting the blush of red that spans my cheeks. Great.

Someone knocks on my door, so I spring into my jumpsuit, zip it and slap the button to open the door. When it slides back, Gabe is on the other side, his grin cocky. "Turns out, girls do like scars. They won't leave me alone about it." His eyes narrow slightly. "Why are you all red?"

"It's hot in there." The door shuts behind me. I tug Gabe down the hallway, and note the others who are making their way down to the Debriefing Room as well. Some of them limp, and some of them hold onto one injury or another, but most of us are okay, and that's good to see. "You ready for this?"

"Guess so. I don't know what they're going to say. We did eliminate a good amount of Dreamcatchers…what more could they want?"

"I don't know. I've given up on figuring these things out." When we reach the Debriefing Room and I look around, it hits me just how many people were hurt or lost today. Our numbers are falling, but the Keeper insists we continue with what we've been doing.

We sit down in our teams, automatically segregating. Mae and Brandon find Gabe and me and sit in the chairs beside us.

"Your head looks much better, Gabe!" Mae reaches out to touch where the cut was. Already, it looks like nothing ever happened. "Wow."

"That's pretty cool." Brandon grins.

A girl sitting in front of us turns around and smiles at Gabe, pointing to his scar. "I agree. It is kind of neat." She holds out her hand to introduce herself, though she's been on our team from the start and Gabe knows well who she is. I roll my eyes at the game she's playing, and cross one of my legs over the other. "I'm Margie."

"I know." Gabe shakes her hand anyway and gives her the same cocky grin that he gave me, which makes me angry. "You did a good job out there, too."

"Only because we had a great leader." Margie goes as far as winking at Gabe, then offers me a jaunty little wave that is pathetic at best. "Hello, Seer Beatrice. See anything new lately? It's been a while since we've heard about one of your Visions."

I level my violet-eyed gaze on Miss Margie. She's quickly ticking me off. "It's probably best that way, considering how accurate they are." I want to tell her about the Vision where everyone is dead in the Meeting Room, piled high in corpse towers, unidentifiable from one another. I think maybe this would amuse her, or at least get her to shut up and turn back around.

"There's been a lot going on. I've not had a Vision myself in a good week or so." Gabe shrugs.

"Funny, I haven't either." Mae looks at me, as if I know the answer as to why no one is having Visions anymore, which I don't. Ever since my Visions became so accurate, everyone thinks I have answers.

"Turn back around," I mutter at Margie, a bit too rudely. But I follow with a polite addition, "The Keeper is ready." And she is.

Dressed in her red robes, as always, the Keeper stands at the front of the room, flanked by two armed and high-ranking members of the Watch. Her raven cries out loudly, and I cringe. The Keeper folds her hands in front of her and regards the three teams with a critical eye.

"Seers from Teams A, B, and C, I am calling you here today to first commend you on a job well done. We have confirmed the eradication of fifteen Dreamcatchers, which is more than we were projecting to take down." The Keeper allows a pause for the cheering that starts. I don't clap. All I can see is the panic in Mae's eyes when the child Dreamcatcher was shot and killed in front of her family. Sure she was killed, yes, but at what price?

"Tomorrow, we will deploy Teams D, E, and F and it will be their turn to find and eliminate Dreamcatchers. This doesn't mean it is a day off for you, though. You will, in your teams, collaborate on what you could have done better, and who were the weakest and strongest links in your teams. I want you to fine tune your performance so next time you step out of the Institution, you will kill with more precision and accuracy." There's a long pause, and then the Keeper smiles. "So, I've brought in some help."

Four Watchmen arrive carrying a young man in a Plexiglas box. The expression on his face is that of calm passivity. He stares at us all with wide, green eyes that seem empty and emotionless. As soon as he is put in front of us, we can all feel it. He is a Dreamcatcher.

"This Dreamcatcher goes by the name Mirage. Tomorrow, while the other teams are running their missions, you will take part in a Training Game, in which Mirage will be set loose in the arena, and the first team to find him and kill him will receive an award."

Mirage doesn't move. He doesn't even blink when it's revealed that he will be our prey. The Seers will be loosed upon him like hungry, eager wolves, and at the end of the game, he'll be just another dead body. A Dreamcatcher who will dream no more.

Someone starts to clap at the news, and everyone else follows suit. The Keeper holds her hands up to silence us as Mirage's box is put down on the ground. "I want you to remember the feeling you have now, Seers. This is what you should have felt while out in the streets of the City. If you cannot feel this, then you'll surely die."

I feel it. It's an emotion that's almost like panic, but there's a strange certainty behind the panic. It's almost breathtaking, and the longer Mirage is kept in the room with us, the more restless I become. I shift uncomfortably in my chair and glance sideways at Gabe, who also seems to be in some discomfort.

The Keeper steeples her fingers in front of her as she circles the box. "The Dreamcatcher's hands will be cuffed in Plexiglas boxes so that he cannot grab hold of you. But, if he touches you in any way, one of the Watchmen—" She gestures to the four who flank the plastic box, and the two who walked in with her. "—will shoot and kill you. This is to simulate your expiration upon being seized by a Dreamcatcher, and to further eliminate the weak Seers who will hold us back."

A collective gasp fills the room, much like when the Keeper announced that we would be using live rounds in the Training Games. For the most part, we've gotten over that. It's become normal now, knowing that you might walk into the Training Games and never walk out. But having the Keeper selectively shooting us if we've been "caught" by this imprisoned Dreamcatcher is on a whole other level.

"Are you kidding me?" I blurt. The Keeper looks at me, pausing expectantly.

Gabe's hand finds mine and he squeezes it. "Shhh. Not now. You'll only get in trouble."

"They'll kill us? What will be next, Gabe?" I want to storm out of here. The feeling from the Dreamcatcher is making me agitated, and the Keeper's news does nothing to sate it.

"Watchmen, you may take Mirage back to his cell. Make sure you toss some food into the box for him. I don't want my Seers chasing weak prey. They need to be fit and on their game if we are to protect our Institution and City." At the Keeper's orders, the four Watchmen hoist the box off the floor and carry him out, presumably to put him back in the brig. After Mirage's removal, the uneasy feeling starts to fade away, and the panic slowly disappears. The Keeper bows her head to us. "You are dismissed. Report to the

Training Games at zero eight-hundred hours." She exits the door she used to enter, taking the Watchmen with her.

"Hopefully you won't manage to get another one of your stupid teammates killed tomorrow," Rachelle yells over at us, waving a hand over her head so we know where she is in the crowd of Seers. As if we care.

"Ignore her," I mutter to Gabe, Mae, and Brandon.

Brandon glowers in Rachelle's direction and pounds a fist into his meaty hand. "One day, she's going to get what is coming to her."

"Yeah, she's not too bright." Mae's insult sounds almost cute next to the anger in Brandon's voice.

"Maybe the Dreamcatcher will touch her tomorrow, and we'll get to see it when she's shot by the Watchmen." I turn to the others and smile, but they aren't smiling back. I frown as we file out of the room. "Sorry. She really gets on my nerves."

⇟

Gabe stares intently at the bowl of apples. He holds a pencil, and sometimes he scribbles furiously with it, and at other times, he's erasing. The bowl of apples remains the same as minutes pass by, and we've gotten no further than we were before.

"Art class is so stupid. So is art homework," Gabe finally blurts and drops his pencil on the table to rub a cramp out of his hand. "Why do we need to know art anyway when our job is to protect the Citizens with our Visions?"

I smirk, having wondered the same question ever since we were introduced to art class back when we were small children, barely able to handle our Visions. "Maybe we have to learn it so we won't be as boring to other people as we would be if all we ever did was See all the time. Maybe it's because we know how to draw apples that the Citizens respect us."

"That is almost the dumbest thing I've ever heard, Bea." Gabe laughs, begrudgingly picking up his pencil again.

"Yeah, well. Just draw your apples and shut up. Homework is homework." We are out in the garden, where it is quiet and no one can bother us. Well, anyone could bother us, really, but no one does. Not even the bodyguards, who have yet to show up today. As the days go on, their watch becomes less and less intense. Perhaps the Keeper is realizing I am not the threat that she thought I was. Or, perhaps, the matter with the Dreamcatchers is taking priority over what I am doing.

I tend to think of the garden as a little piece of color in such a monochrome building. The Institution is made up of blacks and grays, and the City around us is dark and shadowy. Retreating to the garden feels like another world altogether, and I wonder if in the past everything was as colorful and as full of life.

In the middle of the garden is a small, fountain-looking stone structure with a rounded top made of red glass. It looks ornamental, but we know it serves a purpose. It looks rather conspicuous with its ominous crimson color and imposing presence. No one ever bothers with it, though, and we've come to accept it as part of the mysteries that the Institution keeps.

Gabe goes back to drawing for a little while, as do I, and when I glance up, I find him staring at me. "What?" I ask.

"Nothing. I mean…" Gabe looks back down, blushing just a touch. "I mean *something*, but…it's stupid."

"What is it?"

Gabe doesn't say anything at first. "It's just that you look pretty out here."

I put a hand to the raven bottle cap pendant that he bought me.

"Me? Pretty?"

"Don't act ridiculous. I'm sure you know that you're pretty." The more Gabe talks, the more his words taper off at the end, lost in the bashfulness.

I don't know what to say to that, so I fumble with the pendant in my hand and swallow a lump in my throat. "Well…thanks, I guess."

"And you're still wearing my necklace," Gabe points out, carefully changing the subject away from my appearance.

"Why wouldn't I be? I love it." I smile and look down at the raven, perched on a naked tree branch. "I really do."

"Bea?" Gabe asks.

I focus on him as he puts his pencil down.

"I've been meaning to tell you that…well…I um…" He scratches at the back of his neck, his long hair falling over his fingers, tangling within each digit. "I like yo—"

"Seers Gabriel and Beatrice." The Keeper is suddenly standing beside us, her arms crossed over her chest. Her raven sits perched on her shoulder, its black eyes inky and vacant.

"Yes, My Keeper?" We almost answer in unison, though Gabe's words are filled with nervousness from whatever he was about to tell me before.

The Keeper looks at the bowl of apples and then back at the two of us, sitting in the grass, sketchbooks in hand. "You are aware that we have Training Games tomorrow morning?"

"Yes, My Keeper," I reply, and realize in an afterthought that perhaps Gabe and I should have been spending our time studying the other teams instead of drawing pictures of fruit. It's too late for regret, though. The Keeper is already here.

"Team A has been doing very well. I'd hate to see it suffer because you two were negligent in your duties." The Keeper's violet eyes shift to the bowl of apples again.

Because the Keeper is not looking at him, Gabe puts a hand over his mouth to cover a grin. I try not to smile as well.

I flip the cover of my notebook over. "We will make sure to be much more…conscientious in the future, My Keeper."

Gabe snorts and the Keeper narrows her eyes at him. He's made a mistake, and I rub my forehead, knowing that what comes next will not be good.

"Seer Gabriel," the Keeper begins, addressing him gravely. Annoyed. "I have placed Team A in both your and Seer Beatrice's hands because you have proven yourselves to be most capable. Your Visions are strong. Not as strong as Seer Beatrice's, but they are maturing nicely."

She bows down and takes Gabe's chin in her hand, forcing him to look up at her. "But if you continue to act the way you are…if you continue to squander your time away on Seer Beatrice instead of working with her to focus on how to crush our enemy, then I shall have no choice but to keep you two separated."

"I apologize, My Keeper." Gabe says this with conviction, as if he actually means it, but the threatening glint in his eyes tells me something else altogether, and the Keeper probably knows it too.

Only when she is gone does Gabe stand and mutter, "We should get ready for those games now, Seer Beatrice."

I frown. "I hope you aren't mad at me."

Gabe shakes his head in response, leaving me with nothing more than that. He even leaves his art supplies behind, which I scoop up in my arms, along with the bowl of apples, and hurry back inside the Institution to prepare for the next day's Training Games.

CHAPTER EIGHTEEN

Echo and I are standing outside of the barricades. I look behind me and watch a sweeping spotlight trail across the electric fence and down the side of a building. We are playing a dangerous game. No, it's not a game at all. Echo tugs on me and is yelling, and I can see his mouth moving but I can't figure out what he is saying.

I can't hear anything.

Someone behind us shoots a gun, and the crack of the bullet leaving the barrel jars me out of the deafness.

"Beatrice! Hurry! We have to run now!"

I look behind me again and see a line of Watchmen with their rifles pointed in our direction. Behind them, Seers are trying to claw their way through to get me. Despite all the noises and voices, I hear Gabe calling. "Beatrice! Don't leave me!" One of his arms stretches out past a Watchmen's head, as if trying to grasp for me.

Echo pulls on my arm and I lurch forward a couple of steps, stumbling into him. He grabs my face in his hands and stares into my eyes. "We have to run."

"But Gabe…" I whisper, tears forming in my eyes.

"You have to leave him, Bea. We have to run."

"I can't!" I try to rip away from Echo. I want to run toward the fence and crawl under to be with the others. Maybe they will understand. I was under the influence of a Dreamcatcher. Surely, they'd let me return…

Another shot fires and the bullet is so close that I can hear it whizz past my face.

I listen for Gabe, but I realize that he's not yelling anymore. None of the Seers are.

"He is gone." Echo's mouth is close to my ear, and he tugs on me again.

"What do you mean he is gone?" Panic fills my lungs, and I can't breathe any more. I wonder if this is what it feels like to drown.

Echo runs, leaving me no choice but to follow. The farther away we get, the quieter all the noise becomes. Somehow, after only a few steps, we are back in the meadow with the solitary tree. The wind rustles through the fields, and a raven flies overhead, screeching ominously.

"They're all gone." Echo looks to me, his mouth downturned. "They're all gone."

⟡

This time, it's not a dream. I wake up and my eyes are glowing, and before I can comprehend the Vision, the Keeper arrives at my bunk. "We've indicated that you've had a Vision, Seer Beatrice."

I am hoping not. That could not have been a Vision. It would mean that I'd lose Gabe in all of this, somehow. I ran away from him. I left him behind, and I'd never leave him behind. The prophecy leaves me speechless.

"What have you Seen?" The Keeper presses for answers. Of course, I can't tell her the truth. If I tell her that I've been communicating with a Dreamcatcher, I'll be executed for sure. But no one has ever lied to the Keeper before.

Until now.

"I saw guns…and the Seers. And they were trying to fight, but then they all disappeared. They…they were *gone*." I look up at the Keeper, hoping that she's buying this. Praying that she is. All the while, I keep hearing Gabe calling my name, reaching out for me to come to him. I can see his fingers flexing, desperately grabbing for me like a baby reaching for a toy out of its grasp.

"What do you mean by *gone*?"

I shake my head and drag some hair out of my face. I'm sure I look like a mess, having just woken up, but the Keeper is surely used to my freshly awoken state. "I don't know how to explain it. They were there, and then they weren't. They were yelling…and then they weren't."

The Keeper's lips press together. "Hmm. Interesting." She gets to work, typing all of this into her digipad.

"Is Gabe okay?"

"Seer Gabriel, you mean?" the Keeper asks without looking up at me.

"Yes, My Keeper. Is he okay?"

"I don't see why he wouldn't be. I don't keep tabs on every Seer in the Institution, Seer Beatrice. You'll have to forgive me if I don't know what precisely he is up to right now." The Keeper flips her digipad closed and tucks it away under her robes. "Well, if that is all then, I'll evaluate the Vision and see what we can use in our fight against the Dreamcatchers. Surely, there had to be a reason why everyone just…disappeared, as you say."

Does she sound suspicious of me? Does she know I am lying? I simply bow my head, which is beginning to throb from the Vision.

"I will be relieving you of your guard. They are needed for pressing matters. Do not think, though, for one moment that you are not being watched. It is for your own protection. And I want you to mind the time that you are spending with Seer Gabriel." The Keeper rises and leaves shortly after speaking with me, her gracious threat left behind.

The clock reads 7:00 a.m., which means I have exactly an hour to get dressed and meet the others down by the arena for the Training Games. Today is the day we will be stalking a real, live Dreamcatcher, and I feel guilty because of it. How could I in one moment have my arms around Echo and feel him kissing me, and in the next hunt and kill one of his kind?

But then I recall Echo's warning. That we are enemies, despite everything else. We are after each other, and that's something we can't avoid. But I want to avoid it, especially if it means that in the end, I'll have to lose Gabe because of it.

I tug my jumpsuit on and dash out the door, eager to find Gabe and know that he's all right. The halls are filled with other Seers, all heading down to breakfast. I make it to the doors of the cafeteria when I'm suddenly pulled backward by a hand on my shoulder. When I spin around, Rachelle is standing there, looming over me by just an inch or so.

"Don't think that I don't know what you are doing, Beatrice," she says. "I saw it in my Vision."

"Saw *what* exactly? And I heard your Visions weren't much to brag about in the first place, Rachelle. You only barely earned the right to wear the mark of the raven's wings on your face." Rachelle's Visions, like most of the other Seers', aren't as clear as mine. Where others See blurs, or information is skipped in a haze, I can See faces clearly enough to identify them and I can easily mark out events and places. Well, for the most part. There's some deciphering to be done, since not all Visions are direct. Some require you to think them through and piece them out. And that's why we train in the art of Seeing so that we know how to do exactly that. Rachelle barely knows how to do it at all. And though one of her Visions might have caught the Keeper's attention, the majority of them are recorded and filed away, never to be contemplated again.

She crosses her arms over her chest, insulted. "I Saw you, betraying the Institution."

"Did you really?" I can only half believe this. It's not easy to See faces.

Rachelle stumbles over her words, her momentum momentarily thrown off. "I Saw some woman betraying the Institution, and something told me that it was you."

"Something?"

"Yes. A feeling. A strong feeling. Everyone is watching you, Beatrice. They are waiting to see what you're going to do next, you know." Rachelle tosses her chestnut brown hair over her shoulder and it bounces into place behind her. "Or what you will See next."

"Wonderful," I deadpan and continue into the cafeteria. "I had another Vision today, if you want to go and run and tell all of your little friends. You can all put your heads together and think about what I could have possibly Seen. It could have been Team B all caught in a building, surrounded by Dreamcatchers with no way out." Smiling, I turn away from Rachelle altogether, leaving her behind to stew.

I continue back on my original course—to find Gabe. When I reach our usual spot, Mae and Brandon are sitting down, nibbling at eggs and honey biscuits, engaged in cheerful conversation, judging by the smiles on both of their faces. But there's no Gabe. "Where's Gabe?"

"Morning, Bea!" Mae scoots over and pats the chair next to her. "Have a seat. We got you and Gabe a tray." She pushes a Styrofoam tray in front of me. "And I don't know where Gabe is. I guess we thought he was with you."

Brandon has already cleaned his plate, and he looks at mine with his beady violet eyes. "Breakfast was good."

"I can see that." I laugh and push my tray back over toward Brandon. "Here, have mine. I'm not hungry this morning." Twisting my body around, I search the room for Gabe to see if maybe, for some reason, he is sitting somewhere else. And he is.

With Margie.

"He's over there." My tone isn't at all nice.

"Oh, yes! He's sitting with that girl from yesterday. What's her name again?" Mae doesn't seem to latch on to the fact that I'm not happy about this development, not one bit.

Neither does Brandon. "Margie! I think she's pretty."

"Shut up, Brandon," I grumble and tap my fingernails on the table. *Taptaptaptaptap. Taptaptaptaptap.*

Mae stands and starts to wave her arms over her head. "Hey, Gabe! Gabe! Over here!" He looks up in her direction and smirks, but then he spots me sitting there, glowering. "I got his attention."

"Thanks, Mae. You are always so helpful."

Sarcasm is also often lost on Mae and she chirps, "You're welcome!"

Gabe pushes up to stand. They were both sitting on the same side of the bench, which is annoying. He waves at her and turns to walk in our direction, that sure-of-himself grin lighting up his face.

"If he thinks he's just going to come back over here and sit down, he's wro—"

Gabe sits down. "What's up, Mae? Need something?"

My hands ball into fists, fingernails digging into the soft skin of my palm. How can he be so handsome and infuriating at the same time? And how can he not notice how angry I am with him? Or maybe he does notice, but he's just ignoring it. That makes me even angrier and I huff, blowing some strands of hair out of my face.

"Oh, nothing! Beatrice was just wondering where you were." Mae pulls the insides of a biscuit out and starts to squish it into a square.

"Was not," I mutter. Mae giggles.

"Looks like you're angry," Gabe notes, sliding one of his hands over my balled up fist to try and get me to relax.

But I don't relax. I pull my hand away from his and glare in Margie's direction. "What were you doing over there?"

"Talking with Margie."

"But why? You always eat with us. Now you are going to start eating with some twit who thinks a scar you don't even have anymore is cute?"

Gabe touches the place where a very faint outline of the scar still remains by his eye. "You sound jealous."

"I'm not *jealous*. I am annoyed." I am lying, and he knows it.

Gabe pauses before speaking again. "I don't know what you want from me, Beatrice. I try my best to be there for you. I kiss you and you push me away…"

"You kissed her?" Mae pops the bread into her mouth, her eyes wide as she stares between us. "Really?"

"Not now, Mae." I look back to Brandon, who is too busy shoving his face full with eggs, as if something is going to swoop down out of the sky and claim them. "But yes…we kissed."

"Was it good?" Mae leans forward to hear more. "Huh?"

I ignore the question, but the blush I feel creeping up my face is proof enough that it was probably good. No, it was definitely good.

Gabe shakes his head, sliding his tray in front of him. "I don't get you anymore, Beatrice. You always seem like you are hiding something, and you always seem like you're pushing me away at the same time, when all I want to do is help you."

"I know you want to help me, Gabe. I told you that I knew this. But I also told you that…there are just…I can't say some things. Because I have to protect you." I can see Gabe reaching for me in my Vision. I can hear him calling for me, his screams frantic and desperate. His fingers are stretched out, and if he could stretch them farther without the bones popping out of his skin, he probably would. And then, all at once, he's gone. "I don't want to lose you."

Everyone is quiet. Even Brandon's sloppy chewing eventually dies down. The three of them are looking at me, and I look down at the table to avoid their glances. "There's so much more going on than you'd ever understand. I just wish you'd trust me. All of you. Trust me and know that I'm letting you in on as much as I can without us all suffering for it."

Brandon suspiciously looks around him, glancing to the armed Watchmen in the cafeteria, who seem to blend in now that we are so used to them being around. "Maybe we should drop it for now."

"Yeah." I wait for them to finish their breakfasts, my gaze shifting to the Watchmen, who all seem to be watching me and nobody else. Maybe I'm just seeing things. Making it up. If I'm not careful, I'll become paranoid and then everything will be ten times harder than it already is. I'll never be able to go anywhere without having to look over my shoulder. I'll never be able to trust anyone again. In a way, I realize, I already feel like this. I really don't know who to trust anymore.

A buzzer sounds, alerting the Teams that they don't have much time before the doors to the training arena open, and we are thrust into the fox hunt—except our fox is a Dreamcatcher. I can see Mirage, with his hands cuffed in plastic. What if they caught Echo instead? Would I have been forced to hunt him? Am I already hunting him? "Do you think Dreamcatchers have families?" I ask aloud.

"Hmm?" Mae picks her tray up, ready to dispose of it. She's left some biscuit crumbs in the uneaten blob of honey.

"Do you think they have families?"

"I don't know. I've...never really thought about it before." In thought, she chews on her bottom lip, teeth dragging over the chapped pink skin.

"Why?" Gabe stands also, prompting Brandon and I to follow suit. We all head out of the cafeteria, the others depositing their trays in the used trays box. Each one of them clicks together at the bottom of the bin as Seer after Seer slips them into the slot.

"I don't know. It just occurred to me that maybe they do. I guess I assumed that because we don't they wouldn't either...but the Dreamcatchers are nothing like us, so why shouldn't they have families?"

Brandon *huhs*. "Do you think their whole family is made up of Dreamcatchers then? Or is there just one with the gift? And the others are all normal people?"

I hadn't thought about this. Did Echo have his own family? Did he have to leave them behind? Was he taken from them as soon as they realized he had the gift? And was Dreamcatching a gift at all if everyone else also shared the ability?

"Maybe we can ask Mirage before we kill him," Gabe says as we walk down the hall and toward the arena. His words are brutal and make me angry because I can't help but to think that Echo could easily be in Mirage's place. But Gabe knows nothing about Echo and my offense is lost on him.

When we get to the arena, others are suiting up, loading their magazines and getting ready for the game. Rachelle stands at the head of her group and is already giving out orders, her voice stern and unwavering. She must have been appointed the Captain for the day.

I walk over to my locker and open it. As I pull out my gun, ammunition, grenades, smoke capsules and flash bangs, someone comes up from behind me, their shadow looming over mine. I turn around to find it's the Keeper, her hands folded in front of her, hidden under the long bell sleeves of her robes. The raven on her shoulder watches me almost as intensely as she does.

"Beatrice. You will be the Captain of Team A today. It is your responsibility to see to your team and their safety. We will be watching you."

When aren't you watching me? "Yes, My Keeper."

She nods and walks off, the crowd of Seers parting to move out of her way.

I gather my weapons, most of which are held on the belt that I clip around my waist, and then shove all my hair up into my helmet, which is securely pulled over my head. After slinging my gun over my shoulder, I approach the rest of my team. I have to do this whether I like it or not. "Team A, assemble. Now." The other eleven members of my team line up in two rows, one of which is missing a person—me.

The Keeper's voice masks mine, though, as she gets on the

mike. Her voice crackles across the staging room, loud and grave. "Seers, today you will be hunting a real Dreamcatcher, Mirage. He has already been let loose in the arena and given time to hide and prepare. The team who takes him down will receive an award after the game is over. The teams who fail will be punished." As the word "punished" reverberates through the room, the raven cries out, screeching loudly and unfolding its wings to flap them, though it flies nowhere.

"You have five minutes until the doors open. Please use this time wisely."

I look at my team and freeze, having no idea what I could possibly say. Gabe stares at me expectantly, waiting for me to say something. Anything. He waves his hand forward in a "what next" sort of way, and I shrug at him, since I have no idea what comes next.

"Um. Remember to…um…make sure you are *feeling* where the Dreamcatcher is. It's much more important that we follow this feeling than branch out on our own and blindly search for him. The arena is big. There's one of him and thirty-six of us." I am banking on the assumption that Rachelle is yelling at her team about razing the City to the ground until the Dreamcatcher is the only thing left standing. I can't hear her words over the mumbling and general chatter of everyone else, but she points angrily at specific people in her unit and scolds them about something or another.

The red light by the arena door illuminates and spins, and a loud buzzer sounds, warning those by the entrance that it's about to part. We all step back and wait for the doors to open all the way. That frenzied, panicked feeling starts to build in my middle, like expanding dough without a place to rise. Inside the arena, standing in the middle of the main street that splits the mock city in half, is Mirage, hands boxed in plastic. He doesn't move as he stares at all of us with green, vibrant eyes. Why doesn't he run? Why isn't he hiding? All of the teams, ready to lunge into battle, stay still, violet eyes on the Dreamcatcher.

Rachelle uses the moment of shock to fire at Mirage, but as soon as the bullets leave her gun, he's no longer standing where he was. "Where'd he go?" she yells and motions to her team. "Get in there! Go, go, go!"

Where *did* he go? I didn't know Dreamcatchers could just… disappear. But, I'm starting to realize that I don't know much about Dreamcatchers at all. I think everyone is realizing this. "In!" I yell at Team A, and they follow me as I dart down a side street to where the park is. I look back to Team B to see what they are doing, and trailing at the end of their unit is little Elan, his gun bigger than he is. He must have recovered from the previous Training Game when he was shot. At least he doesn't look bothered by his team demotion.

Gabe pushes me, and I stumble forward. "Keep moving, Bea."

"Aren't I the Captain here?" I snap at him and stop in front of a building that is at least four stories tall. With the heel of my boot, I kick the door open and swing my arm. "Get in! Go!" Team A hesitates for a moment, but then they all enter the building, stepping over the remnants of the wooden door. I point to the stairs, "All the way up."

When we get to the top floor, I slam the door shut behind us. "I know you are wondering why we are up here."

"We're going to lose." Tina, a petite girl of about my age, pulls her helmet off and drops it on the floor beside her.

"No, we won't. Listen. We need to think this through. The other teams are blindly running around the city after something that can just appear and disappear. They are chasing a ghost. We have to be smarter. So start thinking."

There's quiet as everyone does exactly that—think. Gabe is the first person to speak up. "How was he caught, I wonder?"

"Good, Gabe. That's a good place to start. It seems that plastic box kept Mirage in captivity, like the boxes that are on his hands right now. But how did they get him into the box anyway?"

Mae waves a hand in the air, like a schoolgirl in a classroom. "Maybe they trapped him! We could trap him too!" She looks at the rest of her peers with a proud smile, as if she just cracked this whole process and won the game herself.

"But how?" Gabe knocks Mae's hopes down a little bit.

"I…I don't know…"

I put my palms on a windowsill and stare outside. At times, I can catch glimpses of the other teams storming down streets, busting into buildings and turning up nothing. They are running around without any direction, and part of me finds it amusing. They are literally chasing after a mirage, which is absurd within itself. "We'll have to lure him."

I'm about to say more, but there's a swish of air that blows through the room, and suddenly Mirage is there, standing at the door. He's taller than I thought he'd be, standing almost at six feet, looming over most of us, even Gabe. His hair is a sandy brown and greasy from not being washed recently. He wears a long, black tunic, the kind that the brig hands out to prisoners.

His presence is more than overwhelming. It makes me want to run away and toward him at the same time. The others feel the same way, and somehow I miss that they all have drawn their guns and have their sights pointed at him. Before anyone can fire, though, I bark the order, "Stand down!"

"What?" Brandon blurts like I've lost my damned mind.

"Stand down!" I think of Echo. How can I save him if I can't save Mirage? But how do I save Mirage if it means that I'll certainly die a traitor afterward? I hear the Keeper's voice reminding me that I'm being watched. Are they watching me now?

I approach Mirage, and he doesn't move. His chin tips downward to look at me the closer I get to him. Gabe stands up when it seems I am too close, but he doesn't approach. Not yet, at least. I look the Dreamcatcher over, and the whole time, I see Echo and not Mirage at all. Do the others see Echo, too? When I look back up into Mirage's green eyes, they are now blue and don't belong to Mirage. I don't understand what is happening. Has he found a way to catch me?

I stare for too long. I hear Gabe yell, "Do something, Beatrice!" And I do.

I shoot him.

A beacon bullet enters his middle and an expanding glowing light fills him, then shrinks. Mirage falls to the ground, dead weight. His blood is on my face and jumpsuit, and soon it begins to pool on the ground by my feet. Team A cheers, and I hear their hands hollowly slapping together as they clap for me and what is certainly an achievement in their eyes. But for me, all I feel is cold and sick. Though the Dreamcatcher no longer looks like Echo, he does look like someone who was, just moments before, standing in front of me, alive.

His blood pools around the rubber soles of my boots.

CHAPTER NINETEEN

Team B and Team C's punishment was to spend the night in the streets of the City, protecting the Citizens from the threat of the Dreamcatchers. They were without food or shelter until sunrise, and when they returned to the Institution to eat breakfast, they were hostile and accusatory toward Team A. Since we won, we had a rare day off, and I spent most of it in my room, thinking about Mirage and Echo and what happened between the three of us.

I want Echo to come to me, so I sleep a lot, but he doesn't and I'm starting to believe that maybe Echo is angry and has abandoned me because of my atrocious act against one of his kind. He knows just as well as I do, though, that we are at war. It's he who keeps reminding me of this, and yet, when it is my side who lashes out, he becomes angry and leaves me here? It isn't fair, and I feel more like yelling and screaming at him the more I can't see him in my dreams.

I also fear what the others saw when I stood there, staring at Mirage as if I knew him from somewhere. I have to find Gabe — he's the only person I trust — and if it comes down to me having to confess to someone about Echo, I'd rather it be him than anyone else. I need to be careful, since the Keeper is watching me, and it might only be a matter of time before she calls me to her and questions me about the incident herself.

The intercom is across the room, so I make my way to it and dial up Gabe's bunk. The speaker rings back at me, and eventually crackles as Gabe's voice comes over it. "Hey, Bea, what's up?"

"I was wondering if you are busy."

"Nah. I was just playing some stupid game on the holo. Want me to come by?"

"Yes. And bring a snack too."

Gabe laughs. "Alright, Bea. I'll be right there." The intercom switches off, leaving me in the silence of my room.

I put my hands on the glass of the window, staring outside at the City beyond. I remember Echo's hands on mine, his lips on mine, and my head slumps forward, forehead resting against the glass. "What have I gotten myself into?"

Some minutes later, Gabe knocks at my door. "Come in!"

The door slides open, admitting him and the tray filled with snacks that he bogarted from the cafeteria. Most of it is wrapped up cookies, crackers and other various unhealthy things that they sell from a separate window at outrageously high prices. If the Seers want to eat unhealthy, they have to do so at the expense of their own pockets. Considering there are very few places for us to make money, it isn't very often someone buys too much. I have to wonder where the heck Gabe got all of these goodies.

"Where'd you get all of that?"

Grinning, Gabe sets the tray down on my desk and shrugs. "Called in a few favors."

"A few favors? What does that even mean?" I pick up a pack of cheese crackers with peanut butter in them. I haven't had these in years, and I anxiously unwrap them, crumbs falling everywhere as I break a few crackers in the process. I shove one into my mouth and close my eyes, lashes brushing against my cheeks. "Mmmm. These are so good."

"Does it matter where I got them? It looks like you're enjoying them well enough."

I open one of my eyes and focus it on Gabe. "Well, it'd be nice to know how I could get some for myself."

"Easy. The cafeteria." Gabe smirks.

"You know what I mean." I push another cracker into my mouth, all too aware of the fact that I am not being ladylike in the least. Not even a little bit. In less than a few minutes, the whole pack of six peanut butter crackers is gone, with only the plastic wrapper left to show for it.

"Damn, Beatrice. You were hungry, weren't you?"

"I could eat that whole tray of snacks, Gabe. Don't test me." I pick up another, a plump, squishy, chocolate cake filled with cream.

"Well, feel free. I don't really eat this crap anyway. Only sometimes, when I really have a sweet tooth." Gabe lies back on my bed, his hands behind his head, feet crossed at his ankles. He stares up at the ceiling of my bunk, left foot twitching back and forth. "So, what did you need me for?"

"I wanted to talk to you about Mirage." I break the cake into two and sit on the edge of the bed, offering him a piece. "And what you saw. Or didn't see. Or what you felt…or anything. Anything you can tell me about what happened, I'd really appreciate it."

"Why? You were there, weren't you?"

I hesitate. Lately, I've been wondering if I was really there or not. Or, if all of me was there, and part of me was somewhere else, which is why I could see Echo in Mirage's place. Maybe it was half a dream. "Yes, I was there. But…I just need to know what you saw, okay? I want to write it down and study it so I have something to present to the Keeper when she calls me, which I'm sure she'll do. She's all about questioning me until I have nothing left to say."

"Yeah. She has been on your case a lot, hasn't she?" Gabe takes the cake and picks at it.

"Yes."

Gabe licks his fingers with a shrug of his shoulder. "What I saw, hmm? Well. All of the sudden that Dreamcatcher was in the room with us, and you were just standing there staring at him, and then you shot him dead."

"You didn't see anything else?" Like Mirage not being Mirage at all?

"Nope. Why?" He finishes the piece of cake and looks at me. "Did you?"

How do I tell him? Or should I tell him at all? If I don't tell him, he'll just get angry with me again and accuse me of keeping things away from him, or me growing apart from him, or something equally ridiculous to me. "Yes."

He leans forward, elbows on his knees. "Oh really? And what did you see then?"

"He changed. His face changed. He was Mirage, and then he wasn't Mirage. I don't know how to explain it."

"Who was he if he wasn't Mirage?"

"I don't know." I lie.

"Strange. I didn't know that they could change their appearances." Gabe leans back on his palms and stares at the ceiling again.

"I don't think he did, if you didn't see it. I…I don't know what it was. I just know that maybe we should not say anything about it past

Mirage's ability to appear and disappear at will. The Keeper will be on both of our cases…and what if it isn't something good? It could land us in the brig."

"Or the gallows."

"Or that." I swallow and sit beside Gabe on the bed. I want to pour everything out to him. I want to grab him and hold him close and tell him that I'm not going to leave him here. I won't abandon him. But I saw it in my Vision…which means that I might very well do just that. Abandon him. I want to apologize and cry and yell all at the same time. But I do none of these things. Instead, he and I sit there in the silence of the bunk, each pondering our own thoughts. If I were a Dreamcatcher, I could probably tell what he was thinking. If I just held on to him for long enough, I could see what was on his mind.

I feel his hand on my face, and it jars me out of my daydream. "It'll be okay, Bea. We'll keep it between us, and if we're asked about anything, we'll just say what we said here. He changed himself, but he didn't change himself, and only you could see it. I mean, maybe you didn't see it at all. Maybe you were just…I don't know."

That's when it occurs to me. "Daydreaming."

"Daydreaming?"

"Yeah…I was thinking of something else. Something I saw in a Vision…and maybe I was just daydreaming and somehow he was able to make me believe he was someone else?" As soon as the words leave my mouth, I realize that I shouldn't have said this aloud. If it was true, then the Dreamcatcher found a way to catch me without touching me. He was able to get into my head through my thoughts, my daydreams, and nothing more. He didn't even have to touch me. "Shit."

Gabe must have been thinking the same. His hand leaves my

face, and his fingers curl around my hand instead. He squeezes it once and shakes his head, dark hair falling about his face. "Don't think about it. Let's pretend we didn't come to this realization and never speak about it again."

I look at him, my gaze catching his so that he can't look away. "Okay."

There's a pause of uncertainty when both of us don't know what to do now. I'm staring at him, he's staring at me, and his touch is slowly warming me as the familiarity spreads up my arm and through my body. It's just like the moment on the roof, and I wonder if he's going to kiss me again. And if he does, where am I going to run off to if I am already in my bunk?

He does kiss me. His lips press against mine, and the softness of them is surprising. I don't pull away this time. Instead I fervently return the kiss. I keep my mouth against his and breathe in his scent, which reminds me of something hungry and needy. The hand that is holding my hand moves up to my wrist, which he holds with some authority and purpose.

I break the kiss, though, and our faces part. Searching his violet eyes, I see him in my mind again, reaching for me, and the warmth inside me turns into a gripping, paralyzing cold. "I'm not going to leave you. Not on purpose."

Gabe's brows lift in surprise. "What is that supposed to mean?"

"It means what it means. I'm not going to leave you on purpose."

"How else would you leave me, then?"

By necessity? By force? Both? "I don't know, Gabe. I just know that it won't be on purpose."

"I don't understand why you're saying this."

"Because…because I saw you in my Vision, and it's been bothering me." His hand slides off my wrist and the mood is killed.

"I left you. I was being pulled away from you. I don't know what it's supposed to mean, okay? I just know that if it happens, it won't be on purpose. I was being *pulled* away…"

"Calm down, Bea."

Am I getting upset? I lift a hand to my eyes and feel my lashes are damp with unfallen tears. Strange. I don't even feel like I'm crying. "I'm calm. You…it's just that you've been saying so much how I've been leaving you out of things, and I want you to understand that this is part of the reason why. I can't figure them out. All I can see is that I'm maybe going to lose you, and I don't know what to do about it. Do you know how frustrating that is?"

"I can't really say that I do. My Visions aren't nearly as clear as yours. I can hardly make out faces half the time."

He's missing the point, and I sigh. "Gabe, come on. I'm being serious here. Whatever is happening in my Vision, I don't want it to happen. I don't want to lose you or anyone else. Especially not you…but *something* is going to happen. Something we won't be able to stop."

"I think that's already happening, Bea." He's right, too. The war has just begun and as Echo said, the Dreamcatchers have not even started their attack yet. We are in for so much more, and yet we have no idea what we are in for at all. Gabe leans forward to try and kiss me again, but this time, I do pull away.

"I…I can't."

"Why not? You just did two seconds ago." Gabe doesn't press the issue, though. Instead, he runs a hand down the back of my head, cradling the base of my neck in his palm. "It'll be okay, Beatrice. You'll see. I'm not going to leave you. No one is going to take you away from me."

If only you knew, Gabe. "I'm sure I'm just overreacting or something."

"Yeah. Overreacting. That's what it is." Gabe and I both know though that I don't really overreact too much. But it's something neutral to say, and it caps our conversation nicely. He stands up from my bunk, hand leaving my hair to scratch at his. "Anyway, I should be going. Are you going to be okay here? Want me to see if Mae can come up? You girls can talk about something girly. Like about how handsome I am." He grins, and I melt a little bit inside. Even in the most confusing of times, Gabe always knows what to say. And even if I've known him longer than most the other people here, I fall for it constantly.

"No, I'll be okay. But feel free to bring more snacks if you want." I smile back at him until he leaves, and then the smile fades away as I'm left with individually-wrapped chocolate chip cookies, chips that taste like onions, and this terrible, ominous feeling that sits low in my gut.

I have to figure this out. What will happen if I don't?

⟡

In the middle of the meadow, I can hear people screaming from the City, though when I turn to look, the City is nowhere to be seen. Echo pulls me along by my wrist, and I stumble forward while trying to pull back. "Stop!" I hear myself yelling the word over and over again, but he doesn't listen, and the screaming behind me becomes more frantic and painful. There are gunshots. Too many gunshots, and then, like the water from a tidal wave, silence blankets the meadow and there's no more noise.

We stop a few yards from the tree—our tree—and I hunch over to try and catch my breath. Tears and sobs choke me, and each time I suck in air, it gets stuck on the grief. I quickly begin to hyperventilate, and Echo leads me to the trunk where I can sit and calm down. Though I can't hear or see the City anymore, I can smell the sulfur from the gunshots, and the scent of burnt meat.

When I find my breath, I immediately start to yell at Echo. "I told you to stop! I told you to stop! Why didn't you stop?"

"I couldn't, Beatrice. If I stopped, you would have been left back there. I couldn't… "

"You could! We have to go back, Echo! Gabe is back there!"

"Gabe is gone."

My heart stops. He said I either had to stay behind with Gabe or run with him. I didn't choose to run with him…he pulled me along. He dragged me out of there. Gabe is gone? Gabe is gone? *"What do you mean he is gone?"*

"I told you, I don't know. He's just gone."

I get sick. The vomit hits the ground and forms a foul-smelling puddle. Echo doesn't seem to care. He wipes my mouth off with a corner of the regal white robes he wears. "We're safe. You're safe. Isn't that what you wanted, Beatrice? To be safe?"

"I want to know what is happening!" The Vision part of the dream starts to slip from me. I've seen this part before, at least most of it. Now, I want answers. *"Why did Mirage look like you, Echo? Why was he himself one second, and the next second he was you?"*

"That was his ability. Some of us can manipulate others into thinking they are seeing something or someone else that is on their mind. It's used to confuse." Echo brushes my knotty hair out of my face, and when I look up, I can see him better. *"He can also appear and reappear when he wants to. Or he could…before you killed him."*

"I had to.*"*

"I know, Beatrice. I don't blame you for this game we are forced

to play."

The stress of what we just ran from overpowers all rational thought. There are questions I want to ask, but I can't stop thinking about Gabe and that sickening smell. I close my eyes and try to focus. "So what is your ability?"

"To leave those I catch with the images, sounds, smells, and thoughts of what they dream. I don't have to kill them."

"You mean, an echo of those things?"

Echo smiles, lifting my chin with the crook of his finger. "Now you have it."

I don't smile back. How can I possibly smile now, after all that we've just run from? How can I smile when I don't know where Gabe is, or if he is even alive? I suspect when I awake from this dream, it will be Gabe and the odor of gunshots and burning flesh that lingers behind.

"Time is running out, Beatrice. Soon, there will be no turning back. You need to start thinking about what you are going to do. What we are going to do in order to save each other." He brushes his soft thumb over my lips. "Be strong and be careful."

Echo's touch is still on my lips when I wake, except that I can't see him. I hear and smell the things that I predicted I would when I woke, and it makes me feel queasy and my stomach turns. I put a hand over my face and close my eyes as I think about Echo and how much time I really have to figure all of this out.

CHAPTER TWENTY

The gallows are filled today. Each of the seven nooses is looped around a Dreamcatcher's neck, or at least, a suspected Dreamcatcher. There are family members screaming from the crowds, their arms extended toward their loved ones. I can't look away from a little boy who can't be more than twelve years old. He is the smallest of the seven, and his noose hangs lower than the others. He stares at his mother as she cries out, held back by others who can barely keep her from running up the stairs to save her child.

Some of those who are going to be hanged are Dreamcatchers. We can feel it. But others have simply been accused, and with paranoia at its peak, it doesn't take much to be sent to the hangman. The little boy's name is Ryan. He supposedly won't give up his Dreamcatcher name. I don't think he is a Dreamcatcher at all. He doesn't stand with the same sort of pride as the others do.

As the executioner reads out the charges, we all listen intently. "Ryan has been accused of traitorous behavior leading to the suspicion that he is a Dreamcatcher. A classmate of his said that he saw him touch another boy's arm inside the closet and cubby room and the boy screamed and fell onto the ground. Ryan's power was not enough to kill the boy, but he has permanently scarred him and has surely tapped into his mind. For this, Ryan has been sentenced to hanging."

Ryan looks at his mother, tears falling down his face, and his bottom lip begins to quiver. His mother, on the other hand, is crying louder than most anyone else, and when she's not crying, she's screaming hysterically for them to let her son go, that he's innocent.

"This is so sad," Mae whispers as the Executioner reads through the rest of the charges. There's a baker accused of catching others and convincing them to pay too much for their bread, and a few others who stand stiff, tall and unblinking, giving away their identity as true Dreamcatchers.

"It is. How many of these are we going to have to watch in a day, I wonder?" I am quickly becoming bored of hangings. It's heartless of me, I know, but this is the sixth one that we've seen today, and there are probably more to come. The Seers, by Institution law, have to witness each execution. Not only does it supposedly strengthen our senses but it should desensitize us at the same time. Judging by my yawn, it might be working. At least for me.

"Don't know, but I hope not many." Mae wipes at the tears in her eyes. "They are just so very sad."

"They are."

The Executioner finishes reading off each of the names and crimes. A few of those up there are actually Dreamcatchers—two women, Seraphim and Imagine, and a man who refuses to give up his name and has to wear a blindfold around his eyes. Eventually, all of their heads are covered in black sacks, so that we won't have to look at their faces when they are strangled to death at the end of their ropes.

From the wing of the stage, the Keeper nods her head, and one-by-one, the doors under the accused's feet open and they plummet below the gallows. Most of the older, bigger ones drop with a sickening *snap*, and they become still at once. But some of the lighter, younger people kick and struggle as they are strangled and suffocated. Ryan is one of the ones who kick the most, and it goes on for quite a long time. Even when we are all dismissed, he is still struggling.

"Return to the Institution knowing that for another day, we've managed to keep the City and the Citizens safe." The Keeper smiles, her arms stretched out as if she were bestowing a blessing upon us. The Citizens—some of them still screaming and crying, others cheering and jeering—also begin to depart.

Something doesn't feel right, though I can't quite pinpoint what it is. I follow Mae to the Institution, which towers many floors above us, looming and ominous. Its main entrance doors remain open, though they normally automatically slide closed after each person crosses through them. There are so many of us, though, probably hundreds, that the guards keep them open and locked to let all of us through. Watchmen stand interspersed in the crowd, holding large machine guns that are pointed downward, but are ready to be drawn within the blink of an eye. They watch over each of us as we pass by, staring for any sign of abnormality or suspiciousness.

And then, something goes terribly wrong. A surge of pain sweeps through us all, and at one time the Seers fall to the floor, their hands on their necks. I feel like the air in my lungs is being squeezed out of me, and I claw at my throat to try and relieve the pressure, or open it so that I can breathe again. Some of those around me have actually done this, and I can spot Seers with holes in their throats, blood bubbling out as they choke to death.

There's no screaming. We can't scream. The Watchmen don't seem to feel what we do and they stand there, guns drawn, looking for something at which to aim, but they can't seem to find what is hurting us. If only I could scream at them, I'd yell that they *have* to find it before we all end up dead.

My violet eyes bulge, and I swear they are going to pop out of my head. When I look at Mae, she is turning a purplish-blue color, and her little fingers are leaving scratch marks on her delicate neck. I shake my head "no" at her, trying to get her to stop before she ends up like the others who thought that opening their throats would help them. Mae doesn't seem to understand my intent, though.

I am Pathos.

I hear a man speaking. Those Seers who are still alive must also hear him, for even in their panic, they are looking around for the source. I glance at the gallows, where Ryan continues to struggle, but everyone else is motionless. Every time he kicks, I can feel a shock of pain pierce through my limbs. My body feels long, like my toes are being stretched out toward the ground, and my head is being pulled up at the sky.

Today, you've made a grave mistake. Though you've been given the gift of Sight, it is obvious that the Seers are indeed blind. You've killed an innocent boy, whose last breaths for his mother come in gasps that will never be heard. My name is Pathos. You shall share his experience and suffer with him.

Someone has to make this stop. I choke for air and can hear Ryan choking for air, too. We are all choking for air. I'm certain that my head is going to pop off the rest of my body. Mae's fingers are inside of her neck now as she claws open an airway. I shake my head some more, but she's not looking at me. She's looking up at the sky, searching it for some sort of release. She gets it soon enough. Blood gurgles up through the hole and after she gives a few desperate, choking gasps for air, her arms fall to her sides and her violet eyes unfocus.

Though I want to scream for her, there's nothing I can do but roll around in agony and will myself not to claw at my neck like the others. Finally, I hear gunshots. The pressure releases, and my head begins to throb as the blood rushes back to my head. The other Seers who are still alive push themselves up and look to the gallows where the Watchmen stand in front of the bodies, each of which has been shot. The blindfolded man has been shot several times. Ryan no longer struggles.

The Keeper pushes herself up off the stage floor, her own neck clawed and bloodied. She looks at us. I look at Mae. Poor little Mae. I crawl over to her and wrap her in my arms, pulling her into my lap as if she were a toddler. The Keeper gives orders to the Citizens to help triage and relocate the Seers. I don't move, though. All I can think about is Mae as she frantically tore open her own throat, unaware that in the process, she'd never take another breath again.

Heavy footfall stops beside me, and when I look up, Gabe and Brandon block out the sunlight, casting a shadow over me and our fallen friend. They too are bloodied, just like the rest of us, with marks at their necks. Brandon has blood trickling from his eye where tears would normally come from. He doesn't seem to notice it, not even when real tears start to pool, flushing the blood down his cheeks.

"Mae…" Brandon whispers her name and drops to his knees beside me. "Oh, Mae."

"I tried to tell her to stop…" I blurt in my defense.

"I know, Bea, it's okay." Gabe kneels down and puts a hand on my shoulder. "We couldn't help it. The Dreamcatcher had us. Or, at least he had one of us." According to what we've been taught, if a Dreamcatcher can catch one of us, he can catch us all. Though we've learned this, we've never once experienced it until now. And after this, it is very unlikely that we will ever forget it either.

"I shook my head at her, but she kept on clawing. I wanted to stop her, but I couldn't stop myself…" Now tears form in my own eyes, and before I can get a hold of myself, I start to sob for the loss of my dear friend. "She's too young to be dead." *This is a war*, I hear Echo tell me. This is a war. No one is protected when it comes to war. Not even Mae.

Gabe wraps his arms around me and Brandon steps forward to take Mae away. She looks so tiny in his arms, so peaceful and loved. I watch as Brandon carries her away to wherever all the dead Seers are being put, then turn myself around so I can bury my head against Gabe and block out my bloody surroundings. The wounds on my neck ache and burn, especially when the air touches the flayed skin. I choke on my sobs, and the sick thought enters my head that maybe Mae felt like this as she was choking to death on her own blood.

"I think it has started, Beatrice," Gabe whispers into my ear, his fingers brushing soothingly against my back. At some point, he begins to rock me, and I close my eyes as the comfort of his embrace settles in.

"I think so, too." I speak into his black robes. It has started. Echo said that we'd know when the Dreamcatchers made their first attack, and nothing has ever seemed as clear as what we've just been through. It can only get worse from here, and I dread finding out exactly what "worse" entails.

"Come on. Let's go get cleaned up." Gabe helps me up to my feet by holding me under my elbows as my legs find my weight again. Around me, there's a sea of bloody puddles and marks from fingers streaking, scratching across the ground. Bodies litter the area, waiting to be carried away, one-by-one. I estimate that at least fifty of the Seers have died in this place alone. I don't know how many more inside might have been a part of Pathos's fury.

When we get to the infirmary, it is packed. The cases range from those able to get around on their own, like Gabe and I, to those who are still choking on their blood and trying to find a way to breathe. Some nurses have plastic tubes shoved into patient's necks, providing them with an airway until they can be sewn back up.

"I don't want to be here," I decide immediately. There's too much going on, and I don't want to have anything to do with it. The smell of fear mixed with blood, piss, and vomit makes me want to get sick myself. Maybe I didn't realize the extent of what fear could do to a person.

Gabe nods his head. "Let's go somewhere quiet." Neither of us is in any sort of medical emergency, so I follow Gabe's intuition, more than content to be anywhere but here. Without complaint, he and I walk out of the infirmary and down the hall, which is also stained with sporadic puddles of blood.

He takes me up to the roof of the Institution, and when he kicks open the door at the top of the stairwell, the fresh air shocks me and makes it hard to breathe. I cough a few times, and Gabe does the same as we both stumble to a black, wrought-iron bench. I collapse onto it and put my head in my hands as tears start to form once more. All of this is too much for me, and though I don't want to appear weak in front of Gabe, I think he understands. First Connie, now Mae. Connie was shot. Mae was driven to the edge.

I lean back into him and close my eyes. "What do we do now?"

"What do you mean, Bea?"

"The Dreamcatchers are coming, and it's only going to get worse. I could see it in my Visions, Gabe. I could see them taking you away from me…" And although I have already told him this, he listens to my worries as if they were new and runs his fingers through my knotty hair, caked in blood. "Why didn't I See this happen to Mae, though? Maybe I could have stopped it…"

"Don't be silly, Beatrice. You know as well as I do that we can't See everything. Nor can we stop everything. Just because we See it doesn't mean that we can prevent it from happening. You know the Dreamcatchers are going to come…you've Seen them come. But no one can stop them from coming. I think we've learned that today."

"She won't stop trying, though." The Keeper's crusade almost seems personal in some ways. If she knows we can't stop them from coming, then why bother sending us out into the City to hunt them?

"No, she won't." Gabe sighs after pressing a kiss to the top of my head. "I'm going to miss Mae, but I am glad that I did not lose you, too. I didn't know where you were during all of that, and all I could think of was getting to you and making sure you were okay."

"You thought of me? During all that pain? Didn't your head feel like it was going to explode?"

"I thought it *was* going to explode, but when I saw those people around me gouging their eyes out to stop the pressure, and clawing at their necks, I wondered if you were already gone. It frightened me." Gabe isn't one to admit to weakness much. He has done so with me only a few times, and I try very hard not to make a big deal out of it, since I'm afraid if I do, he'll stop telling me what's on his mind. And I want him to know that I will always be there for him, as he is for me.

I look up at Gabe so our violet eyes meet. "I'm here, though, and I'm okay. You don't need to worry, Gabe."

"I don't now, no. But I worried plenty then."

Maybe I'm feeling a bit guilty that during that whole episode I never once thought of Gabe. Maybe, in the back of my mind, I knew that he was okay. Gabe is always okay because he's strong and levelheaded and he always knows how to stay calm in situations that seem so uncontrollable. Or maybe, I forgot about him. I couldn't have forgotten about him, though. Why would I put Gabe out of my mind at a time like that? He could very well have ended up dead just like Mae, and I didn't once think about that?

"Well, we're both okay, and that's all that matters. Maybe we should find Brandon and have dinner in one of our bunks tonight?" I ask. "I don't think I feel up to eating in the cafeteria when everyone else is hurt and bleeding."

"And without Mae." Gabe lowers his eyes. "It's going to be so different without her around. She always knew how to find the good in everything—Did you realize that? It's like nothing could ever be wrong in her world."

He is right. Nothing *was* ever wrong in Mae's world. She could find the sunshine on a rainy, cloudy day, and if she couldn't, she'd *make* the sun shine.

"I'm going to miss her." He protectively wraps his arms around me, as if he could stop anything bad from hurting me or taking me away from him.

When I close my eyes again, I can see Mae staring at me with her blank, dead, violet stare and a smile on her face. My stomach twists into an uneasy knot. "I'm going to miss her, too."

CHAPTER TWENTY-ONE

We have come together in the Gathering Room to say our good-byes to those Seers who fell during the most recent Dreamcatcher attack. Brandon, Gabe, and I stand in front of a small wooden casket containing Mae's body. Like the other bodies lying in their final resting places, Mae's has been cleaned and prepared for the viewing process. They took the trouble to tie a large, pink flower around her neck like a choker to cover the gash made by her own hands.

Staring at her brings about a queasy and uneasy feeling. Just yesterday she was standing beside me, watching as the convicted Dreamcatchers were dropped through the gallows and hanged. Now she sees nothing. I don't know where we go after we die. At least, I don't know where we go past the physical sense. After the viewing, Mae's casket will be carried off to the incinerators, where she will be burned in a flash fire hot enough to destroy all that remains of a human when they've ceased to exist.

Gabe snakes his hand around mine and holds it tightly, a wordless show of support. Brandon is devastated and hasn't spoken since he carried Mae's body off the previous day. His eyes are rimmed red, and puffy half-moon circles darken under them. His hands, folded in front of him, are turning purple from holding on so hard, but what he thinks he's gripping, I don't know.

Some are gathered around their friends in much the same manner, some sobbing, others in too much shock to utter a noise. We are all grieving for different reasons, I'm sure. I am grieving for our past. We've entered into war, whether it's been officially declared or not; I think most people can feel that there's no turning back from here.

The Keeper makes her way to the front of the room, her hood pulled up over her head so that her face is shrouded in dark shadow. I've never seen her so solemn, and her presence silently demands the attention of all of us. Her raven flies from her shoulder and circles the room before finding a place to perch on top of a casket cover.

We all look the Keeper's way, and I am suddenly reminded of the Vision I had of the piles of dead bodies in the Meeting Room. Was this what it really was? Not piles of bodies in the Meeting Room at all, but dozens of lined up boxes?

It didn't seem so bad. This was much calmer and less frightening than the prospect of something creeping up behind us and murdering us *en masse*. I turn my head at the cry of the raven, whose wings spread open, then restlessly fold back.

"Today we say good-bye to many great Seers who have met their ends too soon. This is the way of the Dreamcatcher, to sneak up behind us and rob of us our abilities, and ultimately to rob us of our lives. It is a harsh lesson that we've all learned, even myself." The Keeper admits a weakness, and it catches all of us off guard. There's even a quiet gasp, followed by a deafening silence, as the room waits for some sort of reasoning or explanation.

The Keeper offers neither, though. She bows her head low and prays a quiet invocation. "When we send our friends and family off today, may we always remember our purpose and quest in the City. We must protect the Citizens, who lack the ability to protect themselves, and we must defeat the Dreamcatcher threat before they destroy and overtake what we've worked so hard to defend."

We are all silent, washed out from emotion, filled with grief.

After the invocation, the Keeper exits the room and volunteer attendants gather by the caskets to take them all down to the incinerator room. Brandon steps forward to protect the box that holds Mae's body, and when the volunteers approach, he shoves one of them away. "No!"

Gabe winces, letting go of my hand, and moves over beside Brandon to calm him. "It's time for her to go, Brandon. You have to let her go."

"No!" he shouts again and pushes Gabe next.

"Brandon…" I start, but it's no use. I am shoved after Gabe, and after that Brandon once more pushes the volunteers who try and approach the casket. This continues until two Watchmen approach and pin Brandon's large form against a wall, restraining him at the wrists.

"Let go! Let go!" Brandon thrashes, but it's no use. The casket is carried away, and Brandon only settles when he can't see it or Mae's face anymore. A part of me is enraged that I missed my opportunity to say good-bye to her, but I also know that I am selfish for thinking that way. None of us got to say good-bye to her. The Dreamcatchers stole that opportunity from us when her nails ripped into her flesh and peeled her neck open.

Eventually, the three of us are left in a crowd of people who no longer have bodies to mourn. I sigh and turn to Gabe and Brandon, who both stare at the ground in an attempt to hide their own grief. But I don't comment on it. Instead, I turn and start to walk out of the Gathering Room, and the two of them follow like lost little ducklings without anywhere else to go, or anyone else to follow.

I don't have the heart to tell them that I have no idea where I am going either. We wander the halls floor by floor, walking past the Recreation Rooms, the cafeteria, the arena. I think all we really want is to be alone without actually being alone. I can't figure out if Gabe would be angry with me or not if I were to approach him and offer comfort. When I look back at him, he's walking near Brandon, but far enough away that he can brood. Maybe it's me who wants the comforting.

I decide to take us all to the roof, since it's quiet up there and Gabe always seems to be most peaceful when he's standing on the top of the Institution, looking down at the City. In fact, I feel much the same way, come to think about it. We take the stairs and solemnly climb each one of them until there's nothing left to climb. I push the door open and it flings back, exposing a sight that I wasn't prepared for. Gabe and Brandon come to a stop behind me as we stare out into the sky, which looks as if it has fissured down the middle, purples and pinks pulling it apart like a tear in the skin.

"What the hell…" Gabe whispers as several large airships descend over the City. Two thrusters rotate in any direction, helping to propel forward or backward or to hover in place. We've never seen real ships before, but we've read about them in our history books. These ships look old and rickety, with some newer pieces of metal patching up random sections of the hull. One opens fire, and little streaks of fiery light whizz through the air and toward the City's buildings. When they hit, the buildings shake and crumble, and some of them cease to exist as soon as the explosions die down.

Even our breathing disappears.

"What are they shooting at? Why aren't they aiming toward here?" I ask the obvious question, since I don't understand why they'd be destroying random Citizen structures when they could be taking out the fortress of the Seers.

"We have a barrier," Brandon reminds me and picks up a piece of concrete that has crumbled from around the stairwell. He chucks the rock off the side of the building, and it hits an invisible shield that shatters the stone into a million, tiny pieces. "See?"

"Oh yeah."

Gabe isn't buying it, though. "But doesn't the City have one of those, too?"

"I thought so. But, apparently not." Brandon picks up another stone and does the same thing. The invisible shield crackles when the concrete disappears, turning into a fine powder before falling through the air.

"No, the City did have one. It's always been a bit shoddy, though." My words are nearly choked off at the end by the sound of a raid alarm, one I've never heard before in my whole life. All of the City lights are cut off at one time, and we are thrown into a blinding darkness that is only relieved when the ships begin to fire once more. The Institution PA squeals on, and the Keeper begins to immediately hurl orders at us.

"Seers! Your time is now! I need all of you to suit up, gather in your teams, and report to the staging area immediately. You will be deployed with or without your whole team, so do not delay! The City is under attack! Do not delay!" The PA cuts off.

"Come on!" Gabe grabs me by the wrist. We all run down the stairs, taking them two or three at a time. Brandon uses the rails on each side to swing down half the flights, heels hitting the ground with a *thump* before he's back up and doing it all over again. Eventually we get to an elevator, which drops us down more than a hundred levels to the first floor, where the staging area is. It is packed with hundreds of Seers, from Team A to Team Z, all of us ready to fight, even if we really aren't ready at all. Those near the end of the Team alphabet have the least training, and they all look like they have peed their pants judging by the way they stand huddled together like a bunch of toddlers in the cold.

"We're in trouble," Brandon dares to say as we pass them, the words certainly not a compliment. Maybe some of them even *are* toddlers, now that I can get a closer look. They look barely old enough for Institution privileges, which allow you to wander around without an escort.

Brandon, Gabe, and I suit up faster than we ever have before. I pack a few extra beacon grenades this time, as well as some flares, just in case we get lost out in the dark. My machine gun is locked and loaded, and I tuck extended magazines into my combat belt, ensuring that I don't run out of ammo. Hopefully. Gabe follows my lead and does the same thing, and I'm sure Brandon is packed with anything extra he needs, though with his weight and height, he always seems like he just barely fits into his jumpsuit.

The lights on the bay doors begin to spin, illuminating the room in yellows and reds. We can hear the impact of the explosions, which are still far from us, but close enough to rattle the floor at times. I think about all those poor Citizens who have been terrorized the last few weeks with the Dreamcatcher hunt. Now, the Dreamcatchers are hunting the Citizens themselves, and most of them are defenseless, waiting on us to save them.

The doors couldn't open more slowly. It feels like a whole decade goes by before they are wide enough for the teams to pass through. Rachelle is at the lead of her team, which suddenly reminds me that I am probably at the lead of mine. When I spin around, not only are Gabe and Brandon behind me, but the rest of Team A is as well. They are waiting for orders, which even I don't know.

"Stay close and follow!" This should work. I turn and run out behind the other teams, boots crashing on the ground in unison. I have to figure something out before too long. Teams B and C look as though they are heading straight into the heart of the matter, but in my gut, something tells me this isn't the right choice. *What are they shooting at? What are they shooting at?* The question keeps replaying through my mind, and I make a sudden move down a somewhat broad street that veers to the left, leaving the rest of the teams behind. One or two of them follow me, though, which is good, since there will be more of us should we need it.

What are they shooting at?

And then, I See it. The Vision hits me like a punch to my stomach, and I stumble backward into Gabe, who thankfully catches me. I can see the glow of my violet eyes in the tinted face shield of his helmet. I can See the answer to my question. "It's a distraction," I whisper.

The other teams gather around as Gabe gets me back to my feet just as soon as the light in my eyes begins to fade. I swallow from the ache that comes after the Vision. "It's a distraction. We need to get away from the Dreamcatchers and stay by the Institution."

"Why?" I look toward the question and see Elan, his helmet tucked under his arm. He's been moved back up to Team A with us. He looks confident and ready to kill someone. Maybe he's learned his lesson from last time. Kill or be killed.

"Because. That is where they are trying to go. All of us are running toward the ship, but who is staying behind to protect the

Institution?"

The rest of them "oh" in unison. It is so obvious, but yet most of the Seers are currently racing toward the ships anyway. I pull my gun up and nod to the left. "We're going to continue going this way and find ourselves a building that is strong enough to act like a fortress. Anyone have any ideas?"

Most of us aren't very familiar with the City. There are only a handful of Seers who are allowed out on a regular basis. The rest of us are confined to the Institution for our safety. Thankfully, it seems we have one of that handful in our group. A girl with curly red hair raises her hand, waiting to be called on like we are in class. I call on her, and even in the middle of this chaos, I think it's amusing. "What about the bank? It's made of marble, and because it's a bank, there are plenty of secure places inside."

"Good idea," Gabe concedes, his eyes finding mine to see if I agree. I'd much rather Gabe were in charge right now, as he's so much calmer than I am. My heart is threatening to beat right out of my chest, but Gabe is cool and collected, not one sign of fear or apprehension on his features.

We are briefly distracted when we notice a ship pulling up a net filled with Citizens in various states of distress. Some are badly injured, others are screaming for their lives, but they are all swallowed up by the ship, disappearing in front of our eyes.

"I agree." Only because Gabe agrees. I look away from the ship, which has held my attention for long enough. "Let's get out of here and head that way. We'll talk about a better plan when we get there." We run double time down the streets and in the direction of the bank. Behind us, the constant sound of explosions, crumbling buildings and screaming people echoes through the City.

When we get to the bank, I don't regret my decision. The

building is squat and wide, but thick and sturdy. The windows are covered in iron bars, and the door is made of reinforced steel. The security guard allows us in, muttering a thousand "Thank yous" as we file in and set up a perimeter.

"Get the Citizens to the back of the building!" I order first, since they will only get in our way. Some of them are crying and others look at one another with suspicion, fearing there may be a Dreamcatcher hiding amongst them. "Now!"

Gabe leads the group in peeling Citizens up off the ground, where they've lain down to take cover. Some of them are reluctant to stand, so Gabe pokes them in the side with the barrel of his machine gun, a silent threat. Other Seers start to scream at them, "Get up! Get up now!"

"Calm down," I mutter, glancing about to see what else we can set up for our safety. "I want every piece of furniture that moves pushed to the windows and doors." This will make it harder for them to breach, if they try. They'll have lots of debris to climb over, which will hopefully give us the advantage when they are stumbling about. Overhead, a ship hovers nearby, and the ground starts to rumble from the thrusters pushing down the air with incredible force. The sound is nearly deafening mixed with the scraping of desk legs across the marble floor.

"Damn it, they are right there, Bea." Gabe rushes to my side and starts to tug me back toward the middle of the room.

"Stop. We can't run from them. They might not even know we are in here."

I am wrong about that. They drop a bomb that explodes just outside the bank, blasting all of the glass out of the windows. Some of the shards fly inward, hitting Seers and Citizens alike. Screaming erupts on either side of me. I'm too busy watching each of the windows, waiting for Dreamcatchers to come barreling in. But they don't. The ship continues to hover.

"What are they doing?" I whisper.

Gabe lifts his gun, sighting from one window to the next. Nothing happens.

I make a motion to those who were moving the furniture. "Keep going! Move, move, move!"

They hesitantly drag desks, file cabinets and other miscellaneous pieces to the windows, pilling them up on top of one another. The crunch of glass under their feet is almost sickening as the pieces scrape and pop together. Outside, the trees are all bent at strange angles from the force of the blast and from the power of the ship's thrusters. Is there more than one ship overhead?

Then, I spot their next move. Ropes drop from the sky and dangle there, empty and curious. A few minutes later, Dreamcatchers descend from the ship and land on the ground, dressed for war. They also carry guns, though their combat outfits have a few modifications, including gloves that allow their fingertips to be free. A few of the bigger ones carry net-throwers in their grips, nets to catch Citizens and load them into the ships.

"They are starting to comb the City," Gabe whispers to me when he spots the net-throwers in hand. "They are taking Citizens."

Like Echo said they were here to do. "Here they come!" I yell, and Gabe wastes no time pulling me back toward the teller desks, where most of the Seers are set up, their guns resting on the surface, all pointed toward the windows and the doors.

The Dreamcatchers gesture toward our building and do exactly as I expect. They try to breach the windows and the doors by throwing grenades and other explosive devices. The walls crumble in some places, but stay strong and sturdy in others. Stones soar through the building, and we duck behind the desks to avoid being hit by them.

One-by-one, the enemy soldiers climb through the rubble. I hold my hand up, fist closed in the "hold your fire" position. For some reason, I want them to fire first. I want to feel as if we were defending ourselves from the start. Maybe it has to do with the fact that any one of them could be Echo. And what if one of them is?

But the Dreamcatchers don't fire. They make their way over the mess, some of them still standing in the middle of it, and they train their guns on us. There's about twenty of them all together, not much more than my group, and they are all dressed in black jumpsuits with helmets that are similar to our own. Some of them are men, some women, and they all look as if they are different ages judging by their sizes.

We point our guns at them.

"What do you want?" I call out, opening a line of communication, even if it is probably useless. No one ever taught us the art of diplomacy. No one ever said that it was an option. We've been given guns and weapons with the order to seek out the Dreamcatchers and slaughter them. We've been encouraged to climb over their bodies and keep moving forward to seek out more and murder them where they stand. It's not as easy as it seemed, though.

We weren't taught to talk to one another, and even the Dreamcatchers seem confused by it.

"What?" One of them calls back at me, but I don't know which, since I can't see their faces or mouths.

"What. Do. You. Want?" I slowly speak the words. There's a long pause between what I say, and what their next words are. And I immediately regret trying to speak to them at all.

"We aren't here to talk." And then the one speaking opens fire on me, and it's only by the grace of my intuition that I hit the ground before the bullets can lodge themselves into my head. The rest of them open fire as well, and we find that we're pinned behind the desk, unable to get our weapons up to fire back. This is my fault, and I feel guilty and angry all at once. Why did I have to try and talk to them? Did I really think Echo was standing with them? There are hundreds of Dreamcatchers, and only a handful of them are standing right here. What were the odds anyway?

"We have to shoot back!" Brandon blurts and lifts his gun over his head. "Come on! Everyone start shooting back and we can push them into cover!"

I'm glad someone else is paying attention while I'm sitting on the ground like a moron. How could I have messed it up?

The concussion from the force of the net-thrower sounds along with the gunshots, and the weights on the net clatter on the floor by the teller's desk. Citizens start to scream, the tellers themselves now caught for the Dreamcatchers' purposes. We are too far away to help them, and everything happens so quickly that it is soon too late. The net retracts, dragging the Citizens across the floor. I count three of them, and they are dragged away like objects for the taking.

The other Seers react, and each of them raises their gun and begins to blindly fire in the direction of the Dreamcatchers. The effect is immediate, and the enemy fire becomes less and less as they fall back to find cover. It gives us enough time to peek up over the desk and secure a visual of their forces dropping back and hiding behind the pillars of wall left behind after their breach.

Elan drops his gun as a bullet hits him in the wrist, blasting a hole straight through it. He screams in agony and grabs his hand to try and stop the bleeding with the other. The Citizens lose their calm and begin to irrationally scream as well, as if all of them had been hit just when Elan was.

"Hang in there, Elan! Fall back and take cover!" I yell in his direction. I feel some sort of sisterly attachment to Elan. I want to protect him like I did before, but I'm stuck behind a register, firing away at the opposite wall, hoping that maybe I'll hit something in the process.

Eventually, the Dreamcatchers retreat, and the enemy fire stops altogether. They grapple onto the ropes that they had used to lower themselves to the ground, and all at once they are pulled back into the ship along with the captured Citizens.

"Fire! Open fire!" I shout, and we all run to the windows to try and get a good aim on the fleeing Dreamcatchers. Gabe manages to hit one or two of them, and they come crashing down onto the street, each of them making a sickening splatting noise as their bodies break on the asphalt. They are the only two that fall, though, and soon the rest of the Dreamcatchers are safe in their ship.

And that is when it happens.

The ship suddenly drops toward the ground, its artillery pointed at the bank. My eyes widen and I scream at the top of my lungs, "Everyone down! Take cover! Take cove—"

The words get lost in the noise of their cannons charging. I barely manage to get on the ground as the shots are fired, and large balls of flame streak through the bank and hit the opposite wall, blasting a hole straight through it, and anyone who happened to be in front of it. Citizens and Seers instantly turn to ash.

I hold onto my helmet with one hand and stare at the ship as it charges up again. "Stay down!"

Gabe inches up beside me and shouts, "We need to get out of here!"

"I can't leave them behind!" I yell at him, just as the ship fires again, and the bank continues to fall apart around us. "I can't leave them!"

"You have to, Bea! We need to leave! Let's go!" Gabe hooks a hand around my bicep, and his grip is so tight that it hurts.

"Gabe! Let me go!"

But he doesn't listen to me. He makes a motion for whoever is paying attention to follow us, and we run straight toward the ship as the cannons recharge. The low humming sound becomes louder and louder the closer we get to it. Just as the sound stops altogether, in that nerve-wracking silence before the shots go off, Gabe and I and a handful of others slip under the ship and roll into the street. The next round of fire cripples the building and it falls in on itself, leaving nothing but a pile of rubble behind.

"Get up! Keep running!" Gabe darts away from the ship, and when I look behind us, I notice about ten others who have made it, out of about fifty, including the Citizens. Only a few of them run along with us, bloodied and covered in soot, tears spilling from their eyes.

"Have I failed?" I call to Gabe as we race away from the Dreamcatchers and into the heart of the City, specifically where I said not to go. "Was my Vision wrong?"

"Your Visions are hardly ever wrong, Beatrice." But Gabe doesn't say that I didn't fail, and this sticks with me as we scurry into the City like mice.

CHAPTER TWENTY-TWO

More ships descend upon the City. *You will know,* Paradigm said, and now I do. The Dreamcatchers aren't going to turn back now, and they come down on us full force, guns and cannons blazing. The ships are equipped with large barrels that jerk backward before letting go and firing shells big enough to demolish a building in one hit. One of these ships is doing just that, razing the City structure by structure, presumably after their forces sweep them and capture as many Citizens as they can. The surviving members of Team A, including Brandon and Elan, have to duck and weave as we race toward nothing in particular.

Gabe is at the front of the group, even though I'm technically the leader. But I don't mind, and we follow him into the dust and chaos stirred up by all the fighting. There are moments where sharp pains sear up my sides and into my head, and I hear the Keeper lecturing us about how, if a Dreamcatcher catches one of us, we all experience it in some way or another. She never clarified how, exactly, but I know that each rush of pain means another Seer has been caught and killed. They are eliminating us one by one to get to their prize.

We rush into another building, and once we are inside, I realize it's the Widow's house—or the bar that she called home—but she is gone. I run behind Gabe as he weaves through the halls of the home and to a door that is flung open to reveal stairs leading into a basement. Before we can take cover, though, the roof is ripped off of the small home like a lid being peeled off by a can opener. We stand there, exposed to the fire of a large ship that hovers overhead, blowing around all of the Widow's effects. Within minutes, the house is completely destroyed, and about five Dreamcatchers are deployed onto the ground by sliding down the ropes.

"Take cover!" I scream just in time. The Dreamcatchers open fire on us as soon as their feet hit the ground. I roll behind a wall that divides the kitchen from the front room. The stools that used to stand in front of the bar are all tipped over and broken into pieces. Shots from the Dreamcatchers' guns tear apart the wall, so I hit the ground and crawl on my stomach to find a good place to return fire.

I peek around the corner and notice some of the Dreamcatchers aren't even dressed for battle. They are wearing their white robes with the red satin lining, and somehow, none of the robes are dirty from fighting. They are the same robes that Echo wore in my dream.

And that's when I see him. Echo.

He has a large gash in his cheek, to the point where you can see the meat inside, and he is holding his side with one of his hands, blood dripping through his fingers. He shoots in the direction of two Team A members who desperately shoot back at him. And what if they hit him? What if he kills them? Flashes of light illuminate the room as the beacon bullets explode on impact against the walls.

Someone starts to shoot at me before I can open my mouth and tell the other two to cease fire. They'd of course think I am crazy, but I don't care. I wouldn't have cared…if I'd had the chance. I roll on my side and shoot, bullets ripping into tables and sofas, anything they make contact with. I can barely keep my thoughts off Echo, and my aim is terrible.

That's when we hear another, different alarm sound. It startles all of us, even the Dreamcatchers.

A Citizen girl, who was hiding in the rubble, bolts toward the door while we are all stunned. Echo steps forward and trips the girl and she goes tumbling across the ground, all limbs. Echo lifts her by the wrist like a ragdoll, and in just a moment she screams and collapses. He releases her, and when he looks at me, his eyes are a deep crimson color, no longer blue. The gash on his cheek is also completely gone. Healed.

I stare at him, but the Dreamcatchers must have been ordered to depart, as they all turn on their heels and run out of the house.

"Keep firing!" I hear Gabe order. We've all stopped shooting, shocked at what we witnessed.

"He killed her," I whisper to myself, finally fully understanding why the Dreamcatchers are here.

"Keep firing, Bea!" One of Gabe's shots catches the Dreamcatcher who brings up the rear of their group. He falls, and none of the others turn back to try and help him up. They disappear around a corner, and I hold up my hand to signal that we aren't going to chase them down. The Dreamcatchers are gone.

"What's that alarm?" Brandon stops by my side and looks around. "And what is *that*?"

I look to what he's pointing at, a beam of red light that shoots straight up through the middle of the City and into the sky.

"It's coming from the Institution." Elan has his head tilted all the way back and stares at the light, transfixed.

"Yeah, but what is it?" Brandon asks again, but his words die off as a ship rushes through the light and is immediately turned into dust.

"Holy crap!" I blurt, still not understanding what I am witnessing. Another ship or two zooms by overhead, and they quickly change their course, barely avoiding the beam. "I think…I think that's the Beacon! Come on, let's get back to the Institution. It looks like the Dreamcatchers are trying to get to it, and someone should be there to meet them." I look back over my shoulder in the direction where the other Dreamcatchers left. Echo is long gone. Did I save him? Was that all I had to do?

I climb out of the house's rubble, scaling broken bookshelves and piles of shingles and brick. The alarm is blaring louder now, and I can barely make out the moaning of someone to my right. "Wait! Someone's in here." They all stop moving, and we hear the moaning again.

"That way!" One of the other team members calls, leading us down what used to be a hallway leading to a bedroom. Inside the room, the Widow lays crushed under a beam that used to help hold up the structure of her house. No one else knows who she is, but when I remove my helmet and head over to her, it's made perfectly clear that she knows who I am.

"Beatrice." She breathes raggedly, just like the gurgling noises that Mae made before she choked on her own blood and died.

Gabe stops by my side and grabs my arm so I can't approach.

"Is she a Dreamcatcher?" Elan asks.

"Why would a Dreamcatcher know Beatrice's name?" Brandon shoves Elan, nearly pushing him to the ground in the process. Elan winces in pain, still holding his wrist, and frowns up at Brandon. When they are standing next to each other, one looks like a giant and the other a tiny bug, and if we weren't in the middle of a war, I'd maybe laugh at it.

"Everyone knows her name, child." The Widow holds her hand out to me. "You must save us." She coughs up blood and it trickles from the corners of her mouth and down her cheeks. "Save us."

"I don't know how." And I *don't* know how. How did I become the one who has to save everyone else? Why can't it be someone else's burden and not mine?

"You do." The Widow closes her eyes and coughs again, and when she opens them back up, she reaches out and pulls on the chain around my neck, revealing the raven necklace under my jumpsuit. "Beware what you cannot See."

"But how do I avoid something if I cannot See it?" Everything around me seems to disappear as I grasp the Widow's hand, trying to will her to stay alive a little longer. To help me.

"You rely on your other senses, Beatrice. Seeing is only one part of us. Sensing, as you have learned, is another." The Widow looks up into my eyes. "Don't forget that you are more than just your Sight. You are so much more, Beatrice, and you don't even know it."

"What do you mean? What more?"

After a few, raspy breaths and another cough or two, she ceases to breathe, leaving my question unanswered. *Beware what you cannot See. You are so much more…*

Gabe lets go of my arm. "Who the hell was that?"

"The Widow." I brush some of her hair out of her face. "Remember? She was kicked out of the Institution long ago. A Dreamcatcher found his way into her dreams…or her Visions. I don't know which, just that they threw her out to protect the rest of the Seers at the time."

"Lucky her," Elan mutters, and I cast him a curious look, since

I've never heard of a Seer who didn't want to be at the Institution.

I don't have time to pry any further into his words, though. "We have to keep moving. Back to the Institution. Now."

On our way back, we pass remnants of skirmishes that look as if they broke even for the most part. Dreamcatchers, Seers, and Citizens alike litter the ground like pieces of discarded trash, limbs sprawled out unnaturally in every direction.

The closer we get to the Institution, the louder the alarm becomes, and the more intense the light shines. I put my hand up to my brow, or where my brow would be if I weren't wearing a helmet. Even with the tinted visor, the light is too bright, and I have to look away.

When we get to the front doors, they automatically slide open for us then bolt behind once we are inside. One by one we pull our helmets off, faces beaded with sweat and dirt. I wipe the back of my hand across my cheeks and frown.

"Where are we going to set up now?" Gabe leans down, his palms on his knees. He takes deep breaths, his back heaving up and down as he tries to relax.

"Just outside. We can make a barrier in the bay and wait in there in case the Dreamcatchers try to get in. That's probably where they are going since it's our biggest entrance." I glance at what remains of my team and notice that two Citizens have been running along with us. They stare in wonder at the grandeur of the Institution. "Damn it. How'd they get in here too?"

Elan pushes the two Citizens back toward the door. "Consider yourselves lucky. You got to see what very few Citizens ever get to see." With a little push, the doors slide open and the Citizens tumble out. "But you aren't allowed in here. So go find some cover."

"Give them your gun." I order, feeling bad that we are going to hide ourselves away in the comfort of the Institution, while sending two people back out into the war zone with nothing to defend themselves with. It wouldn't be very honorable of us, and to the Citizens, the Seers are supposed to be anything but dishonorable.

Elan pulls the strap of his gun over his head and tosses the weapon out onto the ground. "Stay safe." The doors shut, allowing no time for the Citizens to say anything back. "We're going to get in a lot of trouble for that one." Gabe picks another gun up off the ground and tosses it to Elan.

"One, two, three, four, five, six…" I count the heads of those who have managed to escape the bank, which is only half of my team. Two of them look even more frightened than the rest. They are new Seers, even if they have the raven's wings to mark the sides of their faces. "Six."

"It wasn't your fault, Bea." Gabe knows what I am thinking. He always knows what I am thinking.

"Then whose fault is it?"

"The Dreamcatchers'. Now come on. We need to find a good place to set up in case they come this way." He allows no time for me to retort. Gabe takes off toward the staging area, and we run behind him, trying our best to keep up. He moves gracefully, even when jogging in his combat suit, which is heavy and cumbersome.

I find myself wanting Echo, and part of me hurts that he didn't seem to recognize me or care that I was standing right in front of him. But at the same time, I want to shake him, yell at him for killing something so innocent in order to heal himself. How could he do that to her? In this chaos, though, it's hard to arrange my thoughts into something coherent, and before I can turn back to confront Echo, Gabe leads all of us into something none of us expected.

CHAPTER TWENTY-THREE

The Dreamcatchers have breached the staging area. They swarm like flies on something dead, running in every direction with no clear purpose or plan. They open fire almost immediately, and a few Seers are caught by their gunfire and fall to the ground, some of them screaming, some of them dead.

"Holy crap," Gabe whispers to himself, and I have only a moment to pull him back beside the doors leading into the large bay. The bullets ping off of the walls and my immediate reaction is to put my hands over my head.

"We have to move!" Elan reminds us. I am beginning to like this kid. He's good to have around—I'm just glad he hasn't been killed yet.

Just as we turn to start running somewhere, anywhere, we hear a clamor in the bay. Grenades are thrown and blast shrapnel around the large room, and some pieces catch in the flesh of Dreamcatcher and Seer alike. The two newer Seers with us get hit with shards of metal, and they both fall, screaming in pain. "Help me get them out of here!" I blurt at Gabe, Brandon, and Elan. We drag them out into the hallway, and when I turn around, I see that Rachelle is leading her team right into the middle of the battle. They start to push back the Dreamcatchers with their weapons and explosives.

"She's got 'em." Brandon forgets all about the hatred we hold for Rachelle, his words filled with hope that maybe she's actually doing something right for once. Maybe she'll save us all by this display of bravado.

But like all things having to do with Rachelle, this is not the case.

She runs up on top of an ATV outfitted with large wheels grooved with deep tread. Instead of actually using the ATV for its intended purpose, she decides to make a display of her charge on the Dreamcatchers, and she hangs off the side shooting her gun up in the air and toward nothing in particular. "You'll never win!" she yells, and if we weren't in some crazy situation, I'd probably die of laughter right now at how stupid she looks. It reminds me of old holomovies with bad guys who get way too full of themselves and end up tripping all over their own pride.

That's exactly what Rachelle does.

Clear in the middle of the bay, she continues to yell just as the doors leading to the outside are blasted inward with a force that sends Rachelle off the ATV and the rest of us tumbling to the floor. I scramble to get back on my feet, and when I'm standing again, I look back to find out what happened, only to find that one of their ships has breached the Institution. The ship's hull doors open, revealing a force of Dreamcatchers inside, all dressed in black, machine guns held close to their chests. One of them hangs out just enough so that he can train his sights on Rachelle.

In just two shots, she falls and her screaming about how the Dreamcatchers will never win eerily echoes through the bay.

"Holy…" Brandon starts to say when Rachelle finally lands on the ground, still and bleeding. A Dreamcatcher walks over to her and points his gun at her head, and just like that, Rachelle is gone, and my stomach ties into knots.

"They killed her," I hear Brandon whisper, shocked.

"They will kill us, too, if we don't get out of here!" Elan reminds us all as he ties a tourniquet around his wrist to bandage it.

In organized line formations, the Dreamcatchers disembark from the ship and press forward, shooting down anything that gets in their way. From behind me, Elan says with much more urgency than before, "We have to move. *Now*."

And we do. The four of us race for the lift, but it's Gabe that points out that is probably not a good idea. "Let's take the stairs instead. We could get stuck in the lift and we'd have nowhere to go." He takes my hand and pulls me toward the stairs. He's trembling, and though he might be trying to make it seem like he's just guiding me to safety, the way he holds my fingers tells me that he's just as scared as I am, even if neither of us dares to let it show.

He pushes the door open with such force that it slams into the wall and rebounds, nearly hitting Elan in his face. The boy is quick, though, and he puts both of his palms out to stop it. That's when his eyes begin to glow, and he nearly collapses. Brandon catches him at the last moment, and we wait in the stairwell until Elan's Vision passes. It doesn't take long.

Elan's eyes dim and he comes back around, looking to each of us. "We will be betrayed."

"By whom? What did you see?" Brandon sets Elan back onto his feet as he asks the question.

"We don't have time to analyze his Vision now. We have to get to cover before they get to us." Gabe begins his trek up the stairs.

"Let's go to the Meeting Room, maybe we can find the Keeper there and warn the others."

"The Meeting room is sixteen floors up, Gabe," I point out to him, but I know it won't make a difference. We are running up those stairs, even if I don't want to. My gear weighs down on me and I feel exhausted just thinking about it.

"Well, we better start hauling ass then, shouldn't we?" Gabe takes the stairs as if they moved on their own and all he had to do was stand still. As we rise, floor by floor, it gets quieter, and the mayhem down at the staging area fades out. Do the people up here even know what is going on downstairs?

The internal alarms start to sound, immediately answering my question. They do now.

When we reach the sixteenth floor, the four of us can hardly breathe. Gabe pushes on the bar to open the door, but something pulls at me from the inside, urging me to stop him. "Wait."

Gabe pauses. "What?"

"Something's not right." I can feel it. It's that feeling we get when the Dreamcatchers are close, plus something more that screams at me not to go in there.

"How do you know?"

"Are you having a Vision too?" Elan asks, holding his head from ache.

"No, it's not a Vision. It's just a feeling…"

"Well, if we start to do everything based on feelings in our guts, we won't get anywhere. They'll find the stairs soon enough. We have to go somewhere." Ignoring me, Gabe pushes open the door to the sixteenth floor and steps in. It's pitch black and too quiet. "What the hell is going on?"

"I told you," I angrily mutter and walk by him, purposefully knocking Gabe in the shoulder.

"Watch out." Gabe's voice hovers in the air, detached from his body, which I can no longer see.

"We have to stick together." I rein in my leadership position once more. Jutting my arms out in front of me, I feel around for the others, blindly grasping into the air. I hear a click in the darkness, and the halogen light on Elan's machine gun turns on. One by one, the rest of us remember to turn our lights on, too.

I gesture down the hall toward the Meeting Room. "Maybe they are taking cover in there? I don't know of another room where they could all go to hide and be safe." The Meeting Room is as good as any, with its catwalks for the Watchmen and its size, allowing most, if not all, of the Seers to be in one place at one time. "Let's go look."

Gabe, Brandon, and Elan follow as we move down the hall. I can't help but notice that sometimes there seems to be a foggy nature to the dark space in front of us, but it's hard to tell in the dark. It's probably just the shadows from the four of our bouncing lights, the only luminosity present. When we get to the Meeting Room doors, they are closed, but not locked. I barely step in front of them and the doors slide open, leading into the strangely quiet area. My boots catch on something in front of me, and I nearly trip and fall onto the ground, but I manage to regain my balance before taking the tumble.

Gabe points his light down to my feet. There's a hand there, open, palm up. The light slides back, illuminating the arm, and eventually the side of the body to which the hand belongs. But as he continues to pull his light back, he reveals much more than just one body strewn on the ground.

There are piles of them, all naked, vulnerable…dead.

I notice the foggy quality of the air and put a hand to my helmet.

"They've been gassed. Keep your helmets on."

It's just like how my Vision showed it. Dead bodies stacked in piles...the black fog...how wasn't I able to stop this when I clearly Saw it before it happened? My stomach churns. I need to vomit, but I can't without taking my helmet off. And if I take my helmet off, I'll most likely end up in a pile with the rest of the Seers here.

"They're all dead?" Brandon nudges another body with the toe of his boot.

"That's like...so many of the Seers." Elan whispers, as if afraid to wake them up from their eternal sleep. "They must have sought shelter here from the fighting."

"Or maybe they were called back. We...we should keep moving." Please don't vomit. Please don't vomit. My stomach lurches again. "Now."

Gabe knows something is wrong with me. He looks in my direction, and though I can't see his face through the tint of his visor, I can feel his eyes on me. He's concerned, even if just moments before, he had no intention to heed my warning.

"But where do we go?" Elan puts a hand to his stomach. "I don't feel so well."

There's another ripple of pain, and this time, we all cry out and buckle. "It's getting worse." Gabe clutches the nearby wall, his light falling by his side as he lets go of his weapon. I don't like not being able to see him.

"Pick your weapon back up. Let's move. They are getting closer—it's why we feel sick. It's why we hurt." They are killing more of us. Each time they do, I feel it—we all feel it—and the pains are getting worse. The pain starts down in my toes and radiates through my legs. Then it balls up in my stomach, exploding into my chest, and eventually simmering in my brain until it dissipates and another pain starts in its place.

"Or are we poisoned too?" Brandon poses a good question, but I have no time to think about it. I brush by them and start in a new direction, toward the stairs. The alarm sounds again and before we can get to the well, all of the doors in the building's infrastructure bolt shut. I push the door, but it goes nowhere. I push again, and again, and again, until Brandon stops me. "Bea, we're stuck here."

"I know that! Don't you think I know that?" I kick the door. It hurts my toes.

"Shhh. They could still be up here." Gabe holds his light up so that it's shining on my face. "Let's go check the other rooms to see if they are closed up too. Maybe it's just the rooms that lead to the outside that are locked."

"Good point." Elan points his gun and light down the hall. "What about the Recreation Room?"

"Okay, let's give it a shot." Inside my boot, I flex my hurting toes before setting forth to lead the way. As we move, I think back on the dangerous red light that shoots up from out of the Institution.

The day is winding down, and it feels like forever since we were first set out into the City. "We need to rest." I look back at the others, who walk with an exhausted air about them. If I could see their faces, I'm sure they'd have circles under their eyes, and their skin would look gaunt and pale. When we get into the Recreation Room, it is quiet and no one else is in there. We quickly fortify the door by pushing the sofas and tables in front of it. I move to the intercom system, and Gabe hustles over to the holovision to see if it is still picking up any transmissions.

I punch in the number for the Keeper's office. It's an easy number to remember: One.

The intercom buzzes over and over again but no one picks up, not even an assistant. "Do you think the Keeper was in the Meeting Room, too?" I don't want to ask them if they think she's dead or not. I don't know who is listening, and I don't want the Dreamcatchers to think they've won.

"Who knows? There were hundreds of bodies in there." Elan starts to take off his helmet, but he stops just as quickly. "Do you think this whole floor is poisoned?"

"I don't know, and I don't want to find out the hard way. Why don't you keep your helmet on?" I level a look at him that Elan will never see. Pushing the "one" button on the intercom, I try the Keeper again.

"Do you really think that was the Beacon?" Brandon asks, settling on the floor in front of a wall. He leans back and puts his legs out in front of him, and his posture reminds me of a baby who doesn't quite know how to sit on its own yet.

"Did you see how it just tore through those ships?" Elan shakes his head. "Amazing."

"Yeah, that was something else. Just…sliced through them, like…" Brandon's brain struggles to find a good comparison. If you stare into his eyes, you can probably see all the cogs turning, straining to think of something. "A knife through melty cheese."

Gabe stops by my side. "Did you reach her yet?"

"No, no one is answering." I look up at him, or where I think his eyes are. "I'm worried. Where could she be? Why isn't anyone answering? Are we the only Seers left?"

He puts a hand on my forearm, and although I can't actually feel his skin on mine, it's still comforting. "Calm down, Bea. We'll figure things out."

"Did you see all of those people?" The words catch in my throat. "I Saw it in one of my Visions. I saw them all there…dead.

Why couldn't I stop it? It's just like with the boy on the bridge… what good are these Visions if we can't actually stop them?"

"I don't know, Bea. I don't know. Maybe we haven't figured it out yet."

"Well, we have to figure it out before more people die and there's nothing we can do about it. I don't want to be helpless anymore, Gabe. I want to be able to…to *do* something about it." I'm just as tired as the rest of them. I can feel the exhaustion deep down in my bones. "We need to rest."

"We do." Gabe drops the subject. "How about we take turns? You three go ahead and sleep first, then Elan will take watch, then Brandon, then Bea."

"Sounds like a plan." Elan's words are caught mid-yawn, and "plan" sounds more like "yam."

"All right. But keep your weapons in hand. Who knows what will happen in the morning?" I hug my machine gun as if it were a teddy bear. It's the only thing that can protect me now.

CHAPTER TWENTY-FOUR

I don't expect to see Echo in my dreams tonight. When I'm taken away into unconsciousness, I appear in his arms and he's running away from the City. I bang on his shoulder and frown, "Put me down!"

"What?" Echo doesn't pause, though. He keeps right on running, stumbling at times. I realize that he's bleeding through a jumpsuit, not the white robe he wore when I was awake, and blood soaks into the material by his thigh. It has to be a deep wound to have bled through the layers of fabric, but yet he seems to somehow manage the weight of his own body as he runs, as well as the weight of me.

I am also bleeding. My leg is broken. I know it hurts, but in my dream, I can't feel the pain at all. It must be why he's carrying me, though. I wouldn't just let him pick me up and run off.

Or would I?

"Where are you taking me?"

"I told you, Beatrice. We need to leave this place. We've saved each other."

"I saw you kill a Citizen. You didn't say anything to me. You didn't even look like you recognized me.

"Did you want me to get you in trouble?" Echo looks down at me when he says this, pausing in his running. "I had to ignore you, Beatrice. And I'm glad you ignored me in return, lest we both be executed."

The thought of standing beside Echo on the gallows makes me sick to my stomach. "True. But you still killed an innocent girl."

"And you've not killed any Dreamcatchers, Beatrice?" Echo starts to run again, fleeing the scene as quickly as he can. Ships buzz by us overhead, fleeing the City, but I don't know where they are flying off to.

I don't have anything to say to that. I did kill Dreamcatchers and he was right. How dare I question him when I've been doing the very same thing? "But you...you used her..."

"I had to heal myself."

"But don't you see how that is wrong? She was trying to run... and you came down on her like some sort of predator." My trust in Echo begins to fade. How did I ever trust him in the first place? How did I bring myself to get so close to my enemy?

Echo stops running again and sets me down on a stone post that marks off an ancient road that leads away from the City. "I didn't want to do it, Beatrice. And I didn't want to have to do it in front of you. But if I wanted to live, I had to do it before I bled to death."

Despite him being so near to me, I feel nothing. Nothing that I'm supposed to feel when I'm so close to a Dreamcatcher. Then again, I hardly ever feel anything when he comes into my dreams like this. It's just not the same as when he was standing there in my real life. When he was something tangible and real.

When he was Echo.

"Did you want to see me hurt?" he asks.

"No."

"Do you want to see either of us hurt?"

"No," I reply.

"Then we have to keep moving." Echo picks me up again. "I don't want to lose you, Beatrice. Not after I just saved you. This whole City will come crumbling down, but at least I know that I've rescued you."

I have no idea what has happened, or where Gabe is, or where we are going. But I do know one thing I feel is for certain, "I don't want to lose you either, Echo."

◇

"Attention: All Dreamcatchers are to be shot and killed on sight. I repeat, all Dreamcatchers are to be shot and killed on sight. The Institution is on lockdown. There is no way in and no way out. Those of you who are still alive need to fight to eradicate the enemy threat on each floor. Protect the Beacon."

The intercom switches off. The Keeper is gone once more, hidden somewhere deep inside the Institution, probably for her own protection.

I really want to pull my helmet off to breathe in fresh air again. The hall is still dark, but at least now the sunlight struggles to stream through the Recreation Room's window blinds and we can see again.

"We have our orders," I remind them all. "We have to leave this room and take care of the Dreamcatchers on this floor. Our time here is over." Below us, we hear a fresh burst of gunshots, which breaks the creepy silence of the sixteenth floor. The war has moved from the City to the Institution, where we've all been trapped against our wills, Dreamcatchers and Seers. "It's started."

"It started a long time ago." Elan slaps a magazine into place, locking and loading his weapon.

"You know what I mean." I roll my eyes at the boy, and though he might be getting on my nerves with his pompous attitude, he's still reliable.

"Listen," Gabe begins, waving us to gather around him. "Once we leave here, it's not going to be easy. We can't go back into hiding…we need to be on the hunt."

"This is a depressing pep talk." I'm smiling at Gabe, but he can't see it anyway.

"It might be…but we have to be honest with ourselves here. We might not see each other again, Bea. Not alive, at least. We don't know how many Dreamcatchers are out there…"

My smile fades. "Stop talking like this."

"Someone has to." Brandon turns his head toward me. "He's right, Bea. I think we've learned by now that one minute we can be alive, and the next minute…gone. Just…gone." Like Mae. And Connie.

"I know, but we don't have to keep harping on it." I point at the door. "Gear up and meet there. We're leaving."

Gabe doesn't let me go, though. He leans forward and his helmet clinks against mine. Brandon and Elan leave us alone, giving us space and privacy by walking to the far side of the room and turning their backs.

"What are you doing?" The nervousness I feel leaks into my words, causing them to tremble. I can't look weak in front of him. I'm his leader right now…I'm supposed to be strong for him. I'm supposed to be strong for Team A…all four of us.

"I don't want to leave here without saying good-bye to you."

"I don't want you to say good-bye."

Gabe squeezes my arm with his hand. I imagine that his eyes are closed when he is speaking, unable to look at me as we say our farewells for what could be the very last time. "I don't know what's going on with you, Bea, and you told me to trust you…so, I'm trusting you now, okay?"

"Okay."

"Trust me, too." Gabe reaches out and unlatches my helmet. Reflexively, I reach up to push it down.

"What are you doing?" I blurt at him, frantically trying to latch the helmet back down again. "Are you crazy?"

"I'm saying good-bye to you. Hold your breath." He unlatches his own helmet and pulls it off. With a nod, he signals for me to do the same.

I suck in a deep breath and pull my helmet off as well. It's the first time I've seen Gabe's face in a whole day, and it tugs at my heart that it might be the last time I ever see it again. Especially if I have to go by my Visions, which so far…have all come true.

He leans forward and kisses me deeply, so much so that if I weren't holding my breath already, he would have stolen it away. When I close my eyes and kiss him back, I see him yelling for me, stretching out to me, begging me to come back and get him. I wrap my arms around his neck to hold him as close as our jumpsuits will let us. *I won't let you go, Gabe. I'm not going to let go of you.*

He breaks the kiss first, just as he started it. Neither of us draws in a breath. He helps me replace my helmet and latch it airtight again, and I help him do the same. When we are back in our protective barriers, I already feel so cut off from him, a premonition of something to come.

"This isn't good-bye," I assure him.

"It isn't…but at least we said it, just in case." He taps the pendant that hangs outside of my jumpsuit. "You're wearing my necklace."

"Of course I am. I've never taken it off."

"Are you two done yet?" Brandon turns back around. "Something is coming down the hall."

Just like that, we are thrown back into the mayhem. For a moment, I forgot we were in the middle of a war—that is, until the gunshots echo from somewhere above us.

It's our turn to eliminate the Dreamcatchers from the sixteenth floor. I march in front of what is left of my team. "Remember to keep your line of fire clear. We can't be effective if we are in each other's way. And you can't blame anyone but yourself if you get shot by your own people." Beacon fire. The kind that will destroy you instantaneously. I pause and wait for the shots overhead to stop. "We have to move. We are going back to the Meeting Room. We'll wait for them there."

"With all the bodies?" Brandon sounds like he's not pleased. "Why?"

"Because we are going to show them we aren't afraid, that's why." I look at Gabe, my lips pressed together in a line. "Let's go."

I open the door by hitting the release button with the nose of my gun, pointing it first to the left. Nothing is there. "Clear." The other three move up and cover me as I turn and check the other side. The hall is long and dark, but I can't see anyone. "Clear." When I give the go ahead, the three of them come out into the hall. Brandon and Elan keep their sights aimed to the left, while Gabe and I stand with our back against their backs, guns aimed in the opposite direction. We have all sides covered, reducing the chances of a Dreamcatcher sneak attack.

"As we move down the hall, I want you to open each door and check the rooms. We don't move forward until they are all cleared."

This will be tedious—there are at least a dozen rooms before we get to the Meeting Room. I'd rather it be tedious and clear, though, than sloppy and dangerous. The last thing we need is to have our backs turned and the Dreamcatchers sneaking up behind us.

Each pair of us takes a door, opens it, checks the rooms, and then moves forward after giving the all clear. I am careful not to let the heel of my boot sound on the ground. We need to be stealthy, just in case we can catch them off guard.

We make it to the Meeting Room without any incident. The sunlight streams into the windows that line the very top of each wall. The fog that we thought we saw the night before is gone, but all of the bodies are still there. Their faces are all stuck in haunted, pained expressions, mouths open like they were screaming before they just suddenly expired. I recognize some of them and quickly turn away.

"What happened?" Elan steps around a body, then looks up and around him, searching everything and everywhere with the barrel of his gun. "Where'd all the Watchmen go?"

Brandon nudges a body with his toe. "Here." The corpse is that of a Watchman, dressed in black with blood coming down his arm. "He looks like he's been shot, though. He didn't die like the others."

"He probably shot at the Dreamcatchers and they got him back." Gabe shakes his head. "This isn't right."

I kneel down to get a better look at the Seers. All of their eyes have turned white, as if they were all blind. The girl I am looking at is young, and doesn't yet have her raven's wings tattooed over her eyes. I reach out and close her lids so she doesn't have to blankly stare out at the world anymore. "They did something to the Seers."

"They did?" Gabe kneels by my side and gets a closer glimpse at one of our fallen. "Their eyes…"

I push myself up off the ground and dust the knees of my

jumpsuit off. "It's like they stole our—"

"Power."

A female voice finishes the sentence. We all turn and point our guns at the source: a small woman with flaxen hair and icy eyes. She wears white robes, just like the Dreamcatchers we saw when I first found Echo. "We didn't steal it, though. We stopped it."

She holds up a hand and a deafening, piercing sound blasts through our heads, and all four of us drop our weapons and put our hands where our ears would be. Of course, because of our helmets, we can't get to our ears to protect them from the high-pitched screeching. As soon as we are disarmed, though, the Dreamcatcher drops her hand and the noise stops. "That's better."

"What do you want?" I ask her, but I can barely hear my voice over the ringing in my ears.

"Are you Seer Beatrice?" the Dreamcatcher asks.

"What's it to you?" Gabe interjects when I open my mouth to respond. I decide to keep silent.

"She is the one with the clearest Visions, is she not?" She looks to me. She hardly looks threatening standing like this, but I know her power is in her hands. In just a touch, she can turn me into nothing, and add me to the bodies piled all around the Meeting Room. Or, she can fill my head with that noise, that crippling noise.

"Who are you?" Elan also doesn't allow anyone to answer her question.

"Enigma. I am one of the Dreamcatcher leaders."

"Why did you kill all of these Seers?" Elan keeps up his interrogation.

"Who said we killed them? We've come for our Citizens to take them home. We've come to destroy your corrupt Institution and the Keeper who runs it."

"Home?" Brandon, Gabe, and Elan ask all at the same time.

When she mentions her home, I recall Echo in the meadow with the tree. I feel peaceful just thinking about it, and I wonder if Enigma can tell since she shoots me a look.

"Our home is called Aura. It is somewhere west, where you've never been because your Keeper does not let you go anywhere." Enigma smiles with a tilt of her head. "It's a shame, don't you think? Don't you ever wonder what is outside of this dim, dark City? Don't you ever want to abandon it for a life of light and…dreams?"

"How can we want something we never knew existed?" Gabe rolls his eyes.

I want it. When I close my eyes at night and Echo finds me, he takes me there, and I never want to wake up. I want Gabe to know the feeling of freedom, of not being bound or barricaded by anything. But he's probably never experienced a dream that has taken him out of the City. How do people dream about something they don't even know about?

Elan puts us back on task with another question. "You killed all these Seers to steal the Citizens away. Why do you need them?"

Enigma's smile disappears. She looks too serious in this moment, as if Elan has just asked a question that never, ever should have been asked. I regret him speaking up at all now. I should have ordered him to shut up. I should have handled the questions on my own.

"Oh, little boy, there's so much truth you don't know." Enigma holds both of her hands out by her sides, and from out of the shadows cast about the Meeting Room by the brightness of the sun, Dreamcatchers walk toward her, stopping in a semi-circle behind her. "For example, there was a time when we cohabitated. A time where we walked side by side and respected one another's powers.

But the Keeper at that time grew paranoid, sensing our powers were getting stronger, and she sent us away, casting us out of the protection of the City and into the broken, fragile world."

"Why would she cast you out if you weren't doing something that you weren't supposed to be doing?" Brandon speaks up this time, but his gaze is on the Dreamcatchers who stand behind Enigma. I follow his gaze, and that's when I realize that Echo is standing there with about eight other Dreamcatchers. He isn't holding a weapon, and is still wearing his white and scarlet-trimmed robe from earlier. I notice that not every robe has that scarlet band.

"Because she was afraid. We are two halves, child. You are the half who can see ahead, and we are the half that recalls the past, harvests the Dreams so that we never forget what has happened. But now, we won't ever function together again. Now, we are two cities, two people who stand on our own, fighting for survival."

I listen to her, but my attention is mostly on Echo, who, for once, is looking back at me. I swallow and glance to Gabe, and I'm relieved to know that now is not the time I will lose him. This is not the place in my Vision where he stands screaming at me.

Enigma continues her story, which has us entranced enough that even I forget I am standing in a room filled with dead Seers. "Together, we were strong…but apart, we are weak. The Keeper has to keep the Seers together in one place so that they can thrive and she can watch over them and use their gifts…and the Dreamcatchers need to harvest the Citizens to keep our powers balanced, and to heal us when we are sick. Like now."

"What do you mean, sick?" Brandon asks.

"A virus has started to spread through Aura. First among the Citizens, and now it has spread to the Dreamcatchers." Enigma shoots a sad, fleeting look to the half-moon of her kind behind her.

"And the Citizens? Why do you bother to kill them, then?" Gabe catches me staring at Echo, and I look down at my feet. Hopefully he hasn't realized that there's a familiarity between me and the Dreamcatcher.

"And take them. We saw you take them in nets into your ships," Elan blurts, making sure we don't forget that small detail.

"Because they are our only hope to stop the plague. You only keep them as your slaves anyway…"

"We do not," Elan protests with a deep frown. "We protect them."

"You *think* you protect them." Enigma shakes her head, her long hair falling around her pale face. She looks like an angel.

The four of us are quiet. What she's suggesting takes all of us off guard. All of this time, the Keeper has been deceiving us, leading us to believe that we were the good guys and the Dreamcatchers were the enemy. For all we know, they still could be, and Enigma could be lying to us. But the thought that the Institution has been harvesting the Citizens as slaves is a little too much, especially when those Citizens include the families we've never known.

I look back to Echo, hoping he'll give me some sign not to believe in this woman. He stands so regally, his hands folded in front of him, that he's hardly recognizable as the young man in my dreams. He returns my glance, but there's nothing there telling me to disregard Enigma's story.

"This is stupid," Gabe mutters.

"It's your history, boy." Enigma's tone turns into something agitated.

"According to you, our enemy. Why do you think we'd trust you?"

Enigma's eyes shift to where I stand and she says, "She does."

Echo's stance stiffens.

I immediately shake my head. I don't trust Enigma any more than the others do. "This is all nonsense."

Gabe moves to reach for his weapon, and one of the other robed Dreamcatchers extends his hand. Gabe screams out and puts his hands back over his ears. "Ah! Make it stop!"

I panic and shoot a glare to Echo. "Stop this! You are hurting him!"

Echo says nothing, but there's a tiny glimmer of pity in his eyes.

The Dreamcatcher drops his hand and at the same time, Gabe drops to the ground, still screaming in pain. I rush over to where he is and fall to my knees, collecting him in my arms. He pulls his helmet off and throws it, forgetting about any threat of noxious gasses. Blood drips down his neck from the inside of his ears. I brush his hair back and hold him close to my chest as he continues to groan and claw at his lobes.

"Why'd you do that?"

"Your friend was reaching for his weapon. We are having a civil conversation here, Beatrice," the offending Dreamcatcher replies.

"Don't use my name," I hiss and hold Gabe closer, as if my mere presence will somehow protect him. I'm weaponless as well, so what can I really do?

"She's feisty." The Dreamcatcher laughs and some of the others laugh with him. Echo doesn't, though, and only continues to watch me as I hold Gabe. When I look back up at him, he doesn't seem very moved, nor does he seem happy that I'm with Gabe.

"So now what?" I ask them all, but eventually my question and attention returns to Enigma.

"We are the Guardians of the royal Dreamcatchers. As you have a Keeper of Visions, we have the Harvesters of Dreams. They are a family, and their position is passed down through the ages. It is our duty to destroy the Beacon before it destroys us….possibly all of us. The scientists made it a long time ago in their quest to find a way to reverse the serum. In the Keeper's hands, it is a misused and dangerous power, and we can't risk seeing it wipe out either the Dreamcatchers or the Seers. It is bad enough that you harvest its power and use it as ammunition." Enigma walks toward Gabe and I, and my first reaction is to grab the gun that's not too far out of arm's reach—but if I do, I'll end up like Gabe, and I'm not even sure if he can hear anything anymore. He rocks back and forth, hands over his ears, whimpering pathetically.

"Get away," I warn.

"Trust her." Echo finally speaks up. I narrow my eyes, and despite Elan and Brandon's obvious surprise and discomfort, I listen to Echo, since he's the only other person here whom I can trust besides Gabe and the other Seers. Enigma kneels down in front of Gabe and reaches out to take him by the hand.

"Don't let her touch him!" Brandon blurts and makes a step toward us, but the "tsk tsk" from the Dreamcatcher who incapacitated Gabe stops Brandon in his tracks.

Enigma reaches out and puts her hands on Gabe's, pulling them away from his ears. She closes her eyes, absorbing the pain that is clearly written across his face. Gabe's body begins to heal, and eventually he stops moaning as loudly as he was before. His ears clearly bother him still, as he cups his hands over them, protecting them from whatever is making them ache. As Enigma gets closer to me, I feel that pain which has been present the whole time, now so familiar that I've hardly noticed it.

"Find the Beacon and destroy it if you want to save your Institution and those inside it," Enigma whispers to Gabe and I, as if this operation has everything to do with us and nothing to do with anyone else. "If not for humanity, do it for yourselves."

Enigma stands, her robes falling around her tiny form, the folds rippling like waves on the water. She's so majestic that I have a hard time looking away from her. The nine of them turn and head out of the Meeting Room, but it's Echo who looks back at me and mouths the words, "Save us."

Save us?

I hug Gabe close to me again, and he quietly mumbles, "Where's the Beacon?"

We let the Dreamcatchers go, and we know that somewhere, someone is watching us do it. Gabe, Elan, Brandon, and I stand in the middle of the Meeting Room and all the dead bodies, speechless and confused. So much bumbles through my mind—it is all too much to digest at the same time.

Maybe I shouldn't, but I've decided to trust the Dreamcatchers. To trust Echo. We now have a new goal, despite the Keeper's orders. If she's watching us, she already knows what we know, but if by some chance she isn't then we still have an opportunity to destroy the Beacon before it can hurt us and kill all the Dreamcatchers, including Echo.

But what will happen after we destroy the Beacon? Will they still harvest our Citizens?

I think about the options given to us. Keep fighting the Dreamcatchers and eliminate one cause of this war, or destroy a Beacon that can very well eliminate all of us.

"We are going to find the Beacon," I decide for the group.

"Why? Why are you trusting them? What if destroying the Beacon destroys *us*?" Elan picks his gun up off the ground and checks it to make sure everything is working properly. He shoots some rounds of beacon bullets off in the direction of the side of the Meeting Room, and Brandon startles when they hit the wall and burst in little flashes of glowing light.

"Stop, Elan," Gabe scolds the boy.

"Fine, whatever. Let's go find the stupid Beacon, then, if it will make everyone else happy. I think we're walking into a trap. We have no reason to trust those people, and yet here we are, buying into everything they are saying and walking straight into disaster."

"If you don't want to come, you can always stay here," I offer as I pick up my weapon. "But I figure, we don't really have the option."

"And what if it is meant to protect us?" Elan retorts.

"We learned in class that its power is great and can affect us all. What if the Keeper uses it to only save herself? I mean…where is she anyway? I haven't seen her fighting to protect the Institution."

Elan snorts.

I sling my gun over my shoulder and start for the double doors leading out of the Meeting Room. "That's what I thought. Come on, we're finding this Beacon and putting it out of its misery."

CHAPTER TWENTY-FIVE

The Institution is still in lockdown, which we are quickly reminded of when we try to push open the door to the stairwell and it won't budge. We know we somehow have to get to the center of the building where the Beacon's red light shoots up into the sky, destroying anything that touches it. But how can we do that when we're stuck on the sixteenth floor with no way out?

And for that matter, where did the Dreamcatchers go after they left us?

The four of us walk up and down the hall, checking into rooms, re-clearing them, and then we walk to the next one to do it all over again. Each one of us is quiet, lost in our own thoughts as we try to figure the puzzle out. The Dreamcatchers are getting in and out, so there has to be a way for us to do the same.

That's when Elan makes himself useful again. The brainy kid points up at the vents. "There. We have to go in there." I'm not quite sure this is the way the Dreamcatchers are getting around, but it will have to be good enough for us if we want to get to the Beacon in time, before it destroys us all.

Brandon helps drag some things out of a nearby room that was being used as an office. Most importantly, he pushes out a heavy, metal desk and stacks a filing cabinet tipped on its side on top of it. I climb up the pile of office supplies and push the vent grate up into the metal shaft.

"All right. Let's just follow these down and toward the middle of the building, since that's where the Beacon's light seems to be coming from." I climb up into the vent and push my gun behind my shoulders so I can crawl on my hands and knees.

"I'd suggest heading down to the observatory garden. That's the only outside place I can think of that's near the middle of the Institution. It'd make sense if it was down there. You can hardly get to the garden from the outside of the building." Gabe speaks quietly, probably due to the fact that his ears are still visibly hurting him. He tugs and scratches at them over and over again to try and relieve the pain, then pulls his helmet over his head.

I help Elan up into the vent, and Gabe and Brandon follow up after him. "Sounds like a good plan, mostly because it's the only plan we have. Now, let's go," I say.

We quietly crawl through the ventilation shaft, knees and hands shuffling against the sometimes flimsy and unsupported metal. We keep some distance between us so it won't collapse and send us all down onto the next floor, or Maker forbid, down in between the walls.

As we descend floor by floor, we catch morbid glimpses of spattered blood and strewn bodies through the slits of the vents. Sometimes there are more dead Dreamcatchers than Seers, and sometimes it is the other way around. We continue on our way, even though I feel like I am going to get sick.

The intercom crackles on, and we can barely hear it through

the walls. Still, the message is clear enough. "Seers. We've been watching your progress and are pleased to announce that most of the Dreamcatcher threat has been eliminated. We ask that you find a safe room to barricade yourself in, as soon the Beacon will be activated, and you will have to take cover in order to avoid its overwhelming power."

"Funny that she doesn't mention what it's going to do, isn't it?" Gabe's words are a bit too loud. Brandon shushes Gabe by putting a finger to his lips and "shhh'ing" almost louder than Gabe was talking in the first place.

"We don't even know what it's going to do. Unless you are trusting those awful Dreamcatchers," Elan responds.

The intercom continues to relay the Keeper's transmission. "It's also come to my attention that we have some Seers who may have betrayed our cause. If you come across Seer Gabriel, Seer Elan, or Seer Brandon, you are to shoot and destroy them on sight. That is all." The speakers switch off.

"How come they didn't mention you?" Elan is the first to point this out, and I, of course, don't have an answer for him. I have no idea why the Keeper didn't mention me, but I do know that she's always been strange about my existence in the first place.

"I don't know, but no one is going to be shooting any of us. It's not what we are trained to do. Do you actually think the Seers would turn against other Seers just because the Keeper ordered it?" But, as soon as the words leave my mouth, I realize that is exactly what will happen. Who am I kidding? Of course another Seer would shoot us if the Keeper ordered it.

"Yes." Elan's disappointment is clear, and it tugs at my heart and makes me feel guiltier than ever.

"I don't know why she didn't say my name…but I'm going to do everything I possibly can in order to keep you guys safe. And once we get to the Beacon and disable it, it hopefully won't be much of a problem anyway." Or at least I hope this is the case, but we have no way of knowing what will happen if the Beacon goes off or doesn't go off.

"Let's keep moving. We're almost there." Gabe urges us all to continue, but an awkward silence lingers between us. Why was the Keeper protecting me, I wonder? I am the one who let the Dreamcatcher get near Gabe. I am the one Enigma spoke to and told me to destroy the Beacon. Shouldn't I be the one that everyone should be going after and killing?

And then I remember why I'm not being killed. I remember why I've hardly ever been disciplined, despite the Keeper's sense of threat when it came to me. I'm much too valuable to them. I've the clearest Sight of anyone here, maybe including the Keeper herself. I'm the only one worth anything to her. The only one she can use.

I keep all of this to myself, though. Gabe, Brandon, and Elan won't understand. Well, maybe Gabe would, but he's much too disoriented right now to get everything I want to say to him. It will have to wait until later, if there even is a later.

We make it down to the observatory floor, but before we kick the vent open to slide out of the shafts, we notice that the group of nine Dreamcatchers has also made it down to the Beacon as well. They move slowly, as if every step toward the light is breaking them down. Echo is there, in his red-trimmed white robes. He looks toward the vent, maybe sensing that I'm there with him, even if he can't see me. Elan pulls on my shoulder from behind.

"They know we are here."

"Who cares? We're both trying to do the same thing." This time, I snap quietly at Elan. "Listen. You barely have your wings. You are new to all of this and…"

"So are you! When's the last time you've heard of the Beacon, and the Harvesters, and Aura, and whatever else it is that crazy Dreamcatcher woman told us? Don't act like you knew of all of this ahead of time, Beatrice. You're no more informed than any of us are."

I hesitate, and it's enough for Elan to latch onto. "Unless you did know something…"

Quickly, I shake my head. "I don't know any more than you do, Elan. But I do know that if we don't make our move soon, we might all be lying dead in this vent, and all of our arguing will be for naught. Is that what you want?"

"No," he huffs.

"Me either. So let's go." By the time our conversation is done, the Dreamcatchers are no longer in the hall. I kick the vent out and slide through, hanging to the end until I can safely drop myself onto the ground. I land on the balls of my feet, and a shock of pain sears up my ankles and into my legs. Elan, Brandon and Gabe each jump out after me, and we all pull our guns up, ready to fire.

The humming of the Beacon is loud, like thousands of economy-sized fans all turned on "high" and running at once. Gabe doesn't seem too bothered by the noise, but the rest of us would cover our ears if it weren't for the helmets on our heads. We go the way the Dreamcatchers went, since it's the only way into the garden and observatory beyond.

As I get closer to the Beacon, there's a serene sense of comfort that wraps itself around me, and I turn back to the others. "Do you feel that?" I want to laugh and cry, it feels so good.

They nod their heads and we keep trekking toward the calming sensation. I realize that the Dreamcatchers are not only no longer in the hall, they have disappeared altogether. There are only so many places to hide in this section of the Institution. Where could they have gone?

When I round the corner into the garden, I'm met by a rather strange sight. The Beacon, an extremely bright spotlight encased in what looks to be a large, metal bowl, hums and thrives, spitting a red beam up into the sky. Where did it come from? How have we never noticed it before?

The Keeper stands with a couple of her officials, about five Watchmen and some choice Seers, all highly-ranked. They stand in a line, as if they have been waiting for our arrival this whole time. Her raven is perched on her shoulder, as always, but seems ruffled and frightened.

"Beatrice. We were beginning to give up on you." The Keeper smiles at me, her lips twisted up at the corners like something from a bad dream. Her black robe is caught by the wind, and if I listen closely enough, I can still hear the sound of gunfire somewhere in the Institution. Seers are still fighting for their lives, and here we are, standing beside the very thing that could possibly wipe out all of us.

The Watchmen raise their guns and aim them at Brandon, Elan, and Gabe. I sidestep in front of them all, blocking the shot before it can ever go off. "Leave them alone."

"My child, it's time you say good-bye to your friends. If you want to save the City, this is the only way we are going to be able to get it back." The Keeper's words are soft and comforting, like a mother's lullaby to her fussy child.

"It isn't the only way. They told us about you, you know." I level my gaze with the Keeper's violet stare. I pull my shoulders back and lift my chin to feign confidence. Inside, though, I'm terrified that this is when I will lose Gabe and Echo both.

The Keeper laughs, and as her shoulders jostle up and down, the raven takes off to the sky and starts to fly in circles, watching all of us. "I'm sure they did tell you some sort of silly thing, Seer Beatrice, but you've never been one to believe in such tales before, I'm sure." The Keeper doesn't move from where she stands with her choice guard, but she extends a hand out toward me as she continues to speak. "I will tell you a truth. You, Seer Beatrice, will be the next Keeper. You are my daughter. My blood. You are the one who will ascend to my position when I am gone, and I don't want to lose you before that can happen, or the Institution will have no one to guide it."

I am stunned into silence.

"Beatrice is your daughter?" Gabe looks at me in a new way now, a strange way, as if I'm no longer on the same level he is.

I have little time to react to this revelation before the Keeper—my mother—is speaking again. "The Beacon will be activated to save our people, Beatrice. It is necessary, and sometimes there are sacrifices that must come when the necessary must happen." The Keeper's smile fades away altogether. "And in this case, the sacrifice is that of our people. You will come with us, to ensure that the next generation of Seers grows with a strong sense of Sight. But the others will be left behind."

Elan barks out, "*You* killed all those Seers in the Meeting Room, didn't you?"

The Keeper smiles. "This conversation is over. Activate the Beacon."

Gabe breaks out of line and runs toward the intercom. At the same time, the nine Dreamcatchers come through the door, guns in hand. Their distraction is the only thing that keeps the Watchmen from shooting Gabe down. He hits the "all call" button and quickly screams into the interface, "All available Seers, report to the Observatory Garden if you don't want to die. Hurry!" As the speakers crackle off, the Watchmen open fire, and bullets not only tear through two of the Dreamcatchers standing at the end of their line, but Gabe also falls onto the console and then drops limp to the floor.

"Gabe!" I hear myself scream, but I don't remember my mouth moving. I feel numb, and before I can run over to him, two people grab me from behind and start to carry me backward, dragging me across the ground. "Echo! Echo, help me!"

He hears me, and while the other Dreamcatchers open fire and try to eliminate the Beacon and the Keeper's Seers, officials, and Watchmen, Echo ducks through the chaos and runs my way. Other Seers start to trickle into the garden, one by one, guns ready, but confusion is written all over their faces.

Brandon stands over Gabe's body and points at the Beacon. "Destroy it! It's going to kill all of us!"

The Keeper dials a number in on the keypad attached to the Beacon and the red light switches off and turns a blinding white color. A high-pitched ring accompanies the change of light, and it startles all of us, even the Dreamcatchers, who have to cover their ears. In this quick moment, another one of them falls victim to the gunshots, leaving six of the nine white-robed Dreamcatchers left.

Luckily, though, as I'm kicking and screaming, trying to break free, I notice that other Dreamcatchers have made it to the garden as well. They stand beside the Seers and shoot at the light, which buzzes and flickers on and off with each hit. The metal surrounding it is like armor, and bullets ricochet off the basin and zip across the room in different directions. They change their target when they realize their efforts have amounted to nothing and shoot at the keypad instead.

"Kill the Dreamcatchers!" the Keeper yells, but no one seems to be paying attention to her. The light hisses angrily and struggles to stay alive under its assault. The longer it is allowed to keep glowing, the louder the piercing noise gets, and it physically starts to hurt our ears. Everyone is shooting out of desperation to get it to stop before our heads explode. The Keeper pulls a small pistol out of her robes and holds it to my temple. "If that light dies, so do you."

"I didn't do anything!" I yell at her, still kicking my legs in a futile attempt to somehow escape the hold the Watchmen have on me.

"You betrayed us." The Keeper pulls the hammer back on the gun, locking it.

Just as her finger pulls back on the trigger, Echo grabs onto the Keeper's hand and she seizes up, dropping the gun. Whatever is going on between the two, it seems to be hurting Echo too, and the agony of his face causes me to panic. "Echo! Echo, let go! Let go!"

It's too late, though. Echo has already caught the Keeper, and the violet from her eyes begins to drain into a lifeless grey hue.

"You will regret this, Dreamcatcher." The Keeper struggles to get the words out, and as they are spoken, they are filled with pain and agony.

"I'm doing this for the sake of us all." Echo grits his teeth and hangs on, fingers digging into the Keeper's skin. Overhead, her raven circles and incessantly screeches, its cries shrill and haunting.

Behind him, the Beacon pops and the light sizzles out. The grip it once had on the Dreamcatchers loosens, and they all stagger backward. The Keeper's body hits the ground at the same time, and Echo sinks down into a crouch, holding his head in his hands. He starts to moan, low at first, but then the moaning turns into agonizing screaming.

The raven suddenly stops screeching.

Elan helps Brandon pick Gabe up off the floor, but a puddle of blood remains where it seeped out of him. I look between Echo, who looks and sounds like he could be dying right in front of me, and Gabe, who looks like he's already dead.

The Seers stop shooting just as soon as the Beacon is out, but they warily turn their guns on the remaining Dreamcatchers, of which there are now over twenty. Elan speaks up when I cannot, "We should detain them. All of them. The Dreamcatchers and the Keeper's minions. At least until everything is back together."

At his order, the Seers who were fighting on our side quickly disarm the others and take them into custody. Echo and the other robed Dreamcatchers remain free. We gather around his fallen form, and I crouch down to be closer to him.

"Echo…" I whisper and reach out to him.

"How do you know him?" Elan asks, but I ignore him.

Echo draws away though, shaking his head. "Don't touch me right now. It'll only hurt us both."

"Beatrice! Hurry! We need to get Gabe to the infirmary." Brandon hikes the lifeless body up in his arms, and blood drips down from somewhere in Gabe's jumpsuit. I want to scream at Brandon and ask him who the hell is up in the infirmary when most of us are dead, but thankfully, there's a solution. A young woman, a Seer, steps forward and motions for Brandon to follow her. "I'm a nurse. I can see what I can do for them."

Enigma pulls Echo up by his arms. I hear her whisper something that sounds like "Your Highness," but he's drawn away from me before I have a chance to question it. A hovercraft appears overhead, safe now from the power of the Beacon, and six rope ladders drop down from the sky to hoist up the robed Dreamcatchers, leaving the others behind. They are all gone just as soon as they can be, and there's no chasing them. We take the rest of the Dreamcatchers into custody, as Elan suggested. They are wounded and hurt, and now they are angry that they've been left here while the others got to escape.

At the end of the skirmish, though, I am unsure if any of this was worth it, with Gabe nearing death, and Echo gone.

CHAPTER TWENTY-SIX

For two weeks, I have Visions of Gabe at the border reaching for me, screaming my name. I promise him over and over again that I won't leave him, but Echo drags me away, and Gabe is gone. Then, something strange starts to happen, and my Visions subtly change. Where Gabe once stood at the fence, desperately grasping for me, now he doesn't show up at all. In my Vision, I feel hollow and confused, as if I know he should be there, and for some reason, he is not, and I have no idea why. But I also feel compelled. Compelled to keep going. Compelled to believe that Gabe will understand, that he would want this for me, and that wherever I am going, it will be for the best, for the City, for the Seers...for both of us.

As I sit in front of a mirror surrounded with high-wattage light bulbs, another Seer is painting makeup on my face, and another is doing my hair. My red robes with the red satin trim and the violet eye embroidered over the right breast hang on a hook beside the mirror. These are the robes of the Keeper, which I will be named today, as tradition dictates, but they won't be worn until after the ceremony. My identity as Beatrice will soon become nothing, and I will fill the shoes of a monster.

I especially feel less like myself because Gabe has yet to recover from his coma, and he won't be here today to see me take over the whole Institution. I wear my raven pendant under my robes, close to my being, because it's the only part of Gabe I have to hold on to right now. The only part of him here with me.

"There. Your hair and makeup for the ceremony are all done."

"Thank you." I rise and they back up a step, a sign of respect for my new station. I slip my robes on and clasp the silver hook that rests under my chin. When I look at myself in the mirror, I hardly recognize the face that stares back at me. My eyes have been rimmed in dark eyeliner, and the raven's wings painted over them have been brushed with a luminescent powder that makes me look like I'm glowing.

"You look beautiful, My Keeper." The Hairdresser folds her hands together and smiles at me. "Just beautiful. You'll be a great Keeper, I just know it."

But something in me doesn't agree with her sentiment. I just don't know what it is yet. Maybe it's the fact that Gabe has yet to wake up, that part of my Vision has yet to come true, and that I'm not certain I want to fill the shoes of a woman, my mother, who almost destroyed us all without any hesitation.

"Thank you." I force a smile in return. Over beside the stage, a manager directs me to come since the ceremony is about to begin. I swallow, and it feels like I'm sucking on sand. When I reach the edge of the stage, I catch a glimpse of the audience between the curtains. There's maybe about a quarter of our original population left, and most are recovering from grievous injuries.

"Seers, please rise for the presentation of your new Keeper." The announcement is made, and in unison, the Seers stand from their chairs, seat legs scraping across the ground.

I step out onto the stage, and there's complete silence. It's not customary to clap for the Keeper when she first arrives, only during the designated parts of the ceremony.

My gown is long and black, with a half train that follows behind me when I walk. I stop before a microphone held on a stand decorated with violet ribbons. With a bow of my head in greeting, I lunge forward into my speech.

"Seers, I thank you for coming here today. The City and the Institution are both recovering from a frightful time for most of us. We have seen and survived a war, an accomplishment that we should be proud of; we are still here today, breathing and experiencing the induction of a new Keeper.

"But at the same time, there's a certain…uncertainty that plagues us. In our brigs, we house around fifty Dreamcatchers that we've managed to round up after the destruction of the Beacon. They have been beyond cooperative, but yet we still insist on keeping them captive." I stop here, because there's some murmuring that spreads through the crowd. Maybe they've already guessed that I plan on letting these Dreamcatchers go. This could be the first mistake I make as the Keeper.

"I will be letting them go, and they will go to their homeland of Aura, never to return to the City again without the express permission of the City and the Institution. I will also be conferring awards to those Seers, both alive and dead, who fought in this battle. I know you've lost your friends and loved ones while fighting back the Dreamcatchers, but we've all been deceived, and though I don't expect you to know or understand that now, we will know and understand it in time. All of us."

The silence is too loud. All of their violet eyes are set on me, and none of them look very happy at my proclamation. I press my lips together in a thin line and sigh. "I know you are unhappy with this, but you have to trust me as your new Keeper, that there's logic behind my decisions. In my Visions I've Seen what we are going through…but not all has come true yet. We will have to face something more, and though it is not clear yet, I know that when it happens, we'll all need to be on the same page.

"So allow me to be clear with you. From this day on, the Dreamcatchers are no longer our enemy. We are not friends, but we are not enemies either. We will strengthen our relationship through diplomacy, and if it succeeds, then we will live our lives free of enemy threats. And if it fails, then we will surely prepare ourselves for another war. This time, though, I, as your Keeper, will not be keeping you in the dark about the nature of our history with the Dreamcatchers. We've much to learn…much to discover…much to adjust to."

There's not even a stirring from the audience. I decide that this is a good time for me to stop my speech. "That is all. I thank you for your insistence that I take over the Institution, and I promise you that I won't fail you." *At least, I think I promise that.*

Before I can leave, the raven, which had disappeared after the last Keeper's death, descends upon my shoulder and spreads its wings behind my head. Its talons dig into my skin and I wince, knowing it has probably drawn blood. I exit stage left and disappear behind the curtains before the blood can seep through my dress. As soon as I'm out of view of the others, the talking and gossip begins in the audience. I can't make out anything they are saying, but the general tone is not that of approval.

"I am going up to visit Gabe. Please don't let anyone bother me." This is said to Brandon and Elan, my two newly-appointed officials. They nod in understanding as I hurry off down the hallways to the infirmary.

The infirmary rooms are filled with patients, all suffering from war injuries. Gabe is kept in a side room where it is quiet and not so busy. I requested this room for him in hopes that he'd recover sooner. But in two weeks, there's been no sign of improvement, and when I enter his room, I'm reminded of just how poorly he's doing.

Gabe is hooked up to tubes and machines that beep and buzz at different intervals. I recall how proud he was of the scar that he got back when this all started. Even though he was annoying about it at the time, I'd much rather he had a simple wound like that than this never-ending coma.

I sit down in a chair beside his bed and scoot it close to the arm rail, which I drop down. Leaning over Gabe's body, I rest my head on his chest and hold his hand in mine. He's so warm, but so lifeless. I find it strange that someone can be in both states at one time. I close my eyes, blinking tears from under the lashes, and squeeze his fingers. "Please wake up, Gabe. I can't do this without you."

He doesn't move, though. The machines continue to beep, and a nurse comes in to check on his progress, but nothing else happens. I squeeze Gabe close and rest my eyes. Eventually, I fall asleep.

◇

It is nighttime, and I am back at the barricades, but everything is different now. There aren't any screaming people, though there is a distinct feeling that something isn't quite right. Behind me, the City is in shambles, but the watchtowers are still in place, operated by Watchmen who are much more on guard than before.

"Beatrice..."

I hear him calling for me like he did way back when I didn't even know who or what he was. I head in the direction of Echo's voice—I'll have to cross the barrier and leave the City behind. Someone in the watchtowers sets off an alarm, and a spotlight swoops across the barrier to where I am standing, trying to figure out how to escape. I'm dressed in my Keeper's robes, which are unmistakable to anyone who lives inside the City. Watchmen file from the tower and start to run toward me, but when they realize who I am, they hesitate and their footfalls come to a halt.

"Beatrice…"

Where are you? I search the fields beyond the barrier, but I find no sign of Echo anywhere. I do note a hole dug under the fence, and after swallowing my fear and apprehension, I drop to the ground and belly my way under the barbed-wire. The Watchmen all run forward, yelling at me to come back, but I don't turn back.

"Beatrice…"

I can't turn back.

◇

Brandon wakes me up. "Bea…er…My Keeper?"

I blink out of my sleep, turning my face into Gabe's stomach. After taking a moment to wake up, I brush the wrinkles out of Gabe's hospital gown and rise from my chair. "What is it? I'm sorry, I must have dozed off…"

"I just wanted to tell you that the Dreamcatchers have been released, as you've requested…but, um, they don't know where to go."

"Oh." I didn't think this far ahead. Where will they go without their ships? "Well, I have an idea, but I'll need you to contact the Watchmen and tell them to prepare to turn off the barricades."

Brandon stammers over his words, "W-what? Turn them off?"

"How else will they get through if we don't let them through, Brandon? Think about it…they have no way home, and we don't want them left here."

He nods his head, eyes shifting to Gabe. "All right, I'll let them know."

"Tell them I'll be down in a half hour. Round the Dreamcatchers up in the staging area."

"Yes, My Keeper." Brandon bows his head.

"And Brandon?"

"Yes?"

I smile. "Please don't call me that."

Brandon grins back at me and mock salutes. "All right, Bea."

CHAPTER TWENTY-SEVEN

The sun has set, and the barricades are no longer buzzing with electricity when we get to them. I lead the Dreamcatchers to the edge of the City where a gate provides an opening to the land beyond. A small contingent of Watchmen and Seers stand with their rifles loaded, ready to put down anyone who causes any trouble.

Beatrice...

I look up when I hear my name, but no one is there. Lifting my hand into the air, I signal for the gate to be opened, and an annoying buzzer sounds, activating a yellow light that spins in circles. The Dreamcatchers file out of the City and into the fields beyond, but not one of them has given me any clue as to whether they know where they are going or not. They don't even look at me on their way out.

Beatrice...

The sky turns purple and then black as the sun disappears beyond the horizon. When the last of them is out, the gate is pulled shut behind them and the powerful magnetic lock comes back to life, sucking the door closed. I turn to head back to the Institution, but when I hear my name called again, I stop and look back over my shoulder. Brandon and Elan continue on without me, the both of them chatting about something unimportant.

I have to save you…

I turn all the way around and face the meadow. It's too late for me to walk out the gate, but I have an urge to run away from here before something happens that I can't stop. I take a step toward the barricades.

You save me, and I save you…

"Echo?" I whisper into the night wind.

A Watchman realizes that I'm not behind them and stops the group. Everyone else pauses beside him, then turns when they want to see what he is looking at. "My Keeper?"

I look back at him, but I don't bother turning around to catch up. Instead, I take another step closer to the electric fence.

"Beatrice? What are you doing?" Elan uses my given name instead of the formal title, which earns him a few choice looks from the others. "Where are you going?"

I still don't answer them. "Echo? Where are you?"

Come with me; we need you now. My people need you. You are the only one who can save us…

"But where are you?"

"Who is she talking to?" a Watchman asks.

I see a hole that has been dug under the fence and it brings back my Vision…or was that a dream? Does it even matter anymore? I know I have to go under the fence, but I have no idea where I will go after that. All I know is that I have to find Echo.

I pause by the hole and chew on my bottom lip. Will Gabe ever forgive me for this? Will he understand like I think he understood in my Vision? Will I ever get back home? Though I don't know the answers to these questions, a twisting, wrenching in my gut seems to understand what is going to happen, even if it's not making it clear to me. I just know that something is not right here. I know there's something more. Something that goes beyond my love for Gabe.

Beatrice...

"Beatrice! Come back!" Brandon starts after me, breaking away from the Watchmen.

I shed my Keeper's robes, leaving me in the black gown underneath. It's not going to be easy getting under the fence wearing this, but I haven't another choice besides losing the gown as well and shimmying under naked, and that's just not happening.

Taking one last step to the hole, I kneel down on my hands and knees, flatten myself onto my stomach and start to carefully slide under the electric wires. I say a silent prayer that my gown won't get stuck or all of this will quickly be for nothing.

"Someone turn the fence off before she kills herself!" Brandon frantically snaps, his voice directed up toward the watchtower.

"Beatrice!" Elan yells at me, this time louder, like he is trying to break my trance.

But nothing can keep me from Echo. I'm being pulled to him, like how I felt when I was being pulled by him in my dreams. Nothing can keep me from whatever fate this is. I can't leave Gabe behind, I don't want to leave Gabe behind...

And then, I am on the other side of the fence. I am free. I slowly turn around and look back at Brandon, Elan, the Seers, and the Watchmen, and my heart sinks.

"I don't expect you to understand this now."

"Beatrice! Don't do this!" Brandon continues to run toward the fence. "Come back!"

"I can't." I don't know why I can't. I don't even know why I am saying that I can't. But I do know that I just can't. "I have to do this. We'll understand it in time…I Saw it, Brandon. I Saw it in a Vision. And I Saw that it will be all right. Everything will be all right." I pause and from behind me, I hear someone approaching.

Echo stops near me and puts his hand on my wrist. It doesn't hurt. I don't even feel the pain in my body when he gets near. His fingers slide down my hand and intertwine with my own.

I look over my shoulder at Echo and smile sadly at him. I turn back to Brandon, let go of Echo's hand, and approach the fence. "Brandon?"

He looks at me with all the sadness in his eyes. "Please don't go."

I can't let him shake me. "Tell Gabe, when he wakes up, that I love him."

"Beatrice…" Echo calls for me. It's time for me to go.

I don't give Brandon time to respond. I step back, reach for Echo's hand and allow him to tug me off through the fields and into his world beyond, the world where Paradigm came from, the one she warned us about, the world that threatens our own. *He doesn't know any better…*I hear her in my head. And maybe he doesn't. But neither do I.

The City is behind us, its million million lights flickering in the nighttime, lighting up the sky with an eerie, fuzzy halo that encapsulates all the towering buildings. The Institution stands taller than all of them, and as Echo and I walk away, I look back only once to burn the image into my mind so I won't forget where I left Gabe in my choice to follow Echo.

ACKNOWLEDGMENTS

Nearly two years ago, I sat at my desk and stared at my classroom of 10th graders at Kenwood High School. I decided then that I wanted to write something for them, and LUMINOSITY started to shape from fragmented ideas of dreams and visions. When my book sold after that school year ended, and I told my now former students, they praised and congratulated me and offered me the most amazing support I could ever ask for. Since that time, I've gone to a new school, where I've been met with the same enthusiasm. My students have gone so far as to volunteer to be my beta readers for book two. They are so selfless and supportive. So, before everyone else, I have to thank all those little souls who have filled my life with ambition and promise. My students have given me purpose, and without them this book wouldn't exist. Thank you to all my little ducklings, especially Melinda, Tyriq, Candice, Shyniyah, and Geronimo.

I couldn't have done this without the support of many others, though. My husband, Brandon, for one, has pushed me through this process, lifted me through the difficult times, and supported me through each and every step. My journey has been a long one filled with many ups and downs, but through it all, Brandon has never given up on me. He has stood by my side, helped me work through my plot holes while taking long walks with me through the neighborhood, and has taken me out for peanut butter ice cream at the completion of a manuscript. Brandon, I wouldn't be the writer or the person I am today without your courage.

I would be remiss if I didn't thank Stephanie Dray for her encouragement as well. She has shown me through her own success that I could achieve my own, and she has encouraged me through the thick and thin, acting as my own personal cheerleader. She has never asked for anything but my friendship in return, and as she grows as a writer, I grow as well thanks to her mentorship. I cannot give back to her enough for guiding me down this path. Thank you for not only being such a valuable professional resource, but for also being a constant friend.

I thank my family; my parents, Mom, Daddy, Laura; and my siblings, Jamie, Dan, Kelsey, Ryan—they have always known in their hearts that my passion has been writing, and not one of them have ever cast this off as some pipe dream. Jamie, Kelsey and Ryan were the first to read LUMINOSITY, and though it ate me up inside to have my sisters and brother read my manuscript for the first time, their advice and comments were honest and ever-helpful. Thank you, all of you, for letting me know it was okay to pursue my dream. From my early-morning, colored-in-Crayon newspapers when I was five years old, to this series…dreams are nothing without your family there to help make them.

To my best friends, Gina and Corrine, who have dealt with so much of my nonsense, but still somehow remain by my side. Thank you for being what you are to me—everything.

I want to thank my high school English teacher, Mr. Wild, who ignored my crazy and saw in me what I couldn't see in myself. I promised myself that one day I would write a book that high schoolers would read, and maybe even make a summer reading list if I am lucky. He planted these seeds in my head and helped me to become the writer and teacher I am today.

And finally, to my editors, Liz and Kerry, who took a chance on me and made me feel like I was the best thing since sliced bread—thank you, thank you, thank you.

Get tangled up in our Entangled Teen titles...

Gravity by Melissa West

In the future, only one rule will matter: Don't. Ever. Peek. Ari Alexander just broke that rule and saw the last person she expected hovering above her bed — arrogant Jackson Locke. Jackson issues a challenge: help him, or everyone on Earth will die. Giving Jackson the information he needs will betray her father and her country, but keeping silent will start a war.

Greta and the Goblin King by Chloe Jacobs

Four years ago, Greta fell through a portal to a world where humans are the enemy. Now a bounty hunter, she's caught the attention of the darkly enticing young Goblin King, who invades her dreams and undermines her will to escape. But Greta's not the only one looking to get out of Mylena…

Onyx by Jennifer L. Armentrout

Thanks to his alien mojo, Daemon's determined to prove what he feels for me is more than a product of our bizarro connection. Against all common sense, I'm falling for Daemon. Hard. *No one is who they seem. And not everyone will survive the lies…*

Get tangled up in our Entangled Teen titles...

Inbetween by Tara Fuller

It's not easy being dead, especially for a reaper in love with Emma, a girl fate has put on his list not once, but twice. Finn will protect the girl he loves from the evil he accidentally unleashed, even if it means sacrificing the only thing he has left…his soul.

The Marked Son by Shea Berkley

When Dylan sees a girl in white in the woods behind his grandparents' farm, he knows he's seen her before…in his dreams. Only he can save her world from an evil lord—a world full of creatures he's only read about in horror stories. Worse, the human blood in his veins has Dylan marked for death…

My Super Sweet Sixteenth Century by Rachel Harris

The last thing Cat Crawford wants for her sixteenth birthday is an extravagant trip to Florence, Italy. But when her curiosity leads her to a gypsy tent, she exits … right into Renaissance Firenze. Cat joins up with her ancestors and soon falls for the gorgeous Lorenzo. Can she find her way back to modern times before her Italian adventure turns into an Italian forever?

Get tangled up in our Entangled Teen titles...

Conjure by Lea Nolan

Sixteen-year-old twins Emma and Jack Guthrie hope for a little summer adventure when they find an eighteenth-century message in a bottle revealing a hidden pirate treasure. Will they be able to set things right before it's too late?

Chosen Ones by Tiffany Truitt

The government, faced with humanity's extinction, created the Chosen Ones. When Tess begins work at a Chosen Ones training facility, she meets James, and the attraction is immediate in its intensity, overwhelming in its danger. Can she stand against her oppressors, even if it means giving up the only happiness in her life?

Toxic by Jus Accardo

When a Six saved Kale's life the night of Sumrun, Dez was warned there would be consequences. But she never imagined she'd lose the one thing she'd give anything to keep... Dez will have to lay it all on the line if there's any hope of proving Jade's guilt before they all end up Residents of Denazen. Or worse, dead...